Grandmother, Mother and Me

Memories, Poetry and Good Food

Grandmother, Mother and Me
Memories, Poetry and Good Food

Editor

Donna Clark Goodrich

First Edition

Hidden Brook Press
www.HiddenBrookPress.com
writers@HiddenBrookPress.com

Grandmother, Mother and Me: Memories, Poetry and Good Food

Editor – Donna Clark Goodrich
Cover Design – Richard M. Grove
Layout and Design – Richard M. Grove
Front and Back Cover Photograph Credits

Front and Back Cover Photograph Credits:
Upper Left – Florentine Hardt, mother-in-law of Elaine Hardt
Upper Middle – Elynne Chaplik-Aleskow with her grandmother Fannie Lebedow
Upper Right – Photo by Christopher Grove of Ruth Grove
Middle Left – Sandra Fischer, granddaughters Sydney and
          Olivia Lannom, and daughter Sarah Lannom
Middle Right – Photo by Joshua Gough of Ann Abouchar and daughter Juli
Lower Left – Peggy Cunningham with her grandmother Mary DiNicola
Lower Right – Ida Fernley Culley, grandmother of Joanne Culley
Back cover – Sylvia Neal Nickerson, grandmother of Janet Kivisto

Typeset in Garamond

Printed and bound in U.S.A.

Library and Archives Canada Cataloguing in Publication

     Grandmother, mother and me : memories, poetry and
good food / editor, Donna Clark Goodrich.

ISBN 978-1-897475-94-2
     1. Grandmothers--Literary collections. 2. Mothers--Literary
collections. 3. Canadian literature (English)--21st century.
4. American literature--21st century. I. Goodrich, Donna Clark

PS8237.G73G73 2012   C810.8'035253   C2012-907073-4

In loving tribute to our

Grandmothers and Mothers

for their fostering,

nurturing,

cherishing,

for their encouragement.

Table of Contents

Memories of My Grandmother

Like a Mother to Me

Memories
of
My Mother

A mother,
There to support you,
And hold you up whenever you need her.

—Laurel Stephens

Connie Poole-Wesala

Chocolate Fixes Anything

I looked nothing like my mother Wanda. My father's genes were the stronger. My mother was tall and thin, blonde and hazel-eyed. I was my father's daughter, or so I thought—short, brunette, bushy eyebrows set above large brown eyes.

I was quiet and introspective, given to bouts of dark moods, and often a loner. I took pride in that for years. It made me feel somehow mysterious. My mother's gregarious, outgoing personality, and her insistence on telling total strangers everything she was thinking, embarrassed me. I had no desire to become her. I hated her smelly ashtrays, her constant chatter, her endless cups of coffee, and her large costume jewelry.

Then one afternoon at my dad's eightieth birthday bash, one of my mother's friends found me at the punch bowl and exclaimed, "You look just like your mother!" *Was she suffering from dementia or perhaps cataract affected vision?* I wondered. I smiled politely, patted her hand, and told her how nice she looked. "You haven't changed a bit either," I said.

For weeks after that, her remark left a million questions rattling around in my head. I kept glancing in the mirror trying to conjure whatever essence of my mother she had seen. It slowly came into focus, all the lessons absorbed into my being without my notice. I had hosted the party for my dad and entertained "Wanda-style" the many guests I hadn't seen in years. I chatted and smiled in my one good dress and heard my mother whisper, "I told you, a scarf can make any dress look new."

My brown eyes faded to her shade of hazel following the birth of my son— the red-haired boy my mother said I'd have. She shared this prediction from her hospital bed. She was fifty-seven and dying from lymphoma. I was thirty-two and pregnant with my second child. I simply shook my head, patted her hand, and smiled. I'd already named this baby Angelina.

Eighteen weeks later, as my obstetrician held up a tiny screaming baby boy, he noted my shocked and stricken face and said, "I can't put him back, Mom." We all had a good laugh, and I heard my mother chortle above my bed in the delivery room. "I believe I told you so," she said crisply.

In those thirty-two years, my mother implanted herself solidly. After her friends' observations, I began to see her legacy quite clearly.

Her lessons were many:
– "One good dress is better than a dozen cheap ones." I have taken that to heart.
– "Save as long as it takes to get the expensive piece of furniture." Ditto! I started with Drexler and antiques. My new home looks like a Pottery Barn display.
– "A Democrat can live with a Republican." Been there, done that (twice unfortunately).
– "Parent with a decent helping of discipline mixed with unconditional love." My two wonderful adult children are living proof of that.
– "Women are better drivers." I fly down the freeway as freely as she did the highway between Oklahoma and Kansas.
– "Everything tastes better fried, and chocolate cake can fix anything." I love frying chicken and making cream gravy, although my age and digestive system don't tolerate it so well now. Each year I make my mother's chocolate cake. I learned recently that it is often called Texas Sheet Cake. Being from Oklahoma, she sort of left out that Texas part.

I learned the most important lessons early on, subliminally. As a young girl I watched my mother sit with her best friend and neighbour, Betty, as they drank coffee and smoked cigarettes, complained about husbands, and bragged about kids. I rode with her to her friend, Maxine's, house and watched them chat for hours, saw them laugh while they shopped the Montgomery Ward catalogue, and support each other through daily trials.

When my parents' friends, Claude and Virginia, came over in the evenings, the women would quietly slip from the family room into the bedroom, leaving the men to talk golf and cars. I'd wander down the hall shortly after and settle on the floor as the two women sat on the bed and talked about the important issues of life. Years later I watched them sit together on my sofa, holding hands, and hugging during my mom's last stages of cancer and chemo—not knowing she'd be gone within the next few weeks.

"Women friends are the most precious gift God gives us," she told me. "Treasure them and treat them well." Virginia sat by her side daily until my sister and I took over the death-watch of her last two weeks.

Recently I have spent days and hours sitting with my women friends as they faced cancer and surgeries, knowing that they will be the ones to help me when the time comes in the not-so-distant future. I wonder at the passing of time and see her nod knowingly.

I often feel shortchanged by my mother's untimely death, but she did show me how to die with dignity. We had an agreement before she passed. We were driving through town to an appointment with her oncologist. If she were to die—although she would NOT—but if—she would tap on the window occasionally to let me know she was still around and to reassure me there was a heaven on the other side.

During the first few months following her funeral, she rang the doorbell. It terrified me late at night, and my husband would go downstairs with a baseball bat as I followed close behind. There was no one there, of course, and he attributed it to a loose wire. Later, the tapping began…infrequently, out of the blue, always at the bedroom window. I would hop out of bed and race to the back patio planning to see a woodpecker sharply tapping at the wooden eave above the bedroom window or a tree limb smacking in the wind. The knocking became less frequent with each move. But not too long ago I heard the tap and didn't even bother to get up to look. I just rolled over and said, "Hi, Mom, I'm fine," and went back to sleep.

I have living proof that genetics are stronger than upbringing. I watch my daughter, Michelle, flit around her kitchen like a hummingbird, glass of wine in one hand, stirring a pot with the other. She talks and gestures as she tells a story, and when she walks outside for a quick cigarette, I see my mother in every move. Michelle is fun and active, full of chatter and *joie de vivre*, enjoying life to its fullest. She tilts her head and uses expressions she never had a chance to observe, and she often surprises me by wearing Mom's large clunky pins and necklaces with pride.

Mom must be thrilled at her granddaughter's closet—her shelves lined with no fewer than a hundred pair of shoes. She'd probably want to wear the four-inch Manolo Blahnik's. I swear she did housework for years in high heels. I can hear Wanda outside on the patio, smoking with her granddaughter, praising her independence and her career.

Recently I stood at a checkout in Macy's. The jeans I'd chosen were marked 30 percent off, plus I had a coupon! I knew Mom would be proud. When the salesclerk said, "That comes to $7.36," my mouth dropped. As she showed me all the markdowns, I swear I heard Mom beside me. "Go girl, I need coffee and a cigarette after that!"

I could have used her help earlier this week. I told my son I'd gladly sew a project for him. Two days later I wondered what I'd been thinking. I kept looking up. "I know you're laughing at me, Mother, so stop." Mom sewed all of my clothes through fifth grade when I decided "store-bought" was better, although later, she copied expensive prom and dance dresses we could never afford to buy. I'm sure she was thoroughly embarrassed I couldn't sew three straight seams without glopping up the bobbin.

Both my sister and I have now lived longer than our mother. Each of our fifty-seventh birthdays was a milestone fraught with worry and concern. Would it be our destiny, as well, to leave our own children at such tender ages? Luckily we got our dad's healthy genes, and that anniversary came and passed. We are intended to live longer.

That is something my mother never got to teach me—how to age gracefully. How to be sixty, or seventy, or eighty. She left that to my dad who lived to ninety-three. So I have had to figure that out on my own, and I do so knowing that she will tap that window again soon to let me know she is keeping me safe. In the meantime, I'm baking chocolate cake because she was absolutely right…chocolate fixes anything!

Dorothy Wells

Mother Dear

Where should I begin? First of all I thank God for placing me in the family of His choice and at His timing. Much mystery clouds our understanding, yet occasionally a glimpse of His purpose will shine through. Mother lost her mother to the dreaded TB in 1906, when she was only twelve years old. Grandpa was a Presbyterian minister and needed a wife and mother for his four little children, so he married a lovely lady I knew as Grandma. Our ancestral roots reach into a Calvinistic Scotch Irish background producing integrity, thrift, and family value. The Great Depression further fueled some of these traits, as problems present challenges for character growth.

Father lost his job as a civil engineer and diligently searched out any opportunity for work, often having to be away from home. Mother kept things orderly, using whatever means she could. She was almost always home when I bounded into the kitchen from grade school, calling, "Momma!" Garden produce in the summer and home canned supplies in the winter kept our tummies full, and there was always something to give to transients who often asked for a bite.

Although we lived in the city we had an apple tree, currant bushes, and room for a large garden in the backyard. We learned the work ethic early in life and my brother and sister and I had our assigned chores without any reimbursement (allowance) expected. This was our family and we all shared. Later, when we moved to the farm we had a bigger garden and chickens, cows, pigs and a dog. Winter evenings around our fireplace afforded time for listening to the radio, or Victrola records, while keeping busy with handcrafts and repairs.

Mother sewed and repaired our clothes on her little White treadle machine which she also taught me to use. Chicken feed came in pretty flowered sacks and these became transformed into lovely garments. Hand-me-downs were not resented but greatly appreciated. Recycling was the normal way of life. Crocheting, needlepoint, knitting, and simple quilting provided opportunity for teaching and sharing.

Mealtime in the kitchen, or—when we had company, in the dining room—was usually followed with a time of Bible reading and prayer. Mother often read aloud in the evenings, and we also learned to love reading. I remember playing school with a large blackboard on a wall next to the kitchen, and Mom listened and monitored from her duties as she prepared meals. She always put our interests above hers. Highlights of the calendar year included visits with grandparents, aunts, uncles, and cousins. Family indoor games in the winter included board games such as Monopoly, along with Chinese and regular checkers, Bible Biography, Pit, and marbles. Summer added outdoor croquet and gardening to our exercise. In spite of our need for thrift, we never lacked for simple joys.

Monday was laundry day. An old rocker machine with wringer attachment to the rinse tubs was in the basement. So the big heavy wet clothes had to be carried up the steps to be hung out on the clotheslines. They smelled fresh as they became sun-dried. We also had lines in the basement for rainy days and in the wintertime. Tuesday was ironing day with the old ironing board and simple (not steam) iron put to good use. Wednesday often brought out the smells of fresh baked bread which I took for granted and I now regret that I even resented the fact that we couldn't buy "store" bread like my little playmate had. Thursday and Friday passed quickly with various tasks and then Saturday arrived with its assigned duties. Sunday was the Lord's Day. Perfect attendance pins accumulated as we attended every week. It was also a family day. On nice days we might go for a walk, or just relax around the house. Even homework was discouraged on our day of rest.

Mother suffered with a heart condition but never complained. I really can't recall her voicing any negative words. She plugged faithfully along her pathway and I am truly thankful to her—and to God for giving her to me.

Freda Hatfield Tong

Mama and the Writing Box

One of my earliest memories is of watching my mother write letters. Perched on a kitchen bench, her writing box on her lap, there might be time to dash off a quick note to her cousin Lizzie while the biscuits baked. Of course, biscuits required a hot oven and didn't take long to bake, so she had to keep one eye on the old woodstove, lest she end up with black-topped biscuits. We children hated those, but for reasons we could never fathom, Mama professed to love them.

What Mama referred to as her "writing box" was an old wooden Victrola case, its inner works long gone. On one end of the box was embedded a steel ring which might once have been the opening for a handle used to crank out music from old-fashioned cylinder-type records. The box's hinged cover, added by our father, could be lifted upward. Mama wrote on the flat, smooth top and kept her writing implements inside: pens, paper, and letters from who knows how many years. Sometimes the box was jammed so full that Mama had to press down the cover with her forearm as she wrote, so she would not have to write on a slant.

We seldom saw Mama's cousin Lizzie, to whom most of the letters were sent. She lived in Orono, one hundred miles from Alexander, our eastern Maine hometown. I was probably seven or eight years old before we ever traveled to the central part of the state where she lived. These days, such a trip might take a good two hours. Back in the 1940s, on the unpaved "airline road," it took a much bigger chunk of a day to get there. Lizzie and her family seldom came our way either. They had several children. The youngest was a daughter named Beverly, who was a few years older than I.

Mama had plenty of "pen pals." Her cousin Violet lived in Ellsworth. Mama also wrote to her own mother, who lived in Southwest Harbor at the time. It was Mama, not our father, who kept in contact with Dad's Nova Scotia relatives. We sometimes wondered what news Mama had to share. Our lives, we thought, were pretty simple—sometimes even boring—but writing apparently had its own rewards. Occasionally one of us children would take one of cousin Lizzie's replies and, in a singsong voice, read its initial lines. "Dear Edith," it would usually begin. "Received your welcome letter yesterday. Was very glad to hear from you." We seldom saw the letters Mama wrote as she so often barely finished them before mail time.

Along with the biscuits, Mama had to watch for the mailman. In this rural area, Rupert Day, from a neighboring town, drove the mail car, an old wood-paneled station wagon. We lived near the end of the mail route, so if he passed our mailbox before Mama had addressed and sealed the envelope, she could finish quickly and hurry outside to flag him down on his way back through town. She didn't need a stamp. If she gave Mr. Day the three cents involved, he would pay the postage when he got to the Baring Post Office.

I saw Mama follow this hurry-up routine often, and once decided to try it myself. I was perhaps four years old, and certainly not able to write yet, but I found a piece of paper and made scribbles on each line. I thought my "letter" looked like the ones Mama wrote. I folded it and stood out by the mailbox. When the old station wagon stopped at our box, I handed my letter to Mr. Day and said "Take this to Beverly!" A look of amusement on his face, he said, "I certainly will, dear!"

Looking back, I'm sure Mama was my earliest inspiration for writing! She didn't have time to write those letters—she made time! There may not have been much excitement in our little home or town, but she wrote about incidentals and shared them with her dear ones. As we children grew up and scattered, she kept in touch with us by her faithful letters.

Mama has been gone for more than twenty years now. No one in the family seems to know what happened to her writing box. Still, in memory I can see it clearly, envelopes and bits of paper sticking out from under the lid, and Mama's arm clamping the top down, getting off another hurried note to cousin Lizzie.

Donna Collins Tinsley

Mama Said

I woke up from the dream weeping, "I want my Mama!" I am fifty-eight years old and she has been dead nearly twelve years. Will the need to reconnect with the one who gave me life never end? Is the cry of grief endless?

I first experienced it on the day that she died. It is uncontrollable, inconsolable. Involuntarily, it came from my mouth. A piercing scream to match the piercing pain in my heart. But in my mind's eye, I flash back forty years. I heard that same scream coming out of my mother's mouth at the news of her mother's death. It is nearly a primitive sound.

I was assaulted with thoughts of things I felt I could have done or should have done. In previous months, Mama had stayed with us for a few weeks to recover from several surgeries. We were in close contact but the week before she passed away, my children had been sick and we didn't get to see each other.

Our last conversation haunted me. We had always been close and I usually called to check on her every morning. It was about 8:10 a.m. I was in the midst of Monday morning rush. "Hi Mom, I'm on my way to take the kids to school and thought I'd see how you are feeling and what you are up to."

"I can't talk now, the nurse is here," Mama said. It was a routine house visit to check her post-surgery wound. How I wished I had said, "Call me when she leaves." Because of such a quick call I spoke no meaningful words and felt a lack of closure.

At her moment of death I thought I would be at her side. Although I reached the hospital before the ambulance got there with Mama, she had already passed away.

"Please let me go in," I begged the nurse.

"A doctor has to check her first," I was told. Assuming she was still alive, I waited, but Mama had died at home in her own bed the way she had wanted to go.

It was hard to accept not being with her at the end. I had always tried to be the "perfect daughter." As the oldest child, wasn't that part of my job description? Yet I couldn't control the uncontrollable: There is a time to be born and a time to die.

Many times when I have a dream about her I wake up and try to think of all the happy times we had. Mama was raised in the Deep South and there was always an "old saying" coming out of her mouth. She used to say, "Men will go after anything in a skirt!" but I'm sure we don't want to go there. As a teenage mother, divorced two times, she was probably trying to keep me from repeating her mistakes.

It wasn't easy for Mama to raise four children under the age of nine alone when my stepfather was put in prison. Her own mother and father had already passed away, and she was left on her own when she bypassed advice to put us in a children's home until she could get her life together. Although she was a high school dropout, she was smart enough to know it could take a long time, and she wasn't going to be without her children if she could help it. I will forever be grateful that we were kept together as a family. Just sixteen when I was born she was quite a survivor! She loved to dance and I remember thinking what a pretty mom I had as she danced to "Be-Bop-A-Lula." She adored Elvis, Dick Clark and the American Bandstand, and Chubby Checker, "Everybody do the twist." And everybody did.

Even though we moved often, she always worked and made sure there was food on the table. She had a lot of common sense and was so generous you would think she was a rich woman. Her employers loved her because not only could she work circles around everyone else, she made them laugh while she did it.

Mama used to say, "It's a great life if you don't weaken," "You have to laugh to keep from crying," and "What doesn't kill you makes you stronger."

And she always said, "What goes around comes around." That is what I would like to imitate. That is why I want to sow seeds of goodness, kindness, and love because those are the types of things I want to come back to my family. Bless your children and they will bless you. Love your husband and see what a return you get. It is the principle of "sowing and reaping."

Mama also said, "Only the good die young." This must certainly be true. She died unexpectedly at age sixty-two. Sometimes I try to imagine life with her still here. Many times I have gone over in my mind the things I wanted to do for her when she was alive. Whenever we have a family celebration or are eating at a restaurant, I often wish she were still alive and here enjoying herself. She loved to eat and used to say, "I'd rather die than not be able to eat what I want." Diabetes helped that statement come true.

Mama, if I had you back for even one day, I would treat you like a queen. I would take you anywhere you wanted to go. I would make you whatever you liked for me to cook, carrot cake or the little fancy sandwiches for a picnic. We would find a "Po Folks" restaurant even if I had to drive you from Florida to Tennessee to do it. I would take you to a movie and to the flea market. I would rub your back with alcohol and then lotion and I would wash your tired feet with warm, scented water and my tears. I would pray a blessing upon you and show you how much I love you.

These are thoughts I have when I meditate on my mother. Our relationship had its ups and downs, but it is still the strongest bond on the earth, that mother-daughter connection. I will always remember the things my Mama said and it's funny, but I seem to be saying a lot of them to my own daughters now.

Mama's Favorite Carrot Cake

2 cups self-rising flour
2 cups sugar
1-2 teaspoons ground cinnamon
4 eggs
1½ cups vegetable oil
3 cups grated carrots
¼ cup sour cream

Frosting

1 (8-oz.) package cream cheese,
   room temperature
1 stick salted butter, room temperature
1 (16-oz.) box powdered sugar
1-2 tsp. vanilla extract
½ cup chopped pecans

Preheat oven to 350 degrees. Use nonstick cooking spray on 3 (9-inch) round pans. In a large bowl, combine flour, sugar, cinnamon, and salt. Add eggs and vegetable oil. Using a hand mixer, blend until combined. Add carrots. Pour into pans. Bake for approximately 40 minutes. Remove from oven and cool for 5 minutes. Remove from pans, and allow to cool completely before frosting.

Frosting: Add all ingredients, except nuts, into medium bowl and beat until creamy using mixer. Stir in nuts. Spread frosting on top of each cake layer. Stack cakes on serving plate and serve with love.

Diane Taylor

What's in a Word?

Sometimes a word will take you back. I recently read *The Blue Castle* by L.M. Montgomery, and in the story, several men and women were "hankering" to do things they either had never done, or hadn't done in a long time. It's the first time I have seen that word in print, but it's a word I'm very familiar with because I grew up with it. I didn't use it myself, but my mother did.

Where does "hanker" come from? Where did it go? And has anyone ever hankered for a hanky? Because my mother also used hankies (not handkerchiefs). She was born in 1915 in Tweed, Ontario, to a Manx father and German mother, and moved to Uxbridge with her husband and two girls in 1952, ten years after L.M. Montgomery died. My mom was born a Kissack, which is a very common Manx family name.

I was a teenager in the '50s, and I can hear my mother saying in the month of May, after putting out tomato plants, her voice excited like a child's, heated like a lover's, "Ooooh, I'm hankering for fresh tomatoes!" The word expresses longing, desire, deep delight. Her voice would rise to a high pitch on the "hank" part of hankering, and taper off to a husky contralto on the "toes" of tomatoes almost in sight. Her whole body was remembering the tart and fleshy sweetness. Then, the waiting. The watering, the weeding, the mulching, the staking, the stalking wild tomato worms. Then her joyous "Look!" when the first small green nuggets appeared nestled in the pungent foliage.

The day came in August when the first ripe tomatoes were pounced upon, rushed into the house, and across the kitchen to the sink. I am fifteen again, and can see Mom peeling her first miracle, salting it, then hunching over the sink, reddish-brown hair falling over her cheeks, and chomping down the whole tomato like an apple. She moans and slurps, pink juice and yellow seeds dribbling down her chin, her small-boned fingers gently carrying the soft red flesh of the fruit to her waiting mouth over and over until it is gone. "This is the best way," she purrs, licking her lips, running her hands that are dripping with the blood of the fruit under the cold water tap, then drying them on her apron. The subtle scent of sweet acidity reaches me, elbows on the counter, as I am totally immersed in her immersion.

September is calmer...plates of peeled, sliced, laid-back tomatoes grace every table. Peeled, she explained when I asked once, to maintain the purity of the texture, so that the sensation of softness not be impeded by the intrusive and chewy thin skin. She did this for us, her husband and two girls, for the pleasure of our palates. To honour us. To honour the harvest.

October, just a few frosty foundlings from the field. November, none! No! It's okay, though, because there is the satiated memory. Soon, soon comes the rebirth of longing. And then the time will come when the huntress-gatherer in my mother will emerge again.

I don't know if my mother read *The Blue Castle*. I do know that she read Lucy Maud's collected journals. She told me that this author of *Anne of Green Gables* was unhappy with the constraints and duties of her life as a minister's wife in the small—population a few hundred—town of Leaskdale, which was six miles north of Uxbridge where we were living. Lucy Maud, she said, wrote to escape the judgmental pressures that insisted she be a certain way. She struggled with both depression and the side effects of the barbiturates, prescribed to relieve her psychological pain. But hold on. Is depression a consequence of oppression? Of repression? The Victorian era was still in full swing in the '30s and '40s, and longer, in small town Ontario.

Mom was saying, I think, that here was another woman like herself. A woman who hankered for things to be different. Mona, my mother, wanted to go dancing, to have a man who would consult her before he brought home bright orange carpet for the dining room, to have a cook so she would be freed up from mundane chores to write or read, to continue her career as an RN so she could be doing something useful, to not be counting pennies when other families were buying new cars, to throw out the lisle stockings that never kept her or her girls warm and bring on the slacks. This latter she did. She fired off letters to the school board and local paper stating her case...and won. Mom changed, if not the face of the town, at least the legs.

My mother bought books. Her room was lined with them. She had a relationship with the authors, writing notes to them in the margins. She, like Lucy Maud, was a woman who lived in a time of hankering. They were, as Anne Shirley would say, kindred spirits.

Mom, you died ten years ago, and I don't know if you can see me writing these words. We don't know about things like that, do we? In case you can, let me tell you "thank you" for freeing my legs from lisle stockings and my mind from ordinary thoughts. Books were your window on the world, and that view became mine. You and I are also kindred spirits.

So you see where a word can take you.

Juanita Wier Nobles

Daily Meal Time,
Almost Lost in Today's World

My mother was a superb cook. Evening meals with the whole family were as regular as clockwork, and many of them are still imbedded in my memory. At five o'clock every day, we sat down to a delicious meal. Nobody was allowed to be late and make the others wait. While we ate, we talked. Daddy asked me about school. Sometimes my little brother told about something he did. My grandpa always told us how hard he had worked that day. Mother and my grandmother told about their day too. Jokes and laughter were a part of our family life as we all sat around the table and shared together. We learned about each other as we enjoyed good food and good conversation.

When I ate at my friend's house, no talking was allowed. They listened to the radio while they ate. I preferred the way we did it at our house.

Because of the Great Depression, my parents and my mother's parents pooled their resources, and we lived together. Mother and Mama, my grandmother, worked as a team in the kitchen. Daddy was a carpenter and my grandfather, Papa, was a bricklayer. The men came home hungry and were never disappointed when they saw steaming platters of food, and goblets filled with refreshing iced tea or milk. A pie or a cake awaited us most days, sitting in a prominent position on the kitchen counter. Papa gave Mother $35 every week to buy groceries to feed our large extended family and she always managed to buy nutritious food and make mouthwatering, balanced meals.

Besides my parents and grandparents, there were three children. I was first, my brother came six years later, and when I was eleven, my sister was born. Another sister was born after I was out of high school.

I can still see the faces around that table. At every meal, Papa "saucered and blowed" his coffee. He poured a small portion of coffee into his saucer, blew on it to cool it, then drank it from the saucer. He also ate one food at a time. He ate all his corn, then all his potatoes, then his meat, until he finished his dessert. His bushy, white eyebrows went up and down as he visibly enjoyed his food, while drinking cold coffee from his saucer.

During the lean years of the 1940s, aunts, uncles, and cousins stopped by our house regularly and hung around until a meal was served. They knew good food would be on the table, and there would always be enough for one or two extra people. Once a week, we had liver and onions. Mother insisted that we eat it to build up our blood. I hated it, but I endured it because we children had to eat what was on our plates. For some reason, the uncles and cousins didn't show up on that day. They didn't like that dish, either.

My job was to set the table. The knives and spoons had to be on the left side of the plate, with the forks and a folded cloth napkin on the right. If it wasn't right, I had to do it over. A tablecloth always covered the table. I don't remember whether that was because of Mother's preference for a nice-looking table or if the table was old and scratched and she wanted it covered.

A staple in the part of Texas where we lived was pinto beans and cornbread. At our house, it was served at least once a week and sometimes more often. Mother would wash the beans carefully, but no matter how hard she tried, a wayward stone would be in the bowl. Inevitably, the stone ended up on my dad's plate. When he bit down on the stone, he yelled and grabbed his cheek. Funny, this didn't happen to anybody else; it was always Daddy. Pinto beans, cooked with a bit of bacon or ham and spooned over the hot cornbread, made an inexpensive, filling meal.

One day, while the beans were cooking, Mother said to me, "Juanita, go stir the beans and tell me how they look."

I went to the kitchen, lifted the lid, stirred the beans, then yelled back, "What are they supposed to look like?" I failed that cooking test.

We kept chickens in our yard, and several times a week, chicken was on the menu. My grandmother would go out and chase a chicken until she caught it. Then she grabbed it by the neck and swung it round and round. "Wringing a chicken's neck" was the quickest way to kill it so it could be prepared for cooking. When the head came off in her hand, she threw the chicken down on the ground. I watched as it flopped around until it finally lay still. Then she would pick it up, take it to a table in the yard, and dip it several times into boiling water. Sometimes I helped her pluck out the feathers.

In the house, Mama cut the chicken into pieces, coated them heavily with flour, salt, and pepper, then fried them in grease. We children took turns choosing the pulley bone, sometimes called the wishbone, cut from the chicken breast. After eating the delicious meat, two of us would hold the bone over the table. We closed our eyes, made a wish, and pulled it apart. The one with the longest part of the bone was supposed to get his or her wish.

Nothing was wasted in those days; everything was used to its fullest capacity. A large coffee can sat on the stove, and every morning after cooking breakfast, Mother poured the leftover bacon grease into it. This grease was used to fry meat for supper. Most of the time, any kind of meat was fried and served with creamy gravy. Many vegetables, too, were fried. We sometimes had fried okra, fried squash, fried green tomatoes, and several times a week we had fried potatoes. Cholesterol had not yet become a household word.

Macaroni and cheese was my favorite. Often, I put a serving of mac and cheese on my plate, and asked, "When I finish this, may I have some more?" before I even had a bite.

Our table was crowded with seven people around it. When seated in my big chair, I had a habit of drawing my knees up to my chin. Mother would poke my knee with her fork and say, "Does that knee want a bite?" Of course, my knees went down, and if they came back up, she did it again. She taught me to sit properly at the table, to keep my elbows close to my body, and to wipe my face with a napkin. Sometimes, when I had eaten my meal, I was granted the privilege of leaving the table early if I asked politely, "May I please be excused?" Most of the time, though, I had to stay seated until Daddy and Papa were ready to leave the table. Daddy squeezed Mother's hand after every meal. Then he leaned over, kissed her on the cheek, and said, "Thank you, Baby."

I appreciate my mother's efforts to teach us table manners, and so many more things, in that quieter, less frantic world. My memories of good food are accompanied by the love I witnessed between my parents. That love spread around the table to all of us. Along with the delectable food, it was something I could count on.

Mac 'n' Cheese

8 oz. elbow macaroni.
Boil in salted water. Leave in water for 15 minutes. Do not drain until you are ready to add sauce. Macaroni will puff up and become very large as it sits in the water.

Sauce:

1 stick margarine, melted
3 Tbsp. flour
1½ tsp. salt.
pepper to taste
6 cups warm milk
6 ounces Cheese Whiz (you cannot substitute for this ingredient)

Stir all sauce ingredients together.
Drain macaroni and add it, stirring.
Bake in 9x13 pan for 30 minutes at 350 degrees.
Sauce will continue to set after you remove it from the oven.
Add 8 ounces grated cheddar or American cheese to top and bake 5 or 10 minutes more.

This will be very soupy when you put it in the oven, but trust me, it will be wonderful when it is done.

Texas Corn Bread

Mix dry ingredients.

1 cup yellow cornmeal
1 cup flour
1 tsp. salt
3 tsp. baking powder
¼ cup sugar
2 eggs, beaten
1 cup milk

Make a well and add remaining ingredients. Mix gently. Spoon into hot pan.

This is best if cooked in an iron skillet. If you don't have one, grease a square 8x8 pan in this manner: Put about 2 tablespoons of butter in the pan, and heat the pan in the oven until the butter melts. Then pour in cornbread mixture and cook for 20 to 25 minutes at 425 degrees.

Sherrie Ward Murphree

Perfumed Pride

I can't forget a certain pleasant scent that I grew up with—emanating from my mother. Perhaps I smelled this elegance before I was born.

"Miss Etiquette" described Mother, Dorothy Lorene Mangum, a small town girl from Poteet, Texas, south of San Antonio. At seventeen she graduated from high school and married only weeks later on her eighteenth birthday. Pretty, happy, and naïve sum up her situation. My daddy, Woodson Wilber Ward, was a mature twenty-two-year old college student.

Five years later in 1941, Mother and Daddy moved to Washington D.C. where Daddy worked for the Veterans Administration. By then God had adorned their lives with Janice and Beverly. As payment to the doctor for delivering Janice, my parents gave the doctor a cow. I, the third girl, would be the first in our family born in a hospital.

Mother made mental plans to go see the big city doctor when she suspected her third pregnancy. It became a unique experience for her because she'd never been to a doctor. At that time expressions such as "expecting" or "pg" were sometimes substituted for the word pregnant. When Mother called the doctor's office to make an appointment, the receptionist said, "Bring in a urine specimen." Mother asked Daddy what that meant. This simple act of taking a specimen presented as much dread as labour pains to her—a real challenge for someone so prim and private.

The outhouse she used growing up—and that I used a few times—could not have known the likes of a Chanel No. 5 scent but, by George, the specimen she took to the doctor was going to have a camouflaged smell and look as glamorous as possible. What container could she use?

Resourceful Mother decided on the use of an empty bottle of Evening in Paris that she had on hand. This was the popular perfume of her era, and rest assured Paris was a place she only dreamed of visiting. When we were young children we bought this perfume—actually cologne—as a gift for Mother at a downtown variety store. She believed the bottles too attractive to throw away; therefore, through the years she used these empty bottles as decorations on her dresser.

With a tidbit of trouble, she'd use one of these bottles to collect the doctor's request.

Task completed, she dressed up in heels and hat and boarded the streetcar, the royal blue Evening in Paris bottle with its known-only-to-her contents snuggled in an inside pocket of her purse. A thief would have been disappointed.

At the doctor's office, Mother handed the bottle to the nurse. We will never know what the nurse and the lab examiner must have thought of the unusual specimen container. I'm just trusting they didn't forget the bottle's contents and dab some behind each ear before the bottle got a label. Mother accomplished her mission without spilling an ounce of her pride or anything else. In short, Mother's specimen proved vibrant and I turned out to be healthy.

Thankfully her pride didn't "go before destruction." She wore Evening in Paris for years.

So there you have it, progeny. That's a fragrant anecdotal story about the grandmother and great-grandmother you loved.

Kathleen M. Martin

A Daughter's Memories

When I think of my mum, I think of all her sayings. She seemed to have one for most of life's events. The one I practice most often is, "Start the way you mean to finish."

It is this quote that has prompted me to finish this short story about my mother, Catherine Millar Brown, born October 1, 1909, in a small town in Perthshire, Scotland.

Kate, as she'd be called, was the firstborn of four children. Her father, John Brown, married the widow, Martha McKay Jamieson, who had been left with five children.

I recall the fondness in her voice when she spoke of her father, a kind, gentle man whom she idealized. Her love for the Salvation Army and the Sunday evening prayer meetings always met with favour with her dad.

"Just you go, lass," he'd say, and hand her a few coppers for the collection plate. Kate appreciated this gesture, knowing the jobs to help her mother were being excused.

On her eighth birthday her father gave her a large spiral shell. As a child, I remember Mum allowing my brother, sister, and me to take turns listening to the sea's echo, while carefully holding the shell.

Sadly, I never met my grandfather, for he died when my mum was ten years old. While her mother took on an early morning cleaning job, my mum had the responsibility of getting her younger siblings up and ready for school.

Mum loved poetry and had a phenomenal memory for reciting ten or more verses of poems to us as children at bedtime. The poem titled "Cuddle Doon" told the story of three children who slept in the same bed, and wouldn't go to sleep—each child complaining about another's arms or legs being in the way. The next poem, "Waken Up," told another tale of the mother trying to awaken her children in the morning. I never tired of hearing these poems, or the times Mum went up the knock, a hillock, where picking berries and gathering firewood was fun.

"I always wanted to be on the stage," she'd tell me. "But the closest I ever got to it was scrubbing it." I found this a sad reflection of an unfulfilled dream, for she had settled for "bringing her wants down to her means."

At fifteen years old, when I was in my last few weeks of high school, I said to my mum, "I don't want to leave school. My teachers told yer Granny I was clever, and it was a pity I needed to leave school."

I felt she understood the sense of loss for what could have been for me—and for her.

She had left home around her thirteenth birthday, just as her sisters, Bella and Nell, had done years before. She then went into service for a well-to-do family, miles from home, in St. Andrews. She served as a housemaid, helped look after the children, and cleaned and polished the black lead grate. Working from dawn to dusk, and often during the night, if one of the children awoke, she was allowed only one half day off per week.

The Jamiesons and the Browns never thought of one another as not being a sister or a brother to the other. In reflection, my mum modelled the importance of family. I recall as a child we could say we disliked someone, but never use the word "hate" as a feeling.

Her greatest gift to her children was her stories. Her older brothers, Alec and Archie, were sent off at an early age to live on a farm as a helper. Robert was different; he went into service, and after moving through the ranks of the gentry, later moved to London and became a butler.

Mum adored her brother John, and his gentle, good nature. Her younger sister, Lizzie, the sickly one as a child, had a difficult nature. Mum would say it was because she had been treated as a "hot house plant," and got away with tantrums when she wanted her own way. Lizzie didn't leave home to work in service, but worked in a local laundry. Jessie, the youngest of the Brown children, never left for service due to developing asthma; she lived with my grandmother all her life.

Like her brothers and sisters before her, my mum worked to send money home to her mother. The family unit was ever present in spirit.

When my mum married in 1936 and moved to the city of Dundee, she wearied for her family, the small town, and pastoral surroundings. All her in-laws lived close by, and although she got along with everyone, their dialect and the big city mentality—such as never meeting someone from childhood—made it a difficult adjustment. The lack of the family unit in this large family was also incomprehensible to her, as she manoeuvred through the maze of who had a falling out with whom. It might be brother with brother, sister with sister, or brother and sister, often holding grudges for months, sometimes years. "When one's the fire, the other has to be the water."

Mum worked most of her life. During World War II, once we were all in school, she worked on an assembly line for the war effort. During my dad's five years in the army, Mum was our constant, dependable parent, and our moral compass.

Her background in the Salvation Army was her anchor in Dundee. She'd bribe us children with a treat of chips and peas from a street vendor if we'd go with her to a meeting. Her connection to the Army reminds me of my favourite times, especially bedtime. Mum would shake the tambourine, and with the flat of her hand, tap the wooden frame. We followed her around the kitchen into our bedroom singing Salvation Army hymns such as "Fishers of Men" and "Deep and Wide."

Mum's reputation for having a great memory took her beyond poetry to remembering dates. Not only significant events of the times, but birthdates and wedding anniversaries of nieces and nephews, along with important dates of all her in-laws.

Recently, I came across a letter I wrote to my mum the day before my eleventh birthday. I had gone back to stay with my Aunty Jessie after my granny died. Mum had asked me to do this. I remember not wanting to do it, because I'd miss school and my pals.

In the letter, written in cursive writing, using black ink with a pen with a nib, I offered to loan my mum four shillings to help buy a wedding gift for a cousin soon to be married, and for her not to worry about getting me anything for my birthday. I believe my gesture came through witnessing the kindness of my mum.

In their late fifties, my mum and dad immigrated to Canada, for their children and grandchildren were all here.

When Mum was in her seventies, she sadly began to need care as she developed Alzheimer's disease. The following is an excerpt I wrote based on my thoughts during a visit. I watched her staring at herself in the dressing table mirror, and tried to imagine what she was thinking.

My dark eyes look empty. I'm looking for words I've long forgotten. I'm looking for me. I have dropped snippets of my life. My rich fertile memory has gone, now barren spaces exist. Memory is life's photo album of family, places, and events. My album has pages missing.

I see images of the distant past. I am young. I have bright sparkling eyes. The mirror offers a different image, someone with wrinkles, sad eyes, and grey hair. It's someone I don't know.

Time has stolen my thoughts. Sometimes, the thick mist that dims my mind lifts, just like the sun clearing the mist from the mountaintop. There's a lassie here. I don't know her.

"You're a bonnie lassie," Mum told me earlier that day. "Whose lassie are you?"

"I'm your lassie," I answered, taking her hand. "I get my good looks from you."

Within minutes our relationship was forgotten. Mum then began speaking about her mother and how they had been out on a walk.

When my mum died, we saved her ashes and buried her with her mother and her sister Jessie in Crieff, Perthshire.

Donna Lee Shane Loomis

Mom and Birthdays

When I was a child, birthdays were memorable. Mother knew how to make them that way. I knew she listened for our requests and shopped well ahead of time to provide special gifts. Who doesn't like presents? And ours were exciting both in content and appearance. The thrill was enhanced by the wrapping. Each one had either store-bought wrapping paper or the comic strips from the newspaper.

I don't remember many of the actual gifts but I do remember the love poured into them. Sometimes the hum of the sewing machine could be heard late into the night. At gift time I found Mother's loving hands had made me a new dress, summer short set, or pajamas. She gave the beautiful new garments special touches such as heart-shaped pockets, lace-trimmed collars, or teddy bear buttons, assuring me this gift was made especially for me. Whether the gift was handmade or something she knew I wanted from the store it was always exactly right. I do remember wanting a stuffed cat. It was yellow and so soft and snuggly. Mom was not fond of stuffed toys but she knew I was. So imagine that extra feeling of being loved when one of those beautifully wrapped boxes exposed the coveted cat.

As for food, my sisters and I got to pick the menu for our special dinner and the kind of homemade birthday cake we wanted. Oh, yum! I can taste it even now. My favorites, homemade, of course: chicken and noodles or Swiss steak with her delicious tomato gravy over fresh mashed potatoes. I almost always requested bananas and peanuts as a side dish and chocolate cake for dessert.

Mother learned to cook growing up on the farm where she helped my grandma keep her hired hands fed. The tradition of cooking passed through the generations and offered the most tempting foods ever. The portions served were reminiscent of her farm days and cooking for hungry workers. There was always plenty.

Dinner was a party in itself. Sometimes the guests were family friends like the Opsahls, Roes, and Thomases. Almost always it was Grandma and Aunt Polly. Occasionally, because I am lucky enough to have a summer birthday, it was a party with friends and a backyard picnic with games and, of course, presents.

Anyone who knows me knows that patience isn't my greatest virtue, add the excitement of my birthday and…well you get the picture. A couple of days until my birthday, excitement churned inside me. I could hardly stand still. How would I ever make it two more days?

I must have been driving Mother crazy. I remember being in the kitchen while she was preparing supper and she said, "Donna, would you please find something to do and settle down."

"Mommy, I just can't wait until my birthday."

I remember her knowing smile and simple statement, "I don't think you have any choice."

That wasn't the response I wanted. Couldn't we speed it up somehow?

Even though we lived in the city, Mother continued to work hard, long, farmer's hours. It wasn't until I became a mother that I fully appreciated, actually marveled, at her ability to get it all done and still make your special day seem like it was all about you.

My mouth is watering as I'm writing this. I wish that it was my birthday, I was still a little girl, and Mom was here to cook for me. Granted, I'm an adult now which makes me much more appreciative of what Mom did to make those memories. I can prepare her recipes but for some reason Mom's were just better.

Do you suppose it was the love she tucked inside? I pray as my children and grandchildren grow they, too, will feel that special love through these traditions I've carried on in their lives.

The following is one of my favorite recipes from Mom's file.

Chicken and Noodles

1 whole stewing chicken or frying chicken
1 cup diced celery
1 cup chopped onions
½ tsp. salt & pepper

I remember smelling the simmering chicken. Mother cooked it with some chopped celery and onions to enhance the flavour. It usually boiled all day until the meat was falling off the bone (would also work well in a Crock-Pot), cool enough to strip the bones.

Place the meat back in the broth bringing it back to a boil, then add noodles (recipe below).

Homemade Egg Noodles

You can prepare this recipe the night before so after work you can add to chicken that's been cooking in the Crock-Pot all day.

1 beaten egg
2 Tbsp. milk
½ tsp. salt
1 cup sifted all-purpose flour (enough to make stiff dough)

Roll very thin on floured surface; let stand 20 minutes. Then roll up loosely; slice ¼-inch wide; unroll, spread out, and let dry 1 hour (produces long noodles, you may cut them shorter if preferred). (If desired, store in container in the refrigerator.) Requires a little bit of work and time but nothing compares to the taste. YUM!

Linda Jett

Seeds of Faith

The room's dim lights contrasted with the bright fall day outside. The empty corridor, the walls with no windows, the hum of machines, all enhanced the fact that I was buried deep inside the local hospital. Four pictures later and a brief exchange with the technician, I finished my twentieth annual mammogram.

At home, ten minutes later, classical music flowed from my kitchen. Sun streamed through my dirty dining room window as I sorted through dried, mottled brown stalks spread across the table, looking like summer's sad leftovers. Slowly, I rubbed the outer layers from the dried petals of the money plant that grew beside my front walk. Undressed, the innermost layer shimmered like translucent paper. *Is this how fairy wings look?* I wondered as I arranged them in a vase for our table.

Was it the plants or the mammogram that moved me back through the years to my childhood? My mother adorned our house with these very same plants! She died twenty-three years ago at seventy from breast cancer. Do I grow these plants in memory of her? While my hands stayed busy, I again retreated into a world where I carried on a one-sided conversation with her.

"Mom, I have so many questions, so many pieces of life's puzzle that don't quite fit into my desire for a tidy life. You invested your life in me, your only child. You curled my hair in Shirley Temple curls. You designed matching dresses for me, my doll, and my girlfriend. You read two story books and a Bible story every single night, and then waited patiently while I counted the objects stored under my pillow before you tucked me in with prayer. You comforted me in the night when I cried out because my imaginary gorilla was trying to catch me again. You painted my bedroom walls with nursery rhymes and installed a light on the wall by my bunk bed to scare away monsters lurking in the dark. You sewed circle skirts and laughed as I twirled until I grew dizzy. You praised my efforts when I broke into poetry. You protected my childlike innocence from the world's harsh realties. How much of your reality did I miss in my preoccupation with myself?

"Looking back, I wonder. How did it feel when Dad plowed under the colourful bachelor buttons we delighted in, calling them weeds? How often did his thoughtlessness wound your soul and your desire for beauty? Yet, in your last years Dad's rough farmer hands learned to give you Coumadin shots, each leaving ugly bruises. He cried as he said, 'I don't want to hurt you.' Later you confided that the change in your marriage was worth the years of cancer.

"And me? How many ways did I drive a stake through your tender heart? When I left my first marriage with no explanation, how did you come to terms with the pain caused by my rash decision? Still you chose to love both me and my ex-husband. And years later you found room in your heart to welcome my second husband.

"I seldom saw you cry and I don't remember you ever speaking harsh critical words about anyone, no matter how hurtful their behavior. Instead of growing bitter over life's injustices, you remained sweet. Was it because you poured your heart out to God in private while you tended your gardens?

"Cancer stripped away the protective layers of your personality like a soul shedding its skin, didn't it? Once you faced the fear of death, you seemed quiet, peaceful, and more transparent than I'd ever seen. You shared bits of your life that you'd kept locked away. Together we planned your funeral, laughing and crying, sometimes in the same breath.

"Now that I'm a grandma, I understand why you spent all those hours sewing gifts for your grandchildren—your way of enveloping them in your love. I appreciate your concentrated cooking as you anticipated our visits. Following your death, as I packed your boxes of recipes and cookbooks, I understood that our visits gave you an opportunity to experiment with new recipes, an ingenious way around Dad's meat and potatoes boundaries.

"I tried a new pork tenderloin recipe the other night and longed to share the results with you. Do you know that your love of cooking, sewing, gardening, reading, and creating forms the core of who I am? Now I sew quilts and beanbag chairs for my grandkids and cook muffins for them weekly. We routinely pore through my shelves of children's books.

"But, more importantly, are the lasting effects of your prayers. Over the years I've been comforted, knowing that your prayers exist outside time as I understand it. They still form building blocks in the foundation of my faith, a security that does not depend on circumstances or your earthly presence. How I long to be as faithful in prayer for my growing family as you were."

* * *

Each fall when my I arrange my dried money plants, I ask myself, *Am I following Mom's example? Is my life like this money plant? Am I letting life's circumstances rub off the ugly outer layers, producing seeds of hope for future generations? Can my children and grandchildren glimpse a translucent beauty hidden among the wrinkles, skin tags, lost waist line, and chin hairs when they watch me? I pray my life leaves seeds of faith that guide them through life's trials the way Mom's life still leads me over two decades after her death.*

Lindsay Harrel

Snapshots of My Mother

I was eight. I remember visiting my mom in the hospital for the first time: the familiar stench of urine lingering in the air like an invisible fog; her, lying in bed, tubes stuck in her veins like coiled sleeping snakes. She had lost her short brown hair and her energy from the chemotherapy; she tried spooning the green hospital Jell-O into her mouth, but her hands shook. My four-year-old brother and I climbed up onto the bed next to her, the rough sheets under us; we lay still, afraid to hurt her.

She kept a journal. "I love my family so much. Please, God, heal my body so I don't leave them."

She was healed and lived cancer-free for seven years. She said she saw life as a gift and was "determined to do better."

* * *

My mother loved to give gifts. Once she sat at the kitchen table, leaning over and, holding a tiny wooden angel in her left hand, painted a face on the craft with the thin-tipped paintbrush in her right hand. She was making pins for all the women at work.

I walked into the room; she looked up, smiled her kind of smile: high cheekbones raised almost to her eyes, her thin lips stretched from middle of cheek to middle of cheek.

* * *

I can see her smiling, standing in the tile-floored kitchen, barefoot. A small wooden sign hung on the window next to the stove: "Cooking makes you ugly." She thought it was funny when she bought it, laughed aloud—short, staccato outbursts from the back of her throat, like that of a donkey, but not annoying. Never annoying.

The air smelled of spaghetti and Italian spices. She was cooking for someone in her Sunday school class who was sick. She cooked often for others or wrote them encouraging letters on personally stamped cards.

* * *

She sat in the rocking chair next to her bedroom window reading her Bible, leaning intently over it and scouring the pages for something. I crept quietly into the room, peered at her in secret.

Looking up at me, she shook her head, half-smiling. "I have so much to learn."

* * *

I was a crying thirteen-year-old lying in her arms. Her hands stroked my head, the fingers curving over every ponytail-holder crease in my hair. She sang from a book she'd read to me as a child, her soft tones cracking slightly when she reached the higher notes: "I'll love you forever, I'll like you for always, as long as I'm living, my baby you'll be."*

She looked down, made eye contact with me, said, "I don't like that—you'll always be my baby, no matter what. And I love you."

"I love you more," I whispered, for a moment forgetting my sadness.

"I love you most-est," she shot back, softly laughing.

"I love you more most-est." I loved this game. And here came the grand finale—she'd "win" this round…

"I love you up, down, around and back again." She pursed her lips together in a half-smile.

* * *

She stood next to my dad on Easter. I held up the camera. "Smile. And kiss." They kissed—simple, eyes closed, mouths curved in a smile—longer than it took to take the picture.

* * *

My mother threw up blood in September 2000—and then a whirl of tests and surgery; chemotherapy in a pill; twenty-five pain pills every three hours, every day, for a year: four more years of what some called a life "lacking in quality." But she swept the floor despite the walker she had to use for balance, and she kept on reading that Bible, praying, asking for strength…

Then September 10, 2004. In her dimly lit bedroom she lay on her king-sized bed, the green comforter pulled up to expose her cold swollen feet and thinned legs, outlined like a skeleton's: I could see the shape of every bone. Her arms and hands stretched themselves down her sides, blood resting under the thin skin and spotting like bruises. Her short, shallow breaths came only by sheer mechanical impulse, a car engine sputtering, trying desperately to hold out till the end of the journey.

Now, all I could do was hold her hand, lay there, wait, my dad and brother doing the same. My nana sobbed on the chair next to the bed. "No, God. Not yet. Don't take her. Heal her."

7:20 a.m. Her chest stopped moving up and down, and even though her mouth kept opening and closing (a mere bodily compulsion) for a full minute after, we knew she was gone.

Upon her death, something awakened in me. I realized that she had lived the kind of life we all long for—one full of purpose and compassion—and she had never made it a secret that her strength had come from faith in God. Though her sorrows were great, though the valleys were sometimes deeper than the mountains were tall, though her body had deteriorated—she had lived like there was a reason for it all, something beyond herself.

The words she once spoke to me ring in my head even now: "Lindsay, if only one person comes to know God because of my sufferings, it will all have been worth it in the end."

In the end, I want to really live, just like Mom. Lord, help me. I want to live.

*Robert Munsch, *Love You Forever*
(Willowdale, Ontario, Canada: Firefly Books Ltd.,
text copyright © 1987 by Bob Munsch Enterprises, Ltd.).

Peter Hardt

The Overflowing Cup

My mother is the humble cup,
 Formed by the Potter's hand.
Her heavenly Father had a dream,
 He's used her in His plan.

Because she let Him lead her life,
 Her cup has overflown
With blessing upon blessing
 To all of those she's known.

Elaine Hardt

Mother's Hands

When I was a baby (and she was young)
her hands were soft and smooth;
dressing, caressing,
bathing, and feeding,
doing for me what I was needing.

When I was a toddler (and she was older)
her hands were kind and firm;
caring, sharing
teaching by showing,
helping, and scolding, as I was growing.

When I was in school she grew older still.
Her hands were able and strong;
mixing, fixing,
sewing and mending,
washing, cooking, giving, and lending.

When I was a teen she seemed much older.
Her hands were rough and worn,
baking, making,
driving the car,
running the errands, both near and far.

When I married and left the years passed along.
Her hands were busy still;
raising the others,
my sisters and brother,
always toiling —that was my mother!

Now I am older and she is aging
her hands, misshapen and weak,
trembling, aching,
medicine-taking,
folding in prayer, brushing a tear.

Soon she will be leaving her old, crippled body,
meeting her Maker up there,
raising, praising
with hands made new
serving her Savior eternity through!

Mother's mother was extremely crippled by arthritis, and she died at age thirty-six. Mama started getting crippled after having eight kids. She died at age sixty-one. None of us have that crippling arthritis, for which we are thankful. I wrote this poem for Mother and she died two years later, so I was glad she got to see my thoughts down on paper. She was a dear, sweet, uncomplaining Christian.

Janice Green

Mama's Hands

Last Sunday I was moved by the words of the anthem the choir sang. Being one of the choir members, the words had more time to sink in for me than for most who heard the song only once. The name of the anthem was "His Hands," and it was so touching as it described the multitude of ways Jesus showed us His love through His hands—beginning with His healing and other miracles He performed, including feeding the multitudes and ending with His crucifixion and resurrection. By Sunday afternoon I was reflecting on the song and thinking about other people who have shown love to me through their hands, and it was my mother who first came to my mind.

Mama was the best back-scratcher anyone could ask for. Her nails were smooth and even and she worked from top to bottom making sure not to miss any spots. How many times she scratched my back as a child, I will never know, but neither will I forget.

My earliest memories of Mama's hands were of her sewing. When we lived in Gary, Indiana, in the post-World War II era, she sewed dresses for me out of shirt scraps from a nearby shirt factory. I had some of the nicest dresses that could be worn during those years. My sister Joan, cousins Marcia, Terri, and Vicki, and a neighbour girl and I all benefited from those shirt scraps and Mama's creativity.

With so many brothers and sisters, money stretched only so far. Consequently, not all of Mama's sewing was for pretty dresses. I remember a time when she even sewed panties (or maybe they were bloomers—my understanding was somewhat limited as you will see). I also remember hearing her say something one day to the effect that she wasn't wearing any underwear. So I took it in my young head that when women were grown, they stopped wearing them. I decided that I wanted to be grown like Mama and went outside in my dress—without any panties. It wasn't long before Mama saw me out the window and became aware of the missing garment. She quickly called me in to ask why I wasn't wearing them, and then she explained to me that women didn't stop wearing panties when they grew up, but that she just didn't have any left that were wearable. I suspect it wasn't long after that before she bought or made some for herself. I wonder if those were the panties I remember seeing her make.

Another early memory of Mama's hands was of curling my hair. After Saturday night baths, Mama would towel dry my hair and use bobby pins to set the curls. I was so proud of my curly hair on Sunday mornings.

Not all my memories of Mama's hands were as pleasant, though I recall them with appreciation, as I now understand that they were there for the purpose of developing my character and self-discipline. I'll never forget the time I ran when she called me because I had done something wrong, and I knew she was going to spank me. Instead of getting one spanking, I got two. I have long since forgotten what the first spanking was for, but I never ran from Mama again.

Mama kept most of her spankings within the family, but there were two occasions I recall where she caught off guard an unsuspecting misbehaving youngster that was not her own. My cousin Marcia was one of the recipients. (I think the incident had something to do with the right way and the wrong way to get a shampoo.) The other recipient was a neighbour boy in Rochester, Indiana, who wouldn't listen when she told him to stop doing something that was dangerous to others around him.

Something else that Mama did with her hands was to hold the storybooks she read to us. I remember a Bible story book that she must have read to me quite often. Once I recall being praised in Sunday school for being a good listener. I just smiled, but I really knew I didn't deserve the praise since I hadn't been listening at all, I just knew the answer from the stories Mama had read to me. As we all grew older, I remember other books Mama read to us. I'll never forget her voice ringing out, "Tom, Tom, come home, Tom!" as she read *Tom Sawyer* to us more than once.

Mama's hands were hard-working hands that never quit. When we lived on the farm in Rochester, she worked hard and did whatever jobs needed to be done. They planted, drove a tractor, pulled weeds, picked the harvest, sold vegetables to customers who came to our house, and kept up with meals and laundry for five youngsters. Mealtime didn't come easily either. Before we remodeled the house, she cooked on a woodstove in the old kitchen, stoking up a fire burning wood and corncobs for fuel. Ten years later, when we camped out for two summers (11 weeks and 7 weeks) on Center Hill Lake in Tennessee, she took it all in stride once again. Using only a Coleman camp stove, keeping the small tank on the side filled with white gasoline, and keeping the pressure pumped up, she kept us well fed.

Mama's hands made beautiful music. We have had a piano almost everywhere we lived, and I've enjoyed many wonderful hours around the piano singing with family members and relatives. If Mama didn't have the music, she just played what she could from memory, and she played a little by ear as well. Eventually she bought an organ and has thoroughly enjoyed it. She had other less-known musical talents as well. When I was about seven or eight I was given a ukulele for Christmas. Mama tuned it up, played, and sang. One favorite started out, "I took my gal to the ball one night, It was a fancy hop..." My youngest brother, Paul Wayne, learned the chorus to that song and sang it for us often.

Mama's hands have always been creative. On the farm there was little time for creativity, but as soon as we moved to Lapel, Indiana, her creativity came back to life. She was soon making beautiful candles, floral arrangements, and dried weed arrangements. She even operated her own store in the living room of the upstairs apartment in our house where she sold her lovely arrangements.

She also became the expert on decorating for church events. At the end of my senior year in high school, she made the decorations for a banquet to honor the graduates. The take-home favors were hand-blown painted eggs. Inside each egg was a diorama scene that included a tiny graduation cap and a rolled and tied "diploma," all handmade, of course. I am sure that many of my classmates treasured their eggs for years. After having decorated for banquets for several years, Mama put together a small book called *Pauline's Pretty Party Plans*, showing her different party ideas and how to make them. Daddy helped her to print the copies using the old mimeograph duplicating machine he still had from the time he was a church pastor. The books were advertised in a craft magazine and sold for $1 each.

In Murfreesboro, Tennessee, Mama found other craft projects that she enjoyed. These included cross-stitch, hand decorated stationery, plaster of Paris figures, and many others including a gorgeous type of embroidery, called Brazilian embroidery. But her greatest pride and joy has become her painting. She has practiced and blossomed until her work has become well known in

Murfreesboro. Her paintings have often been displayed in the city library as well as at the Murfreesboro Art League. More recently she illustrated an alphabet book I wrote called *Backyard ABC's*.

Mama has always loved flowers. I don't ever recall a time we didn't have flowers growing somewhere around the house in the summertime. Our house in Murfreesboro has been a haven for Mama's flowers, as her hands have set out little flower beds here and big ones there all over the backyard and on down to the lake. Mama and Daddy have both worked many untold hours making the backyard into a showcase. It has even been featured in the Murfreesboro newspaper.

Mama has always loved to fish. When we moved to Murfreesboro, she was in fisherman's heaven, as she only had to go out the backdoor to throw out a line. The crappies would nest under the shrubs in the corner of the yard, so that quickly became her favorite place to fish (or "feed the babies," depending on the size of her catch). I especially enjoyed fishing for catfish with Mama in the middle of the night. We poled out into the middle of the lake on the detachable pier and dropped anchor. Then we fished to our hearts' content in the moonlight and caught quite a few catfish.

Mama, God bless you and your precious tender hands. And God bless Daddy, too, for encouraging you and giving you the room to grow and to bloom where you were planted.

Note: This article was written in 1999. Mama will be 94 in June and is living in an assisted living facility. She has had a few ministrokes which caused her to lose much of her dexterity, but she still enjoys using coloured pencils to colour in several nature colouring books by Dover Publishing.

Sandra Fischer

Mother's Miraculous Morels

Most people in central Indiana herald spring's arrival when crocuses burst through the soil and buds start peeking their heads out of cherry tree limbs. As a young girl, I learned that such signs were sometimes premature. Cold snaps would revisit between April showers causing early tulips to close their petals in tight protest. Many an Easter would find ladies attending church arrayed in peculiar contrast—winter coats and flowered bonnets. For me the most reliable sign spring had arrived to stay was the day I would come home from school to find my mother standing on the front porch waiting.

"Hurry up," she'd call. "Today promises to be good for a hunt."

I would quickly change to jeans, and hurry out to the old Chevy, its motor humming, Mother at the wheel, ready to head to the woods for our first mushroom hunt. To mushroom aficionados like my mother, finding the elusive, mysterious fruit was her favorite activity. These mushrooms were special, quite different from the button variety at the local grocery. Together we sought the yellow and grey cone-shaped morels, which resemble sponges perched atop ivory-white stems. Growing in wild, moist woodlands for only a short season each spring, morels are a prized delicacy.

My mother's regard for mushroom hunting could be likened to treasure seeking. While there are special conditions which enhance the chances of finding morels, there are no guarantees. Mother, however, had the reputation of being one of the best hunters in our town.

As I recall this family ritual, I remember I did not share her enthusiasm. I thought it to be a wild goose chase. I would have much preferred to stay home and play with paper dolls or go roller-skating rather than tramp through muddy woods, slapping mosquitoes and watching out for snakes.

Yet, despite my disdain for the hunting, I was fascinated by the raw beauty and wonder of the woods. We would fan out in different directions in search of our quest and I would soon be distracted by other discoveries: the feathered bobwhites' reassuring "all-right" calls, the rustle of leaves from a scurrying squirrel, the smell of fresh blossoms. My reverie would be broken by a call signaling someone had found a honeycombed treasure. We would converge upon the spot, hoping to find more of the spikes erupting from decaying leaves and fallen brush.

Mushrooming requires keen eyesight and great patience. Success meant having right conditions and persistence. I didn't see why we couldn't just plant them in the garden and save ourselves a lot of trouble. Mother's answer to that suggestion was that morel mushrooms were rare and so special, that God, in His providence, chose to put them where He wanted. Many times we would hunt until darkness crept upon us and, if we found the places God had put them, we would leave the woods with our sacks filled with rewards. At home, the aroma of our success would fill the kitchen. We enjoyed the savory, nutty taste of the morels in a variety of ways—in soups, sandwiches, or creamed on toast. Our favorite recipe was simply to roll them in flour and fry them in salted butter. To me, eating the morels was the best part of mushrooming.

Mother, however, considered the whole process to be a joyful venture, a pleasurable challenge that brought delight to her each year. Mushroom hunting was her passion and anticipating the season brought hope through many dismal winters, until the year she could not go. Major surgery brought confinement to Mother that year and the doctor ordered limited physical activity for the whole mushroom season. My brothers, sisters, and I undertook the ritual at her urging, but we lacked the heart for it and returned home from each hunt with little to show for our efforts.

Mother accepted her detention with resolve and spent her days reading or checking on her flower garden. One day as she poked among the tulips, she gasped, "Oh, come look!" I hurried to see, thinking a garter snake had startled her.

"Look! Can you believe it?" she cried in excitement.

There amid the flowers was a golden morel, standing tall on its ivory stem!

"Here's another one!"

Before long we had found a dozen mushrooms in the tulip bed.

Mother was right. God sends the morels where He chooses. That year Mother couldn't go to the mushrooms, so He sent them to her.

I still ponder the wonderful mystery of those special mushrooms and how God blessed my mother with their appearance in her garden. It was the first and last time we ever found morels near our house in all the years we lived there, and the only time Mother could not go to the woods to search. I shall always remember them as Mother's miraculous morels.

Recipe for Fried Morels

Slice the mushrooms in half, cutting off the base of the stems. Rinse and clean gently.

Soak them in salt water for an hour or two. Rinse in colander with plain water. Drain well on paper towels or pat dry gently. Dredge in flour or finely mashed cracker crumbs; pan fry in salted butter until golden brown. Serve as a side with any meat (especially good with steak). Can also be served on bread as a sandwich.

Patricia Anne Elford

How Sweet It Was!

My orphaned mother, raised by her aunt and uncle, had been required to mop, dust, scrub, peel, hull, clean, and tidy, but hadn't been allowed to cook or bake. When she married my father and had to learn the secrets of the Findlay wood and coal stove, Dad taught her how to cook meats and vegetables. He prepared the Christmas turkeys. Mom taught herself to bake.

Plunged into farm market-gardening and then backyard gardening, city girl Mom quickly learned how to pickle and preserve. She eventually knew every heat spot of that big stove—when to put which things into the warming closet above, how to keep everything bubbling and stewing and cooking...and bake she did.

Every day was cooking day, but Saturdays were baking days. Once I became old enough to help Mom bake, I was in no rush to go outside to play until our masterpieces had been completed. It was fun! So was eating the raw scraps—a habit frowned upon today.

When I was young, Mom's two-ringed binder cookbook seemed so much bigger, opened out on top of a metal utility table. The recipe book is still as thick, yet not as big in length and width as I remember it. The pages are now erratically serrated by age and use.

When not being used, it was tucked alongside the huge blue pottery mixing bowl, inside the cupboard, directly behind that table. For every luncheon and supper dish there are twelve dessert or sauce recipes—a meal wasn't a meal without dessert. There are also several different recipes for similar items. "Never know when they might be made better." Margarine is substituted for butter and is replaced again by butter as the years pass.

There's a combination of Mom's own careful penmanship, handwritten recipes shared by others, and recipes cut out of magazines or newspapers to be carefully glued in with mucilage that looked like corn syrup. Notes along the side of the pages tell of improvements arising from use. Red checks mark the good. An X slashes through those that "didn't make the grade." At one time, you could have tasted the favourite family recipes by licking the cookbook pages.

Among those special treats were doughnuts, molasses candy, chocolate rolled-oat squares, icebox cookies, oatmeal cookies with date filling, peanut butter cookies, coconut macaroons, gumdrop fruit cake, bread pudding, snow pudding with custard, apple crumble, Yorkshire pudding, *blanc mange*, mincemeat without meat, carrot pudding, boiled raisin cake, butter tarts. I must not forget the pies: raisin, lemon meringue, and butterscotch (topped by bottle-top cream whipped by rapidly turning a handle atop a measured glass container, adding sugar and a touch of vanilla at just the right moment). Drooling yet?

For many, many years there were homemade goodies in the house. After we grew up, each time my brother or I returned home, as soon as Mom and Dad were hugged, the first place we visited was the kitchen cupboard where six metal-lidded glass cookie jars would have been filled with fresh favourites for our visit. Soon, the grandchildren who sprouted up followed our route. How sad was the first time that ordinary store-bought cookies greeted us!

I've chosen to share Mom's handwritten "molasses candy" recipe with you. Frequently, on Friday or Saturday evenings, my brother, mother, father, and I used to gather around the card table. The scene was warmed by a floor lamp which bent over to create a wide pool of light. We played crokinole, board games, and card games. The winner was rich in toothpicks and poker chips until the next game started. The molasses candies, wrapped in twists of white waxed paper, waited in the purple translucent glass dish with its silver metal handle. The light glinted on the handle and shone through the candy dish, begging us to taste the contents. Judiciously savoured, one candy could last through at least one hand of cards. Somehow, it made losing easier to bear and winning so much sweeter.

Molasses Candy

4 cups white sugar
½ cup molasses
½ cup corn syrup
½ cup butter (3/4 cup margarine)
5 Tbsp. boiling water
3 Tbsp. cocoa
2 Tbsp. white vinegar
vanilla – drop or two

Boil all together (except vanilla) until a little bit dropped into cold water turns brittle, or to 300 degrees on the candy thermometer. Add vanilla. Pour into greased pan and mark in squares. Cool. Cut along lines. Place each candy into a small piece of waxed paper twisted at each end.

Bon appétit! Let the games begin!

Linda Driscoll

Lifelines

"Out for breakfast?" John asked.

"Out for breakfast," I replied grabbing a jacket, heading for the door and the brilliant, late-October sunshine. We stood on our little porch for a few minutes, soaking up the warmth, a small attempt to let go of some of the stress of the last few days, and then headed out into the Saturday morning.

As we walked the few blocks to one of our favorite morning haunts—great hash browns—we thrashed over (yet again) all that had gone on during our most recent trip to visit my mum, a three-hour drive down the 401 highway. Debriefing, we called it, probably because each visit felt like a military operation. Every two weeks we would plan coping ploys to get us through our two-day stay and then talk about what went wrong on the drive home—and things always went wrong. My 88-year-old mum was just one of those unhappy people for whom nothing was ever right, a character trait exaggerated by old age, declining health, and an uncanny, innately Scottish ability to turn grudge bearing into an art form. As her only child I was now, understandably, the focal point for whatever she perceived as the current problem. But understanding in my head didn't always translate into understanding in my heart and I felt a bit the worse for wear every time.

We were still fresh from the Friday morning return trip and had lots to sort out. It had been a struggle to accomplish, but we had finally been able to have her assessed through a program I had heard about run by a local hospital aimed at finding ways to help people in her situation find ways to cope at home. Just getting her referred had been a struggle, but a push from her social worker finally convinced Mother's doctor to sign the necessary documents.

Weeks of tests had come down to the basic and obvious fact that she was at a very high level of risk. Her eyesight had been failing for years and now she had been deemed legally blind. She was terrified of having the surgery necessary to repair the problem for fear she would lose what little vision she had left. Her hearing was also failing. The hearing aid made everything too loud, she said. She wouldn't wear it, and she had recently refused to let Meals on Wheels in the door and had sent her care worker packing, probably a result of the dementia which had been creeping into the mix. Add her off-the-charts anxiety level, along with her understandable desire to remain in the home her husband had built all those years ago, and it didn't take much stirring or baking to realize that this recipe was going to need a miracle not to explode. I was pinning my miracle hopes on this program.

"Sometimes you have to make hard decisions," the geriatrician had told me. Sometimes a nursing home is the only option and it would be up to me to sign the papers. If I didn't, and anything happened to her, he suggested, it would be my fault. I hadn't discussed any of this with mum...yet. The prospect terrified her—and the prospect of having to make the decision terrified me.

By the time we got to the restaurant we were almost subdued, exhausted from the talking. We ate in silence and over coffee I told John about a dream I'd had the night before. I rarely remember my dreams and this one was so vivid. I had been dreaming about my mother a lot lately but what stood out about this one was that in this dream she was actually happy. I marveled at the mum I had known as a forty-five-year-old widow, lively, confident, laughing at a joke, obviously enjoying herself. Her beautiful auburn (not red! auburn!) hair was done up in a classic Ann Landers flip. She was wearing a hot pink caftan, and a great big smile. I swear she had one of her favorite Brandy Alexanders in one hand. She was in a group of people but when she saw me, her face lit up with delight as she came over and hugged me. I could feel the physical warmth of her body emanating what seemed to me to be a complete sense of joy.

John laughed, caught up in the memory of my mother as he had first known her. Then he sighed. "Do you get the feeling that one of these days we're going to get the phone call?"

We strolled the few blocks home and opened the door. The light on the answering machine was blinking.

We looked at each other. And we knew.

Raymond Fenech

Childhood, Summer, and the Ghost that Kept us Quiet

One of my best memories of Mum was when I was still a boy of eight years during the endless hot summer days. I recall my father still being employed with the British Services as a Telecom operator at Bin Gemma. He worked on shift basis and therefore even nights. Those days seem like yesterday as my mother and I, together with some of my neighbour kid friends, gathered around her towards sunset. It was the treat of the day listening to some personal experiences of my mother, or of some long lost great uncle or aunt. Storytelling then was not an option for parents because kids were not spoiled for choice when it came to entertainment. Computers, iPods, and mobiles still hadn't been invented and television could be afforded by only the privileged few.

Those long summer evenings, sitting on the front porch of our quaint house of character overlooking Spinola fishing bay, are moments that will live in my memory for the rest of my life. Most of the things I learnt about Christian values and principles and life in general were learnt listening to my parents and absorbing all that I could of the wise words they uttered. Today's kids seem to know it all and the result of their arrogance and presumptuous attitude speaks for itself and is very telling in the way they mismanage and conduct their life's affairs. No one seems to have told them that a person has two ears and one mouth so he can listen twice as much as he talks.

Every evening my mother would sit on her chair and start with the favourite introduction every child would be mesmerized with: "Once upon a time…"

The story—which she recounted numerous times was our favourite—and was probably the reason I came to love the paranormal and ended up becoming a paranormal investigator. It was called "The Ghost of the Parish Priest."

Once upon a time, it was said the ghost of a parish priest haunted a small church situated in a very small village in the south of Malta. The church was very popular with the locality's fishermen and hunters, as the first Mass was celebrated every morning at 5 a.m. to accommodate their need to go about their business early.

The new parish priest, Fr. Simon, was becoming increasingly annoyed with the caretaker of the church, as he was repeatedly finding his personal belongings locked in the cupboard of the sacristy upside down, as if someone had been rummaging through them.

At first, the two had many an argument, but then one day the parish priest decided to take the keys away from the caretaker to ensure that no one but himself had access to the church and to the cupboard. To his surprise, he found his cupboard wide open again. It was quite evident that someone had rummaged through his locker. The funny thing about this was that nothing was ever stolen.

The situation was becoming frustrating to the point that he decided to spend the night in the church and keep a lookout for the intruder. It was well past midnight and Fr. Simon could hardly keep his eyes open. He was almost on the brink of giving up, but decided he would persist in his endeavour.

He must have fallen asleep, when he was suddenly awakened by footsteps. He was wide awake now and realised that he was no longer alone in the church. He hid quickly behind one of the huge pillars and fixed his eyes on the altar. The footsteps came nearer and soon a priest came out from the sacristy, readily attired to celebrate Mass.

Fr. Simon remained in hiding until Mass was said and the intruding priest had left. Although he followed him to the sacristy, he found no one there, except his cupboard, which had been opened again.

The next morning he asked the caretaker if he knew anything about the priest he had seen, giving him a detailed description. From the description, the caretaker said the priest resembled the former parish priest, Fr. Charles, but it couldn't be him because he had died suddenly of a heart attack two years before.

Fr. Simon did not want to stir up any panic among the villagers, so he simply said nothing. That same night he stayed on at the church to keep a lookout for the strange priest. Fr. Simon did not really believe in ghosts, but he was determined to get to the bottom of this mystery. He made sure he did not fall asleep and at exactly three o'clock in the morning, he heard the familiar footsteps. Once again, the priest came out from the sacristy. This time Fr. Simon walked out from behind the pillars where he had been hiding and challenged the mysterious figure.

"Who are you and what are you doing here at this time of night?"

The priest turned round slowly and smiled. His voice sounded as if it was coming from far away.

"I am Fr. Charles and have been condemned to come here every day to say Mass, one of the many I had pledged to celebrate for the repose of the souls of my parishioners. Unfortunately, I died before I could complete my assignment. There are still fifteen Masses to be celebrated before I can rest."

Fr. Simon was extremely scared, but he also knew that this ghostly apparition needed his assistance and would never rest in peace unless he intervened.

"Fr. Charles, go and rest in peace, I will celebrate a Mass in your stead until all fifteen pledges have been honoured."

There was a moment's silence and the ghostly apparition vanished, never to reappear again.

This story used to send wave after wave of shivers down our back and the silence whilst my mother recounted the events could be cut with a knife. I don't ever recall us kids keeping so quiet for so long under any circumstances. But this ghost story worked like magic and would tame us down usually till the end of the evening, or till the next day when the sun rose high into the blue sky and we would be looking forward to go to the sandy beach at St. George's Bay to create our usual havoc and mischief.

The ghost of the parish priest would come to haunt us again in a few days time together with other ghouls and ghosts from my mother's long repertoire of stories, a sadly dying tradition in most homes as computers and television have taken over.

Don E. Cunningham

Mom's Fudge

It was the depression. We learned not to expect much on our birthday. Mom loved children and cooking, so a far richer reward awaited us. She made us our favorite cake and fudge! Mine was peanut butter fudge and a moist chocolate cake flowing with peanut butter frosting!

In grade school, my vocabulary was increasing and my writing progressed. I won almost every spelling bee. In anticipation of my birthday, I put up poetic notes in all the rooms of our home. The short poem read, "Remember the day—the ninth of May."

My birthday finally arrived! Surely, all the family knew it was MY special day. At the end of dinner, I was expecting Mom to place the cake and fudge on the table and everyone to sing "Happy Birthday!" My signs were still up, yet no one said anything. Dinner came and went. We gathered around the radio, listening to our favorite broadcasts. It became bedtime; still no celebration. Disheartened, I brushed my teeth and washed up for bed.

When I came out of the bathroom, all the lights in the house were out. I warily walked through the kitchen toward a wavering yellow light and entered the dining room. There on the table sat a candle lit chocolate cake! In the candles' glow, I could see little lead soldiers—created by my dad and painted by my brothers and sister. They were standing guard over my peanut butter fudge, which was waiting to be shared with all.

The lights flashed on and everyone shouted, "Remember the day—the ninth of May—Happy Birthday!"

The little poem became a memorable one. Growing up it was always the greeting on my birthday. Years later, on my eightieth birthday, I received a birthday card with a May calendar page in it. My youngest brother, Guy, circled the 9 with a red marker pen and wrote across the calendar, "Remember the day, the ninth of May!" My first poem still lingered in his heart!

Being a diabetic I can longer make or eat Mom's peanut butter fudge, but the sweet memories linger. I hope you will enjoy it.

Peanut Butter Fudge

1/3 stick butter
2 cups peanut butter
2 cups sugar
1 14 oz. can condensed milk
1 tsp. vanilla

Melt butter; add peanut butter and dry ingredients with condensed milk over medium heat until they totally dissolve in the condensed milk. Continue heating and stir slowly for about ten minutes. Dip out a small drop on spoon and drop into cold water. If it forms a soft ball, remove pan from stove and set in pan of cold water. Add vanilla. Stir in pot while in cold water until it has a granular appearance. Remove mixture to buttered pan and let sit for 1-2 hours until set. Cut and wrap in waxed paper and refrigerate. It will keep for up to one week in refrigerator.

Hazel Elizabeth Barnes

My Mother
Born on December 12, 1912
Dorothy Cox-Rothwell

the photograph on her dresser
is very old in shades of sepia
with an elaborate gold frame.
my mother is seventeen,
she is sitting on a rope swing
with a board seat suspended in time.
her drop-waisted dress has a large bow
her brown hair cut one length with bangs
shining in the sunlight,
swings forward over her cheeks.
she smiles, her eyes look out at me
a reflection of myself.
the other night she came to me
in my dreams
took my hands and whirled in dance—
strange she never danced in life
but dances now in death.
i remember the perfect pink roses
placed on her coffin as it was lowered,
my legs sinking to the ground.
the rose now pressed has turned brown
i place it next to the photograph
for her to see.

My Mother's Hard Crack Taffy

Recipe of Hazel Barnes Williams

Saturday night at our house was a time to be together. We didn't have much money for entertainment and so we made our own. My sister Katie and I would watch while Mom got out the saucepan for cooking and the popcorn popper. We could already taste it in our mouths, the saltiness of popcorn with butter, and the smooth buttery hardness of taffy. We watched carefully as Mom measured the sugar, butter, and vinegar into the pot. Once it was mixed there was no stirring it. It bubbled away on the coal stove while popcorn popped in the popper. What anticipation we had, it all seemed so slow.

At a certain stage the taffy was ready for testing which was the good part. We poured a glass of cold water, and with a spoon dipped into the taffy we were ready to see if it was at the hard crack stage by allowing it to drip into the glass and form hairs. If it went too long, it had a slightly burnt taste which only added to its flavour. Finally when it was done, it was poured into a greased tin pie plate to cool. Once cooled and hardened, it was hit with the hard end of a knife into small sharp-edged pieces, then it was ready to eat. Along with the popcorn, it was our Saturday night treat enjoyed by all.

This same taffy was made at Christmas and Halloween as a special treat to be shared. We had an Italian neighbour we called on at Halloween who made the same taffy, only hers was burnt black and just as delicious. We always headed to her house to be sure of having some of hers, so special was it. The recipe follows:

Hard Crack Taffy

2 cups brown sugar
5 Tbsp. of water
1 Tbsp. of butter
1 Tbsp. of vinegar
dash of salt

The instructions are above, so enjoy!

Paige Carpenter

Three Photographs

I think the frames were originally silver. I don't remember. They've tarnished to dark pewter. The frames are doll-sized, each about two inches high. They came in a kit with instructions to make a maternal family tree, one frame for each generation.

In the first frame is my grandmother. It's her eighth grade portrait, August 1942. Skinny but pretty, she's barely smiling; my grandmother has always been reserved. Her hair is in tight Shirley Temple curls, and she's wearing a starched striped dress, handmade by my great-grandmother, who spent hours sewing puffs in the sleeves and piping on the bodice. World War II is raging, but my grandmother lives in rural Florida. The war touches her in rationed soap and sugar. No bombs fall on Florida's dusty roads, no air raid sirens break the hot summer silence.

The second frame holds a ninth grade portrait of my mother with braces on her teeth and huge cat's-eye glasses on her nose. It's 1965. America's Leave-it-to-Beaver façade is crumbling under Vietnam and Beatlemania. My mother never protested the war or fell in love with John Lennon. But she's forthright, grinning in spite of the metal in her mouth, and has her generation's passion for truth.

I'm in the last frame. It's a snapshot from my sophomore year in college, 2006. One of my friends caught me laughing on camera, but I'm hiding the laugh behind my hand. I have my grandmother's eyebrows and my mother's eyes. I saw the Twin Towers fall and the Internet rise.

I know these frames and their photographs by heart: the curls in the hair, the wrinkles in the cloth. They're a piece of my childhood, and my mother's, and my grandmother's. I wonder how different we are now from then.

Debbie Schmid

Windows to Her Heart

One summer, while visiting my mom in southern California, I had what I thought was a brilliant idea. "Come on, Mom." I cheered her on. "You can do it!"

"You want me to make four scrapbooks between now and Christmas? Um-m-m, I don't think so." She frowned.

"Why not?" I wanted to know.

"Debbie, it's already July! When do you think I'm going to have time to gather all those photos? I don't even know where they are. Besides, I've never made a scrapbook before, let alone four."

"No worries…I'll help you. It will be fun. We'll make them together."

"When?" she asked, her heart softening to the idea.

"I don't know. How about when you come to Arizona the week of Thanksgiving? We can crank them out then."

Mom looked at me in disbelief. "All four…in one week! Are you crazy?"

"No, not yet." I laughed. "Let's go to the craft store and see what they have in stock."

Before Mom could offer another rebuttal, we were in the van and on our way to a local scrapbooking store. When we arrived, I became so excited I could barely contain myself. It was a crafter's paradise! There were beautiful scrapbooks and novelty papers unlike any I'd ever seen before. And this wonderful new adventure made my heart dance.

For years, my brothers and I had longed for a scrapbook from Mom, containing our childhood memories. Now that our dreams were about to be realized, I couldn't wait to help her make those dreams come true. What an awesome surprise this was going to be for my three brothers on Christmas Day.

After browsing around the store separately for about fifteen minutes, Mom approached me with enthusiasm. "Come here, Debbie. I want to show you something."

While following her through the store, I noticed a bounce in her steps. "Look what I found!" She pointed to a row of specialty scrapbooks and started pulling them off the shelf, one after another. "Do you think Jeff would like this outdoor sports one?"

"Yes. It's perfect for him," I replied. She put her newfound treasure in the cart.

"Here's one with baseball memorabilia on it. Scott will love this," she continued. "And look what I found for Timm—Route 66! Isn't that cool?"

"Wow! These are great, Mom. See, isn't this fun?"

She smiled and continued shopping.

It warmed my heart that she had even entertained the scrapbook idea. But now, she was getting serious about the matter. A few minutes later she held out her two favorite Victorian floral scrapbooks. "Which one do you like best?"

"This dusty pink one is pretty," I commented, pointing to my favorite one. It, too, went into the cart.

After choosing the four albums, we continued filling our cart with a selection of coordinating papers, stickers, and mounting supplies. Clearly, our mission was successful and we were one step closer to the reality of making those four scrapbooks. While riding home, I encouraged Mom again, "See…that wasn't so bad now, was it?" I could tell by the look on her face, she was pleased with her selections.

For months following our initial shopping spree, like a little child, I kept checking in on her progress. "Have you located those pictures yet? Did you find our mementos? Are you getting excited?" Oh, how I looked forward to her visit over Thanksgiving so we could spend more time together and get to work.

Once the week of anticipation arrived, we sat at the dining room table from sun-up to sundown, sorting, cutting, and pasting. Every now and then we took a break just long enough to make meals and take care of our family obligations. Then back to the task at hand. By day three, Mom looked across the table at me and shook her head from side to side. "I can't believe you talked me into this."

I must admit, as the week went on, the workdays grew longer and we became weary. On the last day of her visit, we placed the final pages on each of the four stacks; almost four hundred pages in all! While expressing a huge sigh of relief, we looked at each other, and in unison we chuckled, "I can't believe we just did this!"

Even though I knew what was coming to me for Christmas, I couldn't wait to see the final product. When I opened the box containing my beautiful Victorian scrapbook, tears rolled down my face. Mom had written the most beautiful entry letter, and on each page she wrote personal comments from her heart. As I looked through the pages, a flood of memories filled my mind and my heart felt overwhelmed by her love.

Making those precious scrapbooks with my mom was more than a mad dash to the finish line. While cutting and pasting, we laughed, we cried, and we bonded in ways I never expected. I had been given a wonderful chance to ask her all kinds of questions to which she responded with amazing little stories, stories that I had never heard before. As a result, those scrapbooks were so much more than photographs and memories. They were windows to her heart, to her four adult children, and another beautiful example of her sacrificial love for each one of us.

When I think about my mom, I'm so thankful for her generosity. I could ramble on for hours about the countless sacrificial gifts she's given to me and my family throughout the years. But when I think about our scrapbook journey, I feel warm inside. Each scrapbook was a precious storybook, a tangible piece of my mother's heart, and something my brothers and I will cherish forever.

Thanks, Mom! I knew we could do it! My scrapbook was a beautiful dream come true…and I love you.

Deb Wuethrich

Mom, Memories and Tomato Soup Cake

Sometimes it pains me now to acknowledge that my mother and I were not always the best of friends. I was more of a "daddy's girl" in my earliest years, and when my parents divorced, my sister and I still got to see Mom on weekends. It seemed pretty normal to me to be with our father the rest of the time. But then he died. I was nine years old, my sister eight, when we went to live with Mom. She had started a new marriage, we had a younger brother, and soon another came along. There was a gap of six and ten years between us and the boys, and somehow, a time came when I was more the caretaker of them than Mom was. She had other interests as a regionally known country music entertainer, and sometimes I resented being thrust into the role of babysitter when I'd have preferred to be off with my friends.

An early marriage and a move 350 miles from home, from New York to Michigan, didn't do a whole lot to bridge the gap that widened over time between me and my mom. When our daughter Michele was born, however, things started to soften between us as they often will with little ones. I know my mother's heart went out to me when we learned Michele had a terminal illness. Spinal Muscular Atrophy (SMA) took her life at age eleven, and Mom was as crushed as we were at our loss.

I still lived in Michigan, but we'd write letters and talk on the phone, in addition to visits, with Mom often wondering how she could help in a situation where there is little anyone can do. But she reassured me she was there for us. One summer, my husband and I learned that our favorite group, the Oak Ridge Boys, would be performing at a little county fair near where Mom lived. We invited her to join us for the concert. As we pulled into the motel we always stayed at, we noticed a large bus in the lot. When my mother arrived and came to our room, I excitedly grabbed her hand and squealed, "The Oaks are staying here!"

And she said, "Let's go! I saw a guy playing his banjo in the parking lot."

My husband just shook his head, embarrassed by our schoolgirl enthusiasm. But to me, it was the most fun my mother, the country singer, and I maybe ever had together. Joe Bonsall was very sweet and let me take Mom's picture with him. At the fair, our newfound relationship was further solidified as we spotted a red caboose from the Shawmut Railroad on the grounds. I watched Mom's face as she went back in time, revisiting not just the restored station next to it, but the memories of living in a caboose just like that one during the Depression when her home had flooded. A meal then was creamed corn over a piece of bread. It answered a lot of questions for me: Mom's fear of scarcity, prompting cupboards full of canned goods, and her tendency to never throw anything away.

I learned a lot about her that weekend, including how her name, Joan, was the way they spelled "JoAnne" when she was born. She put the latter spelling in glitter on her guitar so people would pronounce it right when she was performing. Our talks brought us closer and revealed little details of a life. On another trip east the next year, I spent a few hours at her house on a rainy afternoon—the first in years that it had just been the two of us, talking about the past, our fears, and life's dreams and disappointments. We were very much in tune that day.

Mom made it even more special. She'd baked a Tomato Soup Cake, which is a type of spice cake, with peanut butter frosting. She remembered how I'd always liked it as a kid. I hadn't had one in years and ate two pieces.

After that, Mom and I talked frequently on the phone and stayed in touch by e-mail. She said it was a dream come true, us finally being close. Her greatest dream, she said, was that we'd move back home someday and could visit more and she'd have all her kids together more often, as we were at Christmas. One night before I went into a city council meeting for my job as a reporter, Mom called me while I was in the car. "They think I have cancer," she said. She was so upbeat, so hopeful, so full of faith, and told me not to worry. I covered my meeting, got in the car to go home—and then cried. I thought of the old Mary Tyler Moore movie, "First You Cry: The Betty Rollin Story," and recalled how it was one of the first movies that made way for open discussion of cancer. And discuss it we did over the next three years.

Mom did have it, cervical cancer, and endured chemotherapy and radiation treatments, including internal doses. She told me on the phone many times, "God is holding me," and urged me to keep the faith as well. We thought she'd beaten it. For about a year she was doing great. Then, doctors found some inoperable growths on her lymph nodes, and it was back to chemo every few weeks. I remember going home to visit one time, and she popped off the red wig she kept on for company. That day, I saw my Grandma Grey in her, and it was the first time I realized she was no longer as young and vibrant as I'd remembered. I saw the strain cancer had put on her

In early April 2011, after my husband passed away, I drove to New York by myself to spend a couple days with Mom. She was in obvious pain, holding her stomach, trying to avoid painkillers so she would be alert to talk. She was worried about me, a new widow. As sick as she was, she had made preparations for my visit. She'd instructed my sister to bake a Tomato Soup Cake, with peanut butter frosting.

It was hard to leave Mom that time, but before I did, I prayed with her. It brought us as close as we'd ever been. I was back home in Michigan only a few days when my sister called to say Mom had taken a turn and that the end was near. I made plans to make the trip in the morning. That night, my brother put the phone to Mom's ear and I could hear the pinched words through her pain.

"I love you," she said, the only words she could muster.

"I love you, too, Mom. I'll be there tomorrow," I promised.

At 3 or 4 a.m., I awoke because I'd heard a whispered, "Debbie." Realizing I was still in my bed, I closed my eyes again. That was when four very clear words were spoken: "I'm going home now." When my brother called at 6 a.m., I said, "I know."

Somehow Mom knew I would be distressed that I didn't make it home to say good-bye. I can almost see her asking God, "Just one quick stop, please," and it gave me great peace to have somehow sensed her in transition. Much of my family is gone now. One day, I will arrive in heaven and the Lord will reunite me with my husband and child. I'm sure I will also smell a cake baking—an aromatic Tomato Soup Cake. When I follow the scent, I will find Mom waiting with the words, "I baked this just for you. I've missed you. I'm glad you're finally home."

Joan's Tomato Soup Cake

1 tsp. soda
1 can tomato soup
1 cup sugar
½ cup Crisco
1 egg, beaten
1¾ cup flour
1 tsp. cinnamon
1 tsp. nutmeg
1 tsp. baking powder

Blend 1 teaspoon soda in tomato soup. Beat. Set aside. Mix sugar with Crisco, then add egg. Put in tomato soup and soda mixture, and beat well. Add flour for cake, sifted with cinnamon, nutmeg, and baking powder. Put in 8x8 pan. Bake at 375 degrees till done when lightly touched, or 25-30 minutes.

Peanut Butter Frosting

2 cups confectioners' sugar
¼ cup peanut butter
1/3 cup milk
Beat. If stiff, add milk to spreading consistency.

Brenda Black

Love in a Country Legacy

I was only six years old when my grandmother suddenly died. My mom instantly became a young mother of three with no mentor to counsel her through those early days of parenting. She grieved deeply. I remember most how she continued to feel the loss often and sensed her sorrow magnified by all the activities that Grandma missed.

"Your grandma would have loved to have seen you do this," my mom would say when we were showing cattle or horses. Grandma's legacy of country living and her love for both livestock and family survived her in the heart of my down-to-earth mother.

Mom grew up herding turkeys, showing dairy cattle, and riding horses. And by the time her own children were able to sit up, we were horseback as well. As a family, we hauled show horses or beef cattle all over the country. We went on trail rides together and traveled the state with P.O.A. ponies and won top honors in contests and youth rodeos. When home, in addition to the show stock, we raised a few pigs for slaughter, bottle fed some calves, and staked out a goat now and again. All the while, we learned to work together and play together. Even if the chores were demanding, I learned to love this rural lifestyle—the only way my mother or grandmother had ever known.

To this day, I can bury my head into the satiny side of a horse, contending he smells like a heavenly fragrance. I'll roll down my window and drive a little slower past a field of sweet, freshly cut hay. I know how to comb away cockleburs and braid mane. I enjoy a good romp with the dog or challenging the pups with a rigorous game of fetch, followed by lots of praise for their slobbering, exuberant efforts. And, quite frankly, I believe there are few things more adorable in all the universe than a baby lamb, mottled-faced calf, little pink pig, or fluffy chick.

This lifestyle I adore is generations old, with passed-down recipes for canning homegrown produce. It provided tried and true remedies to cure a sick pup or bring a calf back from the brink of death. I have applied family principles and practices for frugal country living because Grandma Elsie left lessons for life in the heart of my mom who did her level best to pass those valuable truths on to the next generation.

I learned from my mom how to care for all God's creatures—great and small—including man and beast. She models loving kindness and demonstrates patience just like her mama instructed.

As I watch my mother age, there is one thing for which I am truly grateful: She has been here to teach and guide and celebrate and contribute to my own life as a country mother. She and Dad have participated in the milestone events that my grandma missed. I can't even imagine their not being part of it. And an unseen woman also left her indelible mark. It was my own mother's mother who fostered this love for country living in her daughter's and her granddaughters' hearts.

The Scriptures put it this way: "Do not forsake your mother's teaching. They will be a garland to grace your head and a chain to adorn your neck" (Proverbs 1:8b-9). I am blessed to be clothed with such wonderful, colourful teachings that cause me to look in the mirror and see a reflection of my mom and remember a special grandma who taught me how to love both kin and critter.

Elsie H. Platt

Childhood Memories

One of my earliest memories of my mother was listening to her stories. She seemed to have an innate ability to derive lessons from many of her experiences.

As a child, I recalled her telling me that we must help each other and not just think of ourselves. Besides, the favour or help we give may be returned years later.

My mother grew up on a small farm in Germany during the early 1900s. Most of the farmers at that time had very little money and the money they did make went back into paying for farm expenses. Although money was limited, there was always plenty of homegrown food to eat. Christmas, however, was an exception. At that time, each child received a small bag containing an orange, chocolate, and some nuts. This was special because it was "store-bought" food.

One Christmas in 1904, when she was six years old, my mother asked her parents for a special doll—one that would open and close her eyes. My grandmother told her she would buy her such a doll if she could, but due of lack of money, she would have to settle for a homemade doll.

That Christmas Eve, the family gathered around the live Christmas tree that had been cut from a nearby woods. As was the custom, it was beautifully decorated with lighted candles. In a short time, the usual long-awaited gifts of oranges, chocolate, and nuts were given to the children. To my mother's surprise, she was handed a large rectangular box, elegantly wrapped. It was the first time she had ever seen, let alone received, such a beautiful box. Trembling with excitement, she quickly opened it and there appeared the most beautiful doll she had ever seen. It made her so happy that she began to cry. My grandmother explained that her brother John had bought it for her because he knew how much she wanted it.

Uncle John visited a few weeks later. My mother said to him, "You gave me the doll I always wanted. Someday, I will pay you back."

"Oh, Marie," he replied, "I don't want to be paid back. I'm just glad to see how much the doll pleases you."

"I will pay you back," she answered. "You just wait and see."

In 1923, at the age of twenty-five, my mother came to America to live. But she continued to correspond with her parents and her favorite uncle.

Then in 1941, the Second World War started and all correspondence to Europe ceased throughout the war years. However, in 1945 when the war was over, people in the United States were able to contact their relatives in Europe. Mother immediately started sending care packages to her family. When sending them packages, she recalled her promise to her uncle, "Someday I will pay you back."

Through her sister, she was able to locate John's new address, and she made up several packages for him containing food, coffee, soap, and other necessities. She worked many hours preparing these packages as they had to be wrapped in sturdy cloth in order to ensure their safe delivery. Because of the lack of food after the war, post office employees often opened packages from the United States to use some of the contents for themselves. Since employees had to work quickly, it would take too much time to undo packages sewn in cloth.

Mother's packages to her uncle did arrive safely and in his return letters he told her how much he appreciated them. Like many people in Europe, almost all of his earthly possessions had been destroyed and he was in need of everything. He said that the packages were a gift from heaven—totally unexpected. Mother said that she had the feeling that he was as thrilled to receive her packages as she was to receive his earlier presents, and especially that beautiful doll.

Even though thirty-nine years had elapsed, my mother was able to keep her promise to Uncle John and pay him back for his many kindnesses throughout her childhood years.

Sylvia Adams

Walking the Great Wall

My mother rearranges our lives,
culling the best, slipping it into suitable frames.
All of our pieces fit neatly into place.
She lies on her bed in the nursing home
and reads, or presses buttons on the remote,
no longer needing to wonder where we are,
to approve our friends, agonize through
our piano études or wait up late.

She's accordion-pleated our histories,
compressed broken arms and hearts,
expanded scholarships, careers.
My brother's bronchial winters have melted away,
Friar's Balsam overpowered
by scented memories, weddings in summer gardens.
My migraine-darkened room opens into
the place that Juliet chose to have her kittens
because she loved me best.

My mother has outlived friends
who might have wanted to know
that my brother and I have grown up;
we're settled and all is well.
She's telescoped years of widowhood
into occasional sighs, wishing
our father could see us now.
The nurse nods politely: "Right, sweetie."
She fetches my mother's slippers,
draws them up over swollen ankles,
helps her to her walker.

My mother doesn't notice the grey in my hair,
forgets my children's names,
or even whose children they are.
They are too many, too tall; understand too much
in their brief, awkward gatherings around her bed.

If she doesn't say much, it's because
she's absorbed in planning a new adventure:
Europe, perhaps, or China, to walk the Great Wall
planting each footstep on ageless stone,
wrapping herself in an eloquent shawl

Glen Sorestad

Ten Years

It is now ten years since you left.
After the ministrokes, the path
your body wobbled down
as it slowed to a final stop,
after the final stroke unworded you
and shrunk your world
to the size of a hospital bed,
your heart unwound until nothing
and no one could wind it up again.
Ten years now I have missed you
daily—the desperate reaching out
for what was so long a part of me,
belated recognition, with its constant
reminder, of how a mother is
heart and core of what a son becomes.
How I miss your easy laugh,
the gentle accord you fashioned
with the small world you knew
and neither demeaned or questioned,
but accepted and lived with as though
it held either everything or nothing
of how life's mystery unfolds.

Alice King Greenwood

Inheritance

My mother's hands are ugly, folded there
across her chest, unnatural and bent
in grotesque shapes. Too many years of care
have etched their devastating marks—years spent
in wringing mops and scrubbing soiled clothes,
in cleaning chickens for each Sunday's meal,
in making jams, and weeding garden rows.

The roughened skin belies a life genteel.
Her hands created pretty things: bouquets
of roses crystal-vased, a crocheted spread,
fine music, summer frocks of white piques,
soft quilts with intricate designs of thread.

Now lovely hands their shrouded casings leave
and pin their velvet gauntlets on my sleeve.

Nell Davidson

The New Bride

She came to this land so strange and foreign
Wed to a man she barely knew.
What were those strange white and black people saying?
She had not even a little clue.

South Africa? Where was that? Where could she run?
All she knew it was a long way from China and the trip was not fun.

"Tee, koffie, melk, suiker, tea, coffee, milk, sugar"
They put her behind the counter of her new husband's family store.
Learning these new languages was strange to her tongue
and for her such a huge chore.

Her mother-in-law was strict and demanding,
which seemed to her both unfair and lacking in understanding.

"You cannot cook, your food tastes terrible"
became an echo that brought the tears and became unbearable.

An old man who worked at a restaurant,
took pity on her and taught her how to cook tasty food
which now slowly began to change her mother-in-law's
oft bad-tempered mood.

Her husband bought a store of their own,
after their three babies came along.
"Tee, koffie, melk, suiker, tea, coffee, milk, sugar"
 now became her joyful song.

Glenn Kletke

The Woman of Border Beds

There were no grand gardens you tended
raspberry canes lifting high their bridal veils
maybe the closest you got to exotic

You were the woman of border beds
little creatures that took up a home there
salvia, marigold, zinnia, begonia.

You saw to their brief summer lives, spilled
water upon them, watched for unwanted insects
snapped off dead glory so on they could shine.

They of what you sang. They your petalled score.
Those narrow little bands of cracked earth.
Bare soil now beneath your vanished hands.

Glenn Kletke

Old Claims

A son so often gets
the dreams, hopes and affections
a mother for whatever reason
no longer pins
upon the man she married.

How the son soaks up
the misdirected sunlight
years until he knows
what has fallen upon him
what he must step out of and beyond.

But the shell she closed him in
the coat she placed upon
his unsuspecting shoulders
never quite leaves the hook
where her need first planted it.

And when last breakage arrives
as breakage must, the old claims
she placed upon him reappear
like shadows and in the rags
of their bent ancient love he weeps.

Beverly Ost-Everley

The Birthday Cake Tag Team

"I can do anything she can, if you'd just let me!"

My mother stared in disbelief as my brother, only ten at the time, stood defiantly in the kitchen, a cake recipe in his hand. The "she" he was talking about was me, only two years older.

"Roger, even your sister has never attempted to make that cake. It takes forty-five minutes just to make the batter, and it has some complicated steps to it. I intended to make it this afternoon, right after I got Mr. Burdett's shirts ironed. He wants to pick them up at five o'clock."

My stay-at-home mother contributed to the family income by taking in ironing and alterations. Dad worked two jobs trying to make ends meet. Today was his birthday, and my mom was going to make his favorite dessert, a special Brown Sugar Spice Cake.

Because Mom frequently had ironing or alterations that were due, we kids had started helping out by cooking dinner. I had recently learned to make meatloaf and mashed potatoes, and both of us could make tapioca pudding, custard, or whip up a boxed cake mix. But, the Brown Sugar Spice Cake, made from scratch, was better left to an adult, or at least someone older than sixteen.

"I don't feel good about this, Roger. I'm on a deadline. If you get in trouble, I won't be able to bail you out," she said, trying to give him one more reason to give up his quest.

"I can do this. I know I can!"

Despite her better judgment, Mom gave the okay, although it wasn't without some anxiety. For a family having problems making ends meet, there were some expensive ingredients being used that couldn't afford to be wasted: buttermilk, cake flour, five eggs. And, some difficult culinary techniques for a ten-year-old, like making meringue.

"If you have any questions, come and see me right away," Mom said, continuing her ironing.

Roger began making the cake. Soon, the mixer whirled in the kitchen while Mom continued to iron.

"What does it mean to separate eggs?"

"I can stop one minute and do that for you, but I won't be able to stop again," she said. Putting the iron to the side, she ran to the kitchen. Carefully breaking an egg, she carefully transferred the yolk between the two halves of the shell, expertly allowing the white to plop into a bowl, and placed the yellow yolk into another bowl. She repeated the procedure for the second egg.

"You'll have to do this again for the meringue. Do you think you can do it? You have to be very careful not to get any yolk in the whites or they won't whip to stiff peaks. You can't get any grease in the bowl either, so be very careful."

Mom went back to her ironing, one ear tuned to the activity in the kitchen, answering questions every once in a while.

"Okay, it's going in the oven," Roger said, turning the timer to forty minutes.

After dinner, Roger proudly brought the finished cake to the table, a few lit birthday candles signifying its purpose. After Dad blew out the flames, he cut a portion of the cake into small pieces, placing them on small plates that were passed around the table.

Mom looked at the cake carefully. It actually looked like it was supposed to. She took a bite. It tasted exactly as it should.

"Roger made the cake, honey."

One eyebrow raised. "Really? It's delicious!"

"See, Mom! I told you I could do it!"

"Indeed you did."

"Can I make pot roast next time?"

"With the pressure cooker? Oh, we are definitely going to have a long talk about that!"

Brown Sugar Spice Cake

1 cup butter
1 cup brown sugar
Two eggs, separated
1 cup buttermilk
2½ cups sifted cake flour
1 tsp. baking soda
1 tsp. baking powder
1 tsp. cinnamon
1 tsp. cloves
1 tsp. salt

Topping (Meringue)

3 egg whites
1½ cup brown sugar
¾ cup chopped nuts (Mom used black walnuts)
¼ tsp. lemon extract

Preheat oven to 350 degrees.

Cream butter and sugar, then add 2 egg yolks. Sift flour, measure, and sift together with spices, baking powder, soda, and salt. Add flour mixture to cream mixture. Whip egg whites of the 2 eggs to stiff peaks. Fold into flour mixture. Pour into oiled 15x10 pan.

Stiffly beat 3 egg whites (you can use the yolks of these for an omelette the next day!). Fold with other topping ingredients. Spread topping on batter in baking pan. Bake at 350 degrees approximately 40 minutes. Cake will be done when top is golden brown and cake is baked away from the pan.

Ardith Hird Davenport

My Mother Is a Quilt

My mother is a quilt, handmade in the quintessential pattern of her years.

Her colours are of those of growing things: flower gardens, vegetables patches, cornfields.

Her design is that of the child she was; it speaks of the strength that comes from intelligence and discipline.

The fabric has been collected, cut, and pieced throughout a history of want, of work, of valuing a job well done.

The wise arrangement of colour and texture have balance.

My mother is lovingly hand-quilted in her mother's frame. The underside of the work reveals meticulous measures of needle-in and needle-out. Perfection is its aim.

Only a corner remains for her to finish. She asks if we will bind the edges for her.

The quilt will spread over laps to warm and comfort those within its length and breadth.

We will turn over an edge. The careful tracing of the quilting pattern will remain visible to the practiced eye.

The complexity of the quilt is masked in its simplicity: It is a work of art, executed by the Master of all that is lovely and complete.

Sheri Pattillo

Mom's Southern Fried Okra & Potatoes

If you ask me which vegetable was on my plate most often as a young West Texas girl, my prompt answer will be "okra."

My grandparents grew fruits and vegetables in a large garden out behind their backyard. The garden seemed mysterious to me with vines and creepy crawlies. However, it thrilled my parents because the harvest was passed along to them when my grandparents would arrive at our house and unload brown paper sack loads from their car's backseat.

Perhaps more often than I liked, fried okra was set before me as a child. Fortunately, my mom cooked potatoes in the mixture, which, in my mind, compensated for the strange feel of okra in my mouth.

Although not exactly heart healthy, in those days this dish was considered a classic in the South. My mom, young and hard working, perfected the dish as follows:

– Wash fresh okra and slice them about ¼-inch thick.
– Beat 2-3 eggs and add a little water to thin the mixture.
– Stir okra into egg batter.
– Cut white potatoes into cubes or slices (no more than ½-inch thick so they cook evenly with okra).
– Cut onion into chunks similar in size to potatoes.
– Mix equal portions of flour and cornmeal to make the breading.
– Dump this breading mixture into a large sack.
– Use slotted spoon to dip okra out of egg batter and into breading mixture in sack.

– Dump potatoes and onions (unbreaded) into sack with okra.

– Shake sack until everything is coated well.

– Add about ¼-inch oil to cast-iron skillet and heat to frying temperature.

– Using a large slotted spoon, move okra, potatoes, and onions to the hot skillet.

– Allow one side to brown, and then turn the ingredients to brown the rest. (Add additional oil, if needed.)

– Cover with lid and cook over low heat until ingredients are done.

– Remove lid; turn up heat and brown again for several minutes.

– Drain on paper towels, salt and pepper, and serve immediately.

Donna Langevin

In Lieu of an Obit

Let's just say our mother
who lived on the east bank of the Mississippi
was as strong-willed as its currents
deep and shallow as its soundings
shifting as its sandbars
constant as its tides

Let's just say her colours like the water
ranged from coffee-brown to sunset-silks
Her moods were eels and catfish
mud storms and lightning
Her voice genteel as the belles
sipping iced-tea on plantations
was also a hurricane

She listened to the blues, gospel, jazz
played on cruise boats and shores
but sang only her own song
We sailed to her rhythm
and she weighed our plans like cargo
blessed or sank our ships

As the years stormed on
we tried to change her flow
She laughed at our levees
ignored maps and blueprints
and like a river goddess, followed her own whims
We worshiped and blasphemed her
sweated, slaved for and fought her
shunned and sought her
Like fields of sugarcane and cotton
she nourished and sustained us
but would not be tamed

In lieu of an obit, let's just say
from willow-supple to driftwood
she was every age
of a life that spanned two continents

In lieu of an obit—its narrow bed and borders
black and white words
that can't sum up a life

let's just say our mother was a river

Debbie Carpenter

My Small Hand in Hers

When I was young Mom took my hand,
For glad adventures she had planned.
Off to the park to play in the sand,
How joyous those times were.
Then to the library we would go,
Where all the books stood in a row.
We'd read them with our eyes aglow,
My small hand in hers.

At Christmastime we'd go downtown
We'd hear the bells, oh what a sound,
With merry shoppers all around,
And decorated firs.
We'd eat in a café, what fun!
Times like these were next to none.
We'd head for home when day was done.
My small hand in hers.

Seasons come and seasons go,
And all too quickly I did grow.
How it happened I don't know,
It all seems like a blur.
Now often I was with my friends,
Yet on Mom's love I could depend,
Still time together we would spend,
My hand now next to hers.

A good man came into my life,
And asked for me to be his wife.
But that did not cause Mom much strife,
Her heart with love did stir.
Children were born and she'd ask me,
If all of us could come for tea.
A family we would always be
Their small hands in hers.

Then came the day by Mother's bed,
I heard the words the doctor said.
All within me filled with dread,
We didn't have much time.
I thought about the days gone by,
And as the teardrops filled my eyes,
She walked the path to heaven's skies.
Her small hand in mine.

Linda Dawn Pettigrew

I Remember Mumma

I want to remember Mumma. She was such a fascinating woman. I've met few as interesting with my own worldly experience and she had none then. Remarkable really, given when and where she was born, her upbringing.

First, she always looked terrific—immaculate, meticulous, stylish, and well-dressed, even when she was destitute. By early morning she was groomed, dressed, and hard at work, cooking for her family. Mumma worked from dawn until bed almost every day of her life.

Second, my mother could make loaves out of fishes: She'd turn a piece of cloth into a beautifully stitched garment; yarn into sweater overnight; and a meagre pantry into a delicious meal. Our table was always set, food well presented. I recall her turning simple pancakes into funny shapes, such as a motorcycle, and make an occasion festive when she had no other means to celebrate a child. We often had only pancakes or baked beans for supper.

It was years later I realized we were poor. Yet, I had the most beautiful garments— clothes that looked good on me were designed and tailored to fit by her.

Mumma loved to read. She read novels, popular and good literature alike; she read cookbooks, style and design, history. She taught herself about antiques— how to identify, classify, refinish, and restore them.

Mumma opened a business in her early forties, still a mother with three children still at home, one with multiple disabilities. My mother was one of a kind, amazing by any standards. How lucky I was to have known her for nearly fifty years.

My Mother's Old-Fashioned Baked Beans

In my family we ate baked beans as a main dish served with bread and butter. In those days the end of a ham bone was a main ingredient (pork and beans). If not covering beans, you will need to add water periodically. Serve with: squash, yams or other seasonal vegetable; delicious over mashed potatoes; also good with cabbage salad.

2 cups navy or northern beans
2 sm. onions, chopped, not too finely
water to cover
2 Tbsp. molasses
2 Tbsp. brown sugar or maple syrup
½ cup ketchup (or tomato paste)
2 Tbsp. cider vinegar
1 tsp. dry mustard
salt and pepper to taste

Soak beans overnight or 5-6 hours minimum. Sort, rinse, and cover with clean cold water, bring to boil. Simmer 1 hour. Rinse again. Put beans in oven casserole at 350 degrees.

Add all other ingredients, water to cover, mix. Stir occasionally, adding water if needed

Bake about 6 hours until tender, with or without cover. Serve with squash, yams, or other seasonal vegetable; delicious over mashed potatoes; also good with cabbage salad. Serves 8.

Theodore Christou

It is Beautiful

This is no time to be ornate. It is beautiful to look upon you, mother.

Your beauty needs neither flowers, nor blush.

You sit in a bathrobe working upon a crossword. Your glasses look crooked, and they sit awkwardly athwart your face. Your hair is disheveled, as it always seems to be when you are worried. Each time that I must travel, you imagine the worst.

Those large blue eyes of yours dart.

You have been awake since dawn, it seems like, cooking. I am visiting for the day, and you've made that day a feast. It is Thanksgiving each day that I visit. I have thanks to give for these moments, albeit brief.

It is beautiful.
And the simplicity of this beauty will later lull me to sleep.

* * *

makoupe, and other stories
i long for mother
as all seems lost and futile
as sleepless nights morph to sleepy days
as unrest escalates

as i forget those stories that steadied me as a child
whenever i sensed angst and fear
which are now both too commonplace
which harass which debase
my mother would hold me
and tell me stories of crafty minded
or of noble hearted feats
of courage of hope

i long for my mother each morning
she of the craftiest mind
of the noblest heart
of brave feats
when i falter in courage or hope.

Cheryl Edwards

All That I Am

The excitement of having Mom move home was getting the better of my sister and me. Gayle was driving, Mom was in the passenger's seat, and I was in the back with Dad—who, by the way, had been cremated seven years before, but we took him everywhere. Since his passing, Dad came to his birthday parties every Thanksgiving and was in all the family photos wearing a party hat.

On this trip I was blaming my backseat driving on Dad because that's exactly what he would have done, giving his girls driving instructions even though we'd been driving for years. We all had a giggle because, after all, the humour in humour is truth. (In the months to come, Dad and Mom would travel to a dog show in Sudbury, their urns safely buckled in the backseat. This is how our family deals with some of life's tragedies. It may be bizarre by some standards, but absolutely normal by ours.)

Time was running out for Mom. She had been diagnosed with ovarian cancer in December 1998. The following September the oncologist regretfully said there was nothing more to be done and that Mom was at the palliative stage. She wanted to be at home at the end so she agreed to leave her apartment and come to stay with my sister.

February 2000 was brutal. The snowbanks were six feet high on Gayle's country road. It was too cold to snow and certainly too brittle for even the hardiest to go outside.

It baffled me how the nurse could predict, with some certainty, that Mom would leave us that weekend. Don't you need tests to know this with certainty? Mom appeared to be resting peacefully. Our homage was about to begin.

Six adult children relived their own lives with Mom and tried to imagine a life without her. She was the glue that held us all together. We each went in to see her to tell her what we wanted and needed to say and, lastly, to say our good-byes.

"Mom, I'll see you soon," I whispered as I bent to kiss her. She didn't ask what I meant. She didn't stir. Her eyes were closed, her forehead chilly, and her breathing quiet. But I knew that she knew I was in trouble. Mothers know these things. Just two days before I had been diagnosed with a cerebral aneurysm and had some difficult decisions to make. Have the surgery or not. After all, this six-centimeter bubble in my head could have been there for years, if not from birth. I knew I was very lucky the aneurysm had been identified by chance, but was I prepared to have a bomb ticking away in my head? The neurosurgeon had told me in no uncertain terms that if I didn't have the surgery and the bubble burst, chances of survival were small, and if I lived, well, I would be faced with so many challenges that I'd wish I had died. The surgery itself was risky.

The end came quickly, and five of her six children were by her side. Some of us experienced feeling Mom's spirit leaving her physical being. Her room transformed from a sick room to a tranquil space, with quiet music in the background. We made the required phone calls for a planned home death and then set out to wait. And think. And wait. And cry.

We sat in the front pew of the quaint country church. It didn't seem that long ago that we had done the same for Dad. Now they'd be together.

I could hear the church filling up. I didn't turn around, but I could feel eyes on me and hear the whispering. I had always resembled our Mom the most. Now the resemblance was almost eerie. I looked much the same way Mom looked when her friends saw her last. My head was shaved and my weight gain was noticeable. What everyone couldn't see was my swollen, closed eye and the raw scar that ran down the right side of my face. No one had really known I had been ill.

I leaned over to my oldest, younger brother. "Terry, I don't think I can get up and speak. I thought I could do it, but I just can't do it."

"That's okay, Shesh," Terry murmured, patting my hand. "I'll read it."

Reverend Sue finished her comments and Terry walked slowly to the pulpit, cleared his throat, and looked into the eyes of Mom's family and friends. He began to read the family eulogy.

"Thank you for joining us today to remember the life of Lillian June Edwards. We'd like to share with you our personal message to Mom....

"Mom, during the course of your illness, the character we always knew you had was illuminated. You faced your biggest challenge—a challenge even bigger than raising six kids, being a Nana to thirteen, and being a wife and good friend to Dad. Your greatest challenge was looking your mortality right in the eye. Not an easy challenge for anyone, right? It was not a task that most of us end up facing. Well, Mom, you somehow did this with style; a style that faced the facts and continued, even though the outcome was inevitable. It was a style that continued to consider your family and friends.

"During the final hours of your illness, more than one of us said to you that it was okay. That you could go. You didn't have to worry about us. You taught us well. We'd be all right. We meant it.

"One of the most important things that you taught us was to keep our sense of humour. Years ago we cut out a poem from the local paper that reminds us of you. It goes like this:

> It's easy enough to be pleasant,
> When life flows by like a song.
> But the man worthwhile is the one who will smile,
> When everything goes dead wrong.
> For the test of the heart is trouble,
> And it always comes with the years,
> And the smile that is worth the praises of earth
> Is the smile that shines through the tears.*

"Thanks, Mom, for your inspiration. Thanks more for your love and acceptance. And, Mom, you once wondered whether Dad would know you when you met again. We trust you've found out by now that all you had to do was smile and you'd turn back the years. Sleep tight. We'll love you forever."

There was silence in the church as Terry moved silently back to the front pew. There were no other speakers that day as we all remembered how Mom had touched our lives.

The rain had stopped as we moved outside to the grave site. I stood there as first Dad and then Mom were carefully placed in their new home. Dad's actual service had been years before so my thoughts that Saturday afternoon, the day before Mother's Day 2000, were all about Mom. Everything she had gone through during her chemo, the courage and humour she showed at all times, really reflected how she lived her life. These were her gifts to me, to all of our family, and in the days to come, I held these gifts close during my surgery and recovery. Call it what you will, but I could actually hear her say to me, "Keep your chin up, Cheri, both of them," and this got me through my own illness.

Our family has changed in many ways since Mom has gone, but it's easy to feel her close to us in times of difficulties and in times of joy. She's in our hearts, our dreams, and our souls. I hope I can follow her remarkable example. I do know, though, that "All that I am, or ever hope to be, I owe to my angel mother" (Abraham Lincoln).

(* "Worthwhile," Ella Wheeler Wilcox)

John Pigeau

"Lucky For Me There Was You"

With your kind & gentle ways,
you taught the cat to yawn.
Named it Strumbus, gave
it a warm, tender home,
& paid for its milk
by collecting bottles in
alleys & ditches.

No one knows how many cats you saved.
No one knows the sum of your love.
No one knows you invented gravity,
the sort of earth-tether that lends hope.

But I do. That last one.

And later, when they wished you
would learn to put your lipstick
on straight—how could they have
known you would take those turbulent,
uncertain leaps for them?
Bend their sour, frightened futures
toward grace?

And now, with so many gone,
their flags lovingly planted,
their porches carefully swept,
their souvenirs & memories generously illuminated
(yes, like snapshots of bright-eyed, yawning cats)
you may be the last one walking
through these late, budding hours,
queen of a new, sacred,
debtless country.

* "Lucky For Me There Was You" is taken from a poem by Dani Couture called "Survival Technique No. 7: Pairs"

Joyce Gero

The Tapestry

Strength and beauty,
honour, yes, and majesty—
with these four words,
her pastor wove a tapestry
of warmth and love.
Gently, he smoothed its silken folds
o'er gleaming oak—
not of a coffin, we were told;
instead, within
a chest of hope our mother lies
at peaceful rest.
In death, as sorrow blurs our eyes,
she comforts yet.
In golden threaded tapestry
she leaves behind
her warmth and love—our legacy.

Peggy Levesque

Dancing with Jesus

"Peggy, come quick!" My sister Anita's urgent call woke me from a deep sleep. "Something's happening with Mom."

I bolted out of bed, rushed to my eighty-year-old mother's side, and sank to the floor beside Anita. In the grey dawn light, I reached for Mom's hand, the parchment-opaque skin soft and fragile beneath my fingers.

Three weeks earlier I had flown from Phoenix to Minneapolis to stay with my mother and relieve other siblings from some of the burden they had unselfishly shouldered for many months. At that moment, though, indescribable gratitude filled me that my sister had spent these last hours with me. Her nursing skills equipped her for the physical process of death far better than I could manage alone.

Mom took a quick, shallow breath and let it out. We waited what seemed an eternity for each new breath, almost holding ours. Finally, she stopped inhaling all together and we knew the life and spirit we so loved had gone.

Tears poured down my face; a sob ripped from my soul at the finality of the moment. We expected it, even prayed for God to release her from the torment that had only increased in the past months. Why, then, the crushing grief, the weight that blocked my breath?

As Anita and I consoled each other, arms entwined and rocking back and forth, my mind sifted through the past.

As much as I loved her, I knew my mother wasn't perfect. She had a way of making her adult children feel totally inadequate. I remembered an incident that occurred just months earlier. She stood beside me, supervising my attempt at making her much-touted chow mein.

"I said an inch and a half, not an inch," she huffed.

Stung by her tone, I looked up from the celery I was slicing. Finally I took a deep breath. "Some things are just not that important, are they, Mom?"

I watched the play of emotions flicker across her face, from surprise to anger to regret and tears. "You're right," she said, her voice trembling. Then she turned and shuffled away.

As usual, an internal battled raged afterward. Was I too hard on her? Should I just ignore those moments that threatened to steal my hard-won self-esteem? She was ill and probably too old to change. Hadn't one of my sisters just told me so? Guilt seeped through the crevices in my resolve to stand firm. I didn't want to make her cry. "I love you, Mom," I said. But I didn't apologize.

Maybe my need for boundaries saved my sanity while I cared for her during the weeks prior to her death. I wondered: Would I have traded away her sometimes snappish remarks if it meant giving up the chance to have her beat me at Scrabble one more time? Or make homemade soup for her? Or simply hold her thin, frail body while we watched her favorite home improvement television show? The answer was a resounding no.

Where had the time gone? It seemed a heartbeat ago that as a grade-schooler I watched her youthful body stand before the mirror, clipping on a pair of pearl earrings.

"You look beautiful," I told her, proud I could lay claim to such a lovely mother.

"Thank you." Face glowing, Mom slipped into her black high-heeled shoes—the ones with the open toes. "Daddy is taking me dancing." Iridescent mauve taffeta swished as she bent down to kiss my upturned nose.

How long ago had age and infirmity stolen that vitality from her?

My thoughts drifted to the years of her annual visits to Arizona. What an adventurous spirit she displayed as she tramped with my family to the Grand Canyon, or the Painted Desert, or Slide Rock in Sedona. Like a slideshow through the years, I could see her cradle my two sons and daughter as infants, chase after them as toddlers. I watched my mother teach my seven-year-old daughter to set the table and, years later, sit with tears in her eyes as her granddaughter's nimble fingers coaxed the poignant strains of "Music of the Night" from the piano.

Within these reflections, and many more, my mother's unshakable spiritual faith, her underlying gentle nature and kind spirit sparkled through the debris of her flaws. And isn't that what I want for myself: that my loved ones won't dwell on my imperfections too long, but look past them to see the glow of Jesus shine through?

As I lifted out and examined each of my treasured memories, the ache in my heart grew just thinking of all the things we would never do again.

"Please, Lord, help me let her go," I pleaded. The excruciating pain of loss cut so deep I wondered if my own heart would stop.

In the midst of my grief, a sense of peace settled in, easing my anguish. In my mind I saw my mother in heaven, her body renewed in strength—no more oxygen, her walker cast aside. With the arms of Jesus firmly around her waist, she danced on the clouds.

Later, as we gathered clothing for her burial, a thought flashed through my mind. On my hands and knees, I dug through the bottom of Mom's bedroom closet and pulled out a pair of black high-heeled shoes.

"What are those for?" my sister asked as I blew off years of accumulated dust.

"These are dancing shoes." I grinned, my heart almost light, as I set them on the stack of clothing destined for the mortuary.

Did I believe my mother would ever really wear them? Of course not. For me, those shoes symbolized the new life God had in store for her, in spite of her frail human body, in spite of her failings.

Now, during moments of piercing sorrow, I picture my mom, all dressed up and wearing her black high heels. Dancing with Jesus.

Karen S. Chow

Dumplings for Dinner

On Sundays, my mother implemented a routine that became a family tradition. After we returned from church and Chinese school, my sister Erin and I would nap and wake to the aromatic smells of soy sauce, sesame oil, green onions, and ginger. It was our cue to wash up and join my mom and dad in the kitchen to make dumplings. We stood around the counter for almost an hour, chatting, laughing, making dinner together.

When Erin and I first learned how to make dumplings, we formed a small assembly line. Since she was the youngest and not as skilled with her hands, she peeled off a layer of thin wonton skin and dipped her spoon into the mixture of ground pork to form a small ball. She placed the meatball on the thin dough and wetted the sides with a finger coated in water, then passed the prepped dumpling to me. Taking up the outer edges, I folded the skin while watching my mother's magic act—at least, it seemed like magic, she did it three times as fast! We set the finished art pieces on wide-brimmed plates. When the plate was full, all of the "mini boats" lined up in concentric circles, my dad launched them into the sea of boiling water and attended to the saucepot.

We sat down at the dining table to eat these steaming pockets of love, accompanied by their friends: black vinegar and soy sauce.

As I grew older, the three ladies of our family simultaneously mixed the ingredients and spooned meat (with chopsticks like my mom did) and watered edges and folded the dumpling skins. When my brother was old enough, he was welcomed to the kitchen counter, too, saddled with the elementary task of spooning meat with a teaspoon.

Sunday dinner became an act of habit, a secondhand thought. We reminisced about our week, discussed the news, whiled away the time with gossip. It took only twenty minutes to make the dumplings then.

After I moved into a college dormitory, I made it a point to come home once a month for Sunday night dinner. I missed it too much. Any whiff of soy sauce in the cafeteria would bring me right back to the kitchen counter at home.

Our family tradition carried on until my father passed away. His wasn't a sudden death. It was a prolonged six-month affair of radiation treatments and hospice care, deteriorating health and extended hospital visits. My mother, sister, brother, and I were weary. And we didn't make dumplings the Sunday after the funeral. In fact, we did the opposite, scattering emotionally to the four ends of the earth for a while. We didn't talk about the funeral. We didn't reflect.

However, a few weeks later, my siblings and I had the itch. We wanted dumplings! And this time, the three "kids" made all of the dumplings, and my mother watched the boiling pot. At first, the ritual felt odd without my dad. But slowly, old habits returned and we found ourselves talking, even chuckling. A memory would pop up about my dad and we referred to it without feeling sad.

A little cooking therapy was apparently all we needed. It was comfort, in all ways.

This simple tradition that my mom, probably purposely, instilled in our family is something that I want to pass to my own daughter, so that someday, she can also take comfort in dumplings for dinner.

Dumplings

1 lb. ground pork
½ head of cabbage, chopped finely
3 stalks green onions, chopped
2 Tbsp. ginger, peeled and chopped
3 cloves garlic, minced (optional)
1 egg
1 Tbsp. soy sauce
1 Tbsp. sesame oil
1 tsp. salt
½ tsp. pepper
1 lb. wonton or gyoza skins, thawed
water
black vinegar (for dipping)
soy sauce (for dipping)

Mix ground pork, cabbage, green onion, ginger, garlic (optional), egg, soy sauce, sesame oil, salt, and pepper in large bowl.

Spoon about a tablespoon of meat mixture onto one wonton or gyoza skin.

Use finger to wet edges of wonton or gyoza skin with water. Fold edges together as you wish, making sure all sides are sealed shut (use more water if needed).

Place finished dumplings in water, heat on high. Bring to a boil, then add about ½ cup lukewarm water. Bring to a boil a second time, then add another ½ cup lukewarm water. At the third boil, strain dumplings, and serve.

Judith Cleland

The Recipe Card

Holding the recipe card in my hand,
it is a day, like this one, clear, breezy.
Yesterday's humidity gone, a picnic kind of day
and I can taste potato salad.

The card says "SALAD DRESSING—(Blood Clinic)"
No mention of potatoes, but I know
that was its purpose, although a note elsewhere
says, "same sauce for dandelion, endive and beets."

I also know that when I came home from school
on Wednesdays my mother would not be there.
It was her Red Cross, Blood Clinic day,
folding bandages for soldiers overseas.

This memory is filed among the tantalizing mysteries
that were not explained to young children,
along with the sonorous radio voice of war,
and hushed conversations among adults.

The taste of potato salad, anticipation of
a backyard gathering, aunts, uncles, cousins,
croquet on the lawn amid fragrant peonies
and food, food, food. All of it as clear as this day.

I stand, just as she did, my wooden spoon
patiently, constantly stirring the old fashioned recipe
in the double boiler until it thickens,
perfectly smooth and creamy.

Today it is my mother watching me,
the echo of her wisdom telling me
"A job worth doing, is worth doing well."
and I am reminded to savour the journey as much as the goal.

Linda Patchett

The Grain Givers

there is a sense of being cared for
that exists only in childhood

like an infant, feverishly suckling
from her mother's breast

slivered berry lips
perched on the dark fluid nipple

eyes periodically looking up
to ensure she is still there

i use to revel in that feeling of need
"mommy— my leg bites!"

my dampened spirit bolstered
by the tingling of silky kisses

gliding along my scraped shin bone
her gentle voice crooning—"a—l—l better!"

her tireless arms laden with riches
as she unwrapped a different package

for each ailment, and now—
shattered—i reach out

but there are no healing hands
to reach back in—to cup my own

this is the place girls go to
when they are no longer little

the internal agony swells
like a budding womb in heat

until finally, there is release
out into the void

when i return—a woman—i shoulder a different name
without daughters, i am left without women in my life

i carry the sun on the rumpled flesh of my back
and shake droplets of sweat

into the ground where another seed grows
i harvest and serve every last granule

to the wee men who grunt
while they pass through my kitchen

i run ragged to staunch their bleeding
all the while, wishing for granddaughters

for it is the women who silently carry
the blood of their mothers—

the women who are The Grain Givers—
givers of life

the prenatal cord
like a long shaft of wheat
still joins us,
still grows

to create attached distances

Rita Grimaldi

Rouge and Blush

When I was small I looked up to my mother. I looked up and saw her rouged cheeks and her smile. Then when I was twelve she became ill and I looked down at her in her bed. She was pale. Her cheeks were white. She had no makeup on. When I was fourteen she died. The undertaker put rouge on her cheeks but she wasn't the same.

Now I think, what if things had been different? What if she had not become ill?

What if we could have stood facing each other as adult women? Would she have stood there and said to me, "Rita, what a fine career you have had; how many children you have looked after. And Rita, how well you spin your yarn and what beautiful colours you make in your dye baths. And Rita, what beautiful tapestries you weave and what fine stories you tell."

But she cannot stand here and say these things. Still I can stand here with blush on my cheeks and say them for her.

Anna Yin

Mother

around the globe, you search
for two dots, connected
by a flight line. Distance
becomes a long string
to knot nostalgia;
Fingers nudge a blue
sphere—home beckons
like an aching moon.

You surprise me, drawing
concentric circles. Your pen drifts,
traces solar systems,
that revolve around the same point —
you say, that's our home!

Laughing at your crazy map,
I prune our family tree.
All of a sudden, a wind blows.
I see rings rippling across
your grey hair,
and leaves fall to roots.

Lois A. Wraight

Eminence Grise

I love the streaks of grey
in my hair
that have come to mark
the passing of my years.

I love it that now
reaching lightly into
my eighth decade
my hair is nearly all grey.

I love it that this morning
cleaning my hairbrush
I rolled the loose hairs
around my finger.

I love it that I saw in memory
my Mother performing
this same grooming task
and I became Daughter, watching.

I love it that the circle
is nearing completion;
this Daughter
becoming her Mother.

Stella Mazur Preda

My Mother's Kitchen

walls whispered untold secrets
tired linoleum painfully scarred
creaking floor boards played ominous tunes,
sinister and creepy
even as morning light tickled
window panes and frolicked with shadows
best of all
that old kitchen floor tilted downhill
several inches
      from one end
         to the other

on cold winter nights
we roller-skated circles
up and down its slopes
worked up an appetite
for Mother's old-fashioned
sugar cookies

on hot summer days
hazy stagnant air
hung with the aroma of spices
and simmering sweet fruits
as Mother boiled and bottled
homemade jams

Mother was at her best
in that crooked kitchen
where walls whispered
sunlight danced with shadows
and the old floor tilted
        downhill

Mom's Sour Cream Sugar Cookies

1 cup butter
3 cups all-purpose flour
1 cup sugar
2 egg yolks
¼ cup dairy sour cream (full fat for better flavour)
1 tsp. vanilla
½ tsp. baking soda
½ tsp. ground nutmeg (optional)

Beat butter in large mixing bowl until softened. Add half of flour, as well as sugar, egg yolks, sour cream, nutmeg, vanilla, and ¼ teaspoon salt. Beat until well combined. Beat or stir in remaining flour. Mix well. Divide dough in half. If necessary, cover and chill until dough is easy to handle.

Roll half of dough at a time on lightly floured surface to ⅛-inch thickness. Cut with desired cookie cutters. Place on ungreased cookie sheet.

Bake in 350 degree oven 5-7 minutes or until edges are firm and bottoms are lightly golden. Transfer to wire racks to cool. When they are completely cool, they can be iced if you wish.

Note: My mother never iced these cookies. Despite the fact that there is a cup of sugar, they are not sweet if you don't ice them. Wonderful with a glass of cold milk or good for dipping in coffee. When we were children, they were our favourite cookies.

Poem – "My Mother's Kitchen" was previously published: In My Mother's Kitchen anthology (New York: Penguin Books, May 2006), as well as Tower Poetry Society / Decup 2001—Winter Anniversary Edition

Memories
of
My Grandmother

*What children need most are
the essentials that grandparents provide
in abundance.
They give unconditional love, kindness, patience,
humor, comfort, lessons in life.
And, most importantly, cookies.*

—Rudolph Giuliani

Donna Wootton

Sarah (Kastner) Wilhelm, My Grandmother

My maternal grandmother died in 1989 on Ash Wednesday, a week after my father passed away. I grew up in an idealized world not experiencing death, then in the space of a week, I lost a parent and a grandparent. Shock. Grief. Mourning. They were both great storytellers. Charismatic. The focus of attention. I felt a void with their departure.

My grandmother Sarah was a farmer's wife who outlived her husband by nearly two decades. He was so quiet and unassuming I can't ever remember him speaking, but probably my father talked with him, engaged him in conversation, made him laugh.

Sarah collected eggs in the early hours from the chicken coop. They were still warm when she brought them into the summer kitchen, opened her apron, and put one in my hand. Then she would tell me about wringing the chickens' necks, how they ran around the yard headless before they collapsed. I pictured the scrawny-legged creatures, all body and feathers, no sound, just a confusion of movement churning up the dirt.

Sarah was a baker; she made her own bread. I liked to watch the loaves rise under the white towels placed near the back of the woodstove before she put them in the oven. As they were baking, the smell of fresh bread filled the farmhouse. Never using a recipe, she also baked pies—mostly apple, picked from her own orchard. She said when they had hired help, she would bake a dozen in the morning after serving breakfast. Once, when I was a young mother, I spoke to her on the phone, proudly saying I had baked an apple pie that day. Then she listed the chores she had done. She wasn't bragging, just sharing. Still, I felt like a lazy city dweller.

Sarah also grew vegetables. I have fond memories of pulling the long, green pods off the tall, spindly stalks to pick out the round peas, then popping them in my mouth. The new potatoes that came out of the earth peeled themselves when boiled. I remember the explosion in my mouth of freshness when eaten hot. They did not require added flavours like salt or butter. The flesh of those potatoes was like melted butter.

My grandmother also used the cabbages she grew to make sauerkraut. She shredded them by hand, tossed them in a bowl with salt, then packed them into blue earthenware pots. I tried to replicate this hap-dash method at home. The limp vegetable simply grew moldy, never reaching the stage of fermentation.

Sarah was a strong woman, but in death she looked frail inside the satin-lined coffin. It was open for the viewing at the funeral parlour, but closed the next day at the church. The priest wore white satin for the funeral service, a ritualistic event. He sprinkled holy water and incense over the coffin while chanting incantations. The ground was frozen so Sarah had to rest in the mausoleum over the winter.

I returned to the farmhouse after the service with relatives, friends, and neighbours. Outside the back door to the farmhouse was a pump. The well was no longer in use, but the pump remained as a reminder of more self-sufficient times. The backdoor led to the mudroom with one set of stairs going up to the summer kitchen and another set leading down to the root cellar in the basement. It was damp and dark, smelling of earth, just like the ploughed fields outdoors. Sarah's preserves lined the shelves. She was gone, but her produce was still edible. I placed a variety of pickles on serving plates, and with every bite I pictured her arthritic hands. They were gnarled with deformed joints but she kept working until the end.

In 2006 I produced a collection of six short stories. On the back cover is an aerial view of my grandmother's farm. In the first story a character named Hilary teaches piano to the narrator's daughter. Of Hilary the main character says,

> "Understand, she was used to the domestic side of life. She'd grown up on a farm outside Walkerton where the water turned lethal. It was that nasty episode, the scare over the safety of municipal water that caused her to reveal her past to us. She showed Breanna and me the aerial photograph taken of her family's farm, the farm her older brother still worked. He'd inherited the place when her brother died. Was there malice in

her voice when she said it had lost its value over the e-coli scare? That's what I detected. Sheer malice. With political overtones. Yes, malice against the politicians whose budget cuts had undermined the quality of water and had harmed trusting citizens, then devalued honest people's property."

Malice was not a tone I remember in my grandmother's voice. Mostly I remember her chuckle. My father, too, had a memorable chuckle. Chuckling storytellers.

Jean Ann Williams

Nanny and Me, Punkie Jean

My grandmother, Nanny, peered over the top of my see-through plastic oxygen tent, which she had set over her sofa. I worked to catch a decent breath in my lungs. She frowned down at me with anxious eyes. Did she see the elephant that I felt on my chest?

I had returned from the hospital just hours before, from yet another asthma attack. As was the normal agreement between my parents and Nanny, she took me into her home and would nurse me back to health. My family and I lived too far from the nearest hospital, which was in Nanny's town. The current asthma attack was by far the worst. I had been under an oxygen tent in the hospital, but never before at Nanny's.

From the beginning, after my birth, Nanny was a second mother to me. While she waited for my mom and me to come home from the hospital, she set up a bedroom for us in her home. We lived there for two weeks, where Nanny taught my fifteen-year-old mother how to care for a baby. Nanny prepared a dresser drawer for a bed, padding it with soft blankets. My relatives carried newborn me in it from room to room to keep a close watch. I often wonder if other babies started their life in a wooden box meant for clothes.

As I looked through my clear tent where steam helped me to breathe, my six-year-old self wanted to smile and reassure Nanny that I would be okay. I did attempt to make my lips crease up, but it took complete concentration to work my lungs. As her brown eyes locked onto mine, it gave me strength to breathe in and out as she did.

Nanny rarely left my side on that stay, but when she had to leave, my aunt took over. Standing guard like only a thirteen-year-old would, my aunt never took her eyes off of me. At one point, everyone gathered around, Nanny, Papa, and my aunt and uncle. Their serious expressions and murmurs of "gasping for air" frightened me somewhat. The next part seemed odd, for I either dreamed it, or I really did hover above and look down on my body. I guess I'll never know, but being so young, I didn't understand on that day I could have easily gone on to Paradise.

After I healed enough to venture out, Nanny dressed in her finest clothes, including hat and gloves. She said, "Punkie, we're going to the bank."

I sat on the seat of the car next to Nanny. Good at pretending, I imagined we were going on an adventure far away from my sick bed and to a place called The Bank. The bank turned out to be a tall building with nice ladies who gave Nanny money. Even though Nanny didn't introduce me, they called me Punkie. I stared up at my grandmother a bit shocked. Only Nanny and Papa ever called me by my nickname, not even Mother or Daddy.

I found out years later that everybody in Nanny's town was related to nearly everyone else. They probably knew more about me than I understood about myself.

After the bank, Nanny pulled up to a department store where fancy women's dresses stood on mannequins in the display windows. Nanny held my hand, guiding me along through the open double doors and deep into the rack of clothes. A lady greeted Nanny. "Hi, Edith. You have your little helper with you today." I waited for her to call me Punkie, but she did not, for Nanny didn't stop long enough to carry on a conversation.

Nanny turned, and we entered the girls' section. She picked out a dress and shiny black shoes, and a hat and coat the same colour as hers. To complete the outfit, she bought me a pair of gloves. Just like hers. I have a photograph of us standing side by side in front of the same bank on another day in our matching outfits.

Even though Nanny didn't offer hugs and kisses like my other grandmother, she kept me by her side like the most special child in the whole universe. I learned a lot from her by watching. The best pie maker in town, she allowed me to stand on a stool and "help" her bake. I stood on that stool many times in her kitchen, while she prepared delicious meals and desserts.

The best fun, though, came from Nanny's dressing room. My grandfather, Papa, had a thriving business, and he enjoyed buying Nanny the latest fashions: clothes, jewelry, and shoes. I still remember the day Nanny said, "Punkie, you may play dress up with anything I have in my closet."

I took it for granted all granddaughters had the same right to comb through their grandmother's closets and drawers. I especially enjoyed Nanny's purple dresses and her high heels. In her dressing room, she had two doors leading in and out with mirrors attached to the doors. I loved to adjust the doors in such a way that I saw multiples of myself dressed in stylish clothes.

Have you ever tried walking in heels much too big? You fall down a lot and bruise your knees. Always ready when I needed her, Nanny doctored my skin with the stinky, ouch stuff, topped off with a bandage. With all the care she gave, it felt as though she'd kissed my hurt away.

I had the best life until the summer before my ninth birthday. It was then I found out my family and I were moving five hundred miles north to Oregon. I believe my heart cracked a little, because Nanny and Papa could not go with us. Even though they came to visit during the summers, too soon Nanny passed away before my thirteenth birthday. She thought of my future, though, before she left.

Five years later and soon after my wedding, Papa arranged for my husband and me to meet with him, saying he had something important to give me. When we arrived, he pulled an envelope from his coat pocket. "Here," he said, "this is from Nanny."

My mouth dropped open. I was staring at an envelope with Punkie written across the middle of it. I looked at my papa. He said, "Go ahead and see what she gave you."

My fingers trembled, as I fumbled with the seal and tore it open. My heart caught in my chest: no letter inside as I had hoped. I blinked, not understanding what I was seeing, but soon tears rolled down my cheeks. I gazed into Papa's eyes, unable to speak.

"Nanny got this ready for you before she died," he said. "She told me to give you the hundred dollar bill when you got married."

I sobbed into my papa's chest, mumbling about how I missed and needed her. "Papa, why did she have to die?"

He sighed. "I sure don't know, Punkie."

The money Nanny set aside for my wedding gift saw us through my husband's unemployment, until the small city where Nanny had lived and died hired him as a police officer.

I could never forget Nanny. She made such a positive impression on me, and after forty-five years, I still dream about her. At the end of the dream, I'll remember she has gone to the spirit world and I'll wake with sticky eyes wet from my tears. At those times, a burden will fill my chest like the one I felt when recovering from an asthma attack on Nanny's couch, or when we drove away to Oregon and left my nanny behind.

Several years ago my young son died, and my world grew dark. I told myself to breathe in and breathe out. Before the memorial service, the same aunt who guarded me all those years before came to my home. She said through tears and a quivering voice, "Nanny told me to come." I responded by grabbing her in an embrace and sobbing into her neck.

I saw Nanny's love in my dear aunt's eyes.

Cassandra Wessel

A Pinch of This and That

Grandma's house sizzled in summer like bacon frying in a pan. She was baking biscuits—light, fluffy, melt-in-your-mouth biscuits. Triple digit temperatures, in combination with her cranking oven, soundly defeated all efforts to cool her kitchen. Every year she valiantly fought the heat by plunking her box floor fan in front of her open screen door. In the opposite doorway, between kitchen and dining room, she placed a one-legged oscillating fan in a vain attempt to cool both rooms. A ceiling fan in the living room groaned as it slowly moved sweltering air from one corner of the room to another, air that smelled of biscuits and crude oil from the rig next door.

The rig's perennial chugging added to the cacophony of the whirring, chattering fans that significantly overwhelmed most attempts at conversation. Still, the six-year-old chatterbox, Cassie, tried. "How come you live next to that dirty old rig?"

"Oil rigs chug away all over Oklahoma City. Can't get away from them."

"How do you stand it?"

"A body can get used to a lot of things, honey child."

Cassie's attention wandered around the plain kitchen. In the middle of the aging room, a porcelain-topped table groaned beneath the weight of bags and bowls that cluttered every square inch. Among them, a bowl heaped high with freshly churned butter had a serving spoon plunged into it. On the other side of it stood a quart jug of buttermilk. Next to the table, an old spindle chair was occupied by a fifty-pound sack of flour.

Cassie leaned upon her elbows studying her grandmother, and squirmed. Her rickety slat-back chair creaked to the rhythm of her swinging legs. She watched as her grandmother shuffled, house slippers flip-flopping with bunions painfully protruding, along the opposite side of the table. A red paisley handkerchief, pulled tight around her henna-dyed hair, vainly blocked perspiration from following the folds in her face. Sweat quickly plastered several unruly wisps to her rouge reddened and flushed cheeks, streaking them.

Cassie wondered why her grandmother bothered with makeup, and decided not to wear it. She thought it looked odd. Besides, she could not tell where face powder left off and baking flour began. Her grandmother did a lot of things that puzzled Cassie. She wondered why she tied a flour sack apron around her fleshy frame as her sweat-drenched dress was already soiled. But when she rolled the sleeves of her calico housedress well beyond her elbows, Cassie soon discovered why.

Her grandma plunged her hands up to her elbows into the flour sack and picked out a depression era pottery cup heaped full of flour. Then she emptied it several times into a pottery bowl the size of a bathtub. Next, she added ingredients from various boxes, bowls, and bags scattered across the tabletop. Thrusting her hands into the mix, as Ma worked the dough, she said, "Child, mind you don't overmix biscuits."

Cassie nodded, but her mouth watered. She asked. "Can I have a grape soda pop with my biscuit, Ma?"

Everyone called her, "Ma," never "Grandma." She would brook no appellation indicating that she was aging. Ma wanted to be ageless, thus the makeup, but age refused to concede. Cassie persisted. "How old are you?"

"Old enough to know better than to ask a woman how old she is."

"Aw, come on, Ma, p-l-e-a-s-e, tell me how old you are?"

"Honey, y'all keep asking me silly questions and these biscuits will never get baked. Shoo."

Waving her flour-covered hands, Ma baptized her with white powdery fluff. Cassie ducked, but did not leave. Instead she watched with awe as Ma deftly lifted a ball of floured dough onto the board, rolled it and flipped it like a half moon. Taking a clean and floured number 2 tin can, she punched out biscuits placing them upon a baking sheet, instructing, "Be careful not to handle them too much. Y'all do, and it'll make them tough."

The word "them" was always said with two syllables. Although Grandma was a Normal School graduate and had been a country school teacher, as hard as she tried, she never could rid herself of her Oklahoma twang. Similarly, try as Cassie might, she never did learn Ma's secrets; not her age, or how to make biscuits like hers. Years after she had become a grandmother herself, she still experimented with biscuit recipes trying to duplicate Ma's, but she never could quite figure out what was missing. Could it be the sizzling Oklahoma heat?

Mother Jackson's Low Fat Biscuits

1½ cups white all-purpose flour
½ cup whole wheat flour
1 tsp. baking soda
2 tsp. baking powder
½ tsp. salt (optional)
3 generous Tbsp. nonfat plain yoghurt plus whey
Sufficient milk to make 1 cup when mixed with yoghurt
6 Tbsp. Canola oil (for flakier biscuits use low fat margarine)

Sift dry ingredients together. Mix well. Make well in dry ingredients. Pour in liquid mixture and stir until all flour is absorbed. Dough should cling together without being sticky. Take care not to overwork as that makes for tough biscuits. Dump onto parchment paper. If sticky, lightly flour surface. Shape into an oblong bulk. Roll with a rolling pin until about 1 inch thick. Fold in half. Punch out biscuits with a biscuit cutter. Place on ungreased cookie sheet and bake for about 12 minutes at 450 degrees or until golden. When baked, remove immediately from cookie sheet and place on serving dish.

Hint: A 2½-inch can (well washed and dried) can be used instead of a biscuit cutter.

Joanne Sandlin

Spaghetti, But No Meatballs

Nothing could pry me from my own private tree house escape that Grandpa built just for me in the big backyard oak tree. It was the perfect place to go with a candy bar and a stack of comic books. Carol and Billy were my neighborhood best friends, but they were busy today so it was time to climb up to my own private world.

The one thing that could get me to budge was the smell of Grandma Claudina's cooking after she had been to her garden to gather herbs that she mixed with freshly chopped garlic, olive oil, and real butter. Sometimes she let me help her in the kitchen where she created what I thought was food magic. One day she whispered her secret ingredient put into every dish: She seasoned everything she cooked with love! She made comfort food before it was called that—especially spaghetti.

Her spaghetti was not ordinary spaghetti with tomato sauce and meat that people associate with spaghetti. Hers didn't have any sauce at all, but it didn't need any. What it didn't have in it, it made up for in twice the flavour. Hers melted right in your mouth.

Grandma Claudina was from Gudo, Switzerland, near the northern Italian border. She came to America sailing out of France in 1906 at the age of twenty, through Ellis Island, New York, as an immigrant with one trunk carrying all her possessions. One invisible ingredient in that trunk was her cooking skills. After crossing the United States by train, she settled in California's central coast with other Italian immigrants who worked on farms and as domestic workers.

I always thought the family that hired Grandma must have eaten very well!

Drifting in through the tree house I thought I smelled her spaghetti that was like no other. Sniffing again, I knew I was right! Gathering my books and candy wrapper, down the steps I went. Her spaghetti also meant fresh from the garden butter lettuce gently tossed with her special oil and vinegar dressing made fresh each day, and thick slices of crusty sourdough bread. I could hardly wait! There was always room for anything from Grandma's kitchen. Sometimes it was polenta, a traditional family firm cornmeal topped with slowly simmered beef stew, always served on special occasions. Of all the mouthwatering dishes she lovingly created, however, my favorite was the meatless white spaghetti tossed with fresh herbs and bread crumbs. Who needed meatballs?

I burst into the kitchen greeted by her warm smile, tied on my apron, and headed for the silverware and dishes to speed up tasting that special dish! People leave many kinds of legacies, but family recipes and warm memories of meals shared last a lifetime as each generation savors family favorites!

Cooking and sharing meals with Grandma and family gave me a love for cooking that carried over into adult life. In 2003 I published my own cookbook, *The Front Burner with Family and Friends*, as well as writing and sharing recipes through newspaper columns for fifteen years in two different communities. And I always remembered to add the secret ingredient to every dish: love!

Grandma's Pasta with Herbs and Breadcrumbs

(Measurements are approximate and created from memory. This recipe is
 very flexible.)

1/3 - ½ cup olive oil
2½ - 3 cups breadcrumbs (made fresh is best)
3-4 large garlic cloves, finely chopped
grated Parmesan cheese
¼ - 1/3 cup finely chopped parsley
Salt and fresh ground pepper to taste
Other herbs to your taste finely chopped may be used.
¾ - 1 lb. broken spaghetti or linguine, cooked al dente and drained

Heat the olive oil over medium heat using a large sauté pan.

Add breadcrumbs and sauté until golden brown. Watch carefully, about 5
minutes. Add garlic and sauté it about 2 minutes. Take pan from heat; add cheese,
parsley, salt, and pepper. Stir well to combine. Add cooked pasta and stir to coat
with pan mixture over low heat. If too dry, a little olive oil may be added. Sprinkle
with extra cheese, if desired, and serve immediately.

This dish is easy, fast, and filling, and can be used as a main or side dish. It
is still a popular dish served throughout Italy. Although Grandma made it
without meat because they were too poor to afford it, you may add a bit of
chopped prosciutto. One of the great things about this dish is that it is versatile,
allowing for adjustment to personal tastes. Don't forget to add that special
ingredient just before serving!

Annmarie B. Tait

Hooked on Hats

Hello everyone. My name is Annie and I'm a hat-aholic. There, the hard part is over. I know it's weak not to take full responsibility for my addiction but the hardcore truth of the matter is: It's not my fault! No really, it's not!

The first picture I ever saw of my grandmother was her wedding photo taken in 1920. In this picture she looked stunning, dressed in a dark suit with a narrow waist and a full skirt all piped in a delicate white cording. But, as gorgeous as all of that was, it fizzled in comparison to the phenomenal wide- (and I do mean w-i-d-e) brimmed hat with the huge velvet bow that truly was the crowning glory of the whole outfit. In the photo it dipped slightly to one side and framed her face, perfectly setting off her beautiful eyes and beaming smile. Through the bow in the front was a hatpin probably eight inches long with a large black ball at the end studded with shiny crystals. Clearly this photo captured one of the happiest days of her life. Whatever Pop-Pop looked like I don't remember. I have never gotten past that hat.

"Who is this?" I asked my mom as I handed her the picture, practically drooling over it.

"That's Mom-Mom and Pop-Pop on their wedding day," she said.

"Do we still have the hat?" I asked with my fingers crossed.

"You'll have to ask Mom-Mom, but I doubt it."

The next time we went to Mom-Mom's I barely crossed the threshold before I blurted out, "Mom-Mom, can I try on your wedding hat? Can I? Please. Can I?"

"Oh Annie, I got rid of it years ago," she said. Then she turned right around, winked at my mother and said, "She's hooked," and they both laughed out loud.

At the time I didn't know what all that was about. The laughing that is. But from the moment I saw Mom-Mom in that drop-dead gorgeous hat I knew the crown of my head would rarely feel the warmth of the sun henceforth and forevermore. Amen.

From then on most visits to Mom-Mom's included pulling all of the hatboxes out from under her bed and from every nook and cranny where they were tucked away in Mom-Mom and Pop-Pop's bedroom. Together we sat at her dressing table and tried on all manner of millinery, including wide-brimmed sun hats, fedoras, pillboxes, upturned brim hats, cloches, and even some called sailor style. Most were constructed of felt or straw but all were adorned with a vast array of accessories including little veils, velvet bows, spring flowers, and ribbons galore. Each hat prompted a conversation between us about all the imaginary fancy parties and events we soon would attend, leaving the other guests in awe of our beauty and good taste. None of the dress-up tea party events I shared with any of my little girlfriends remain in my memory with the sentiment and clarity of those precious times I spent with Mom-Mom. I was only five or six years old then.

Years and years later when I was in my twenties, and Pop-Pop had been gone for years, Mom-Mom could no longer maintain her own home and moved into a nursing home. As we were sorting out the house my mom assigned me the task of cleaning out Mom-Mom's bedroom. Just as I suspected all of the hatboxes were gone by then.

After packing up her clothes I turned to go and, just as an afterthought, I went over to the dressing table and sat down one last time. Looking in the mirror I wandered back in time and reminisced about our happy times together. Lost in thought I unconsciously opened the top drawer of the dressing table. As I looked down I caught sight of a beautiful black hatpin about eight inches long with a glass ball at the top studded with shiny crystals pierced through a lovely velvet bow. I picked up Mom-Mom's wedding hatpin and held it in my hands as if it were the crown jewels. I still wonder if she intentionally left it there for me to find.

Today it sits on my bureau among my other hatpins in a lovely china hatpin holder that also once belonged to Mom-Mom. It's not sitting there as a mere decoration. Oh no. I wasn't kidding about being a hat-aholic. I too own oodles of hatboxes and each holds a masterpiece. In fact I rarely leave the house without a hat on. Granted, most times it isn't one of my special occasion bonnets but always a felt beret in winter, a straw sun hat in summer, or something befitting the weather conditions whatever they may be. Mom-Mom hit the nail on the head. I'm hooked.

Dominic Spano

A Gift from Grandma

I used to think my grandmother hated my grandpa. I'm probably the only kid in school who ever felt like that about his grandma but I don't feel that way anymore. It's just that every story I've ever read said that grandmothers are the most loving creatures on earth. Three years ago, my grade five teacher even brought a plaque to hang on the classroom wall that said, "Grandchildren are a person's reward for reaching a ripe old age"—or something like that.

My grandmother, however, always acted like anything but a person who deserved a reward—at least when it came to Grandpa. For one thing, she was taller than him and had a habit of calling him "Shorty"; and sometimes, towering over the sink peeling potatoes, or leaning over the stove to slide another pie into the oven, she'd suddenly pester Grandpa who was minding his own business, asleep on the couch in front of the TV, an open book about to slide off his lap.

She'd say stuff like: "Hey old man, the lawn needs mowing. Get that flat butt of yours out there and make it good for something other than passing air." Or she'd ask him if his sore fingers were keeping him from answering his brother's letter—stuff like that.

"Yes, dear," Grandpa always mumbled, snapping out of a loud snore. "I may be stirring the pot but you're the one making the stew." I never understood what he meant by that.

"That's the good hubby," she usually threw in with a wink that seemed to say, "I fixed his butt."

Only I don't think Grandpa's butt needed fixing; and it wasn't flat, either.

As for his snoring, she often complained to my mom about it.

"Land sakes, Linda, you'd think a 747 was coming in for a landing right there in our bed."

"Well, Martha," Grandpa once told her through a laugh that never made sense to me, "all I know is that you'll miss my sonic booms when I'm no longer here." I would have thought that he'd be angry.

"I doubt it," she said, always wanting the last word. "Since when does the other end elicit a 'he shoots-he scores'?"

"Not always," Grandpa said. "I sometimes hit the post."

"Oh go on with you," Grandma said, shooing him away. And he laughed so hard that his eyes watered. It really confused me. But I don't think Grandma should have been making fun of Grandpa like that. I had seen him play hockey and he wasn't very good. For a guy like him, hitting the post should have gotten him a pat on the back.

Anyway, whatever the chore, Grandpa always acquiesced and, after finishing, he would go out for a walk in the nearby park. Sometimes, he'd even grab his fishing rod, beckon me with his own wink, and together we would stroll down to the river where we could cast our poles underneath the bridge. How Grandma could be mean to my grandpa was a mystery to me—a mystery that grew deeper when he died.

Grandpa never woke up one morning and I remember feeling numb. I was eleven years old and I knew I would never see him again. I also remember thinking that Grandma must be relieved not to have to scold Grandpa for falling asleep in front of the TV anymore. But to my surprise that was not her reaction at all. In fact, she stopped being the grandma I knew. She stopped baking and she spent most of her time doing what Grandpa used to do—sit on the couch in front of the TV. Only she didn't fall asleep. She just sat there, staring at the screen, never changing the channel. Sometimes she lingered next to Grandpa's picture on the stand inside the balcony door and lit the vigil candle—every morning it had to be a fresh one. She said it made her feel closer to him somehow; that it felt too much like she was leaving him behind otherwise. Afterwards, she always went back to the couch.

Grandma's changed behaviour began to worry my mom and she made an appointment for Grandma to see the doctor. But Grandma refused to go.

"Well, you can't spend all your time brooding on that couch," Mom finally told her. Strangely, Grandma got up, grabbed her shawl and went out the door.

"Follow her," Mom told me. "Make sure she's safe."

I watched Grandma go into the park and take the very same route that Grandpa used to. I ran up to her.

"Grandma, are you okay?"

She didn't respond.

I shook her arm. "Grandma, you're scaring me. Are you okay?"

She pointed that long, bony finger of hers towards a tree. I followed her and we ended up sitting on the bench next to the tree. It was funny-looking, with intertwining branches that were begging to be untangled. Fluffy white petals were on the ground all around it.

"Are you there, Horace?" she said after a while, calling out Grandpa's name. "Those petals you used to like in my hair...I think they're dying off...just like me."

I was shocked to hear those words and we both sat in silence for a long while—until I noticed the silhouette of someone striding towards us on in-line skates. It was a woman in white shorts and blue top. Grandma caught me staring and shook her head. She turned to look at the tree and nodded a few times.

"Give me ice skates anytime. Remember those Wednesday nights at the arena?" she suddenly said.

"What do you mean, Grandma?" I looked around to see if anyone else was there. She continued to stare at the tree.

"Every couple hand in hand, striding to the exact beat of the tunes: song...sung...blue[1]...On speed skates too! I'd like to see these kids try their fancy moves on those long blades."

She sighed. "You left me behind, Horace. And I'm tired."

This time my shock overcame me. "Grandma, don't talk like that. You still have us."

The in-line skater smiled and waved as she flashed by. "Good morning. Enjoy the beautiful day."

Grandma half-raised her hand, as though not interested in reciprocating the friendly gesture. Instead, she leaned over to gather two white petals into her palm. She brought her hand up to my face so I could take a closer look. "Your grandfather and I were young once and these meant something special to us."

I closed her hand around the dying flowers. "You mean something special to us, Grandma. Let's go home. Mom's waiting."

"Wait." She reached under her shawl. "Here, take this."

Grandma clasped my hand in both of hers. When she pulled back, she left a small brooch in my palm. It looked like a sheaf of wheat.

"Your grandfather gave it to me. He said it's from The Little Prince[2], something from one of those nonsense books he was always reading."

"Wow! I, uh…" I stared at the trinket in my palm, not really knowing what to say. Our grade seven teacher had read us the story and I knew exactly what it meant. Sharing this particular token with my grandfather made my eyes water.

"It's okay," Grandma said. "Just accept it."

"Gee…"

"Don't give it another thought. Let's go home."

Grandma never woke up the next morning and I wondered if she had worked it out that way with Grandpa. Three days later, the church was packed as everyone paid their respects, clutching the little remembrance card with Grandma's particulars on one side and a prayer on the other.

"I don't think I really knew her until now," I told my mom, struggling with my composure.

Mom answered with a nod. "She was a complex person."

"But it's just not fair. I missed my chance."

"Who is to say what's fair? I got acquainted with my mother mainly through my dad's relationship with her. All I know is that they were born for one another and that's why she missed him so much. I guess it was her time."

On the pulpit, the reverend had begun to speak about Grandma. "You know, my brothers and sisters," he said, "Martha continued to volunteer here at the church even into her later years. Horace used to tease me, saying that I should either start charging her rent or else just send her home to him. Well, Horace—" I thought I heard the reverend's voice crack. "Today I'm sending her home to you."

That day I understood exactly why Grandpa was never mad at Grandma and why he stirred her pot.

He, and all those other people in church, liked her stew.

[1]A reference to Neil Diamond's "Song Sung Blue"
[2]A reference to Antoine de St. Exupery's *Le Petit Prince*

LeAnn Rowse

Chicken for Dinner

The early morning air was cool and crisp. A rooster crowed, coaxing me from my warm, cozy bed on Grandma's screened front porch.

I wandered around to the backyard just in time to see my grandmother enter the chicken coop with a "chicken catcher," a long wire with a hook on the end just big enough to snag the chicken's ankle. Curiosity propelled me toward her, and it didn't take long before she noticed me watching her.

My grandmother was a woman of few words, but when she spoke, I obeyed. "Come here," she said. I followed, not sure what was in store. It didn't take long for me to find out. Grandma spied the chicken she wanted, and with a swift practiced hand, the chicken was taken captive. "Here, hold it," she commanded. I found myself holding a squawking, flapping chicken by its yellow, rough, scaly legs. Grandma spotted another one, and soon had it captured as well. "Here, hold it," came the next command. Now I was holding two squawking, flapping chickens!

"Follow me!" I had a pretty good idea what was to come as I followed Grandma to the chopping block. She took one of the chickens from me. "Sorry to do this to you, old biddy," she said to the chicken then whack, off flew its head. Grandma gave it back to me, then took the other one and said, "Sorry to do this to you, old biddy." then another whack and its head flew off. "Here, take it," she directed. The only thing worse than holding two live squawking, flapping chickens is holding two headless, flapping chickens with blood spurting all over the ground and me!

"This is getting rather messy," I thought as I held them as far away from me as possible. So far, my leisurely early morning stroll was a far cry from what I imagined.

"Come." I obediently followed Grandma to her porch where she had buckets of scalding water awaiting the chickens. After she had dunked them to her satisfaction, she gave one back to me, and showed me how to pluck feathers. I pulled and yanked out feather after feather. The wet feathers stuck all over my hands and clothes, joining the blood spatter. I didn't realize chickens had so many feathers!

After all the feathers were plucked, Grandma loosely rolled up a newspaper and set it on fire. She turned one chicken at a time over the flames until the pinfeathers that were too small to pull out were singed off. Then Grandma gave me a chicken, and following her lead, I stuck my hand into the chicken's body cavity pulling out all the nasty contents such as intestines, heart, lungs, stomach, and gizzard which was full of gravel. The innards were slimy, gooey, and stinky. I felt like gagging! By now, I was covered with blood, feathers, and slime. With the chickens cleaned, Grandma finally let me go. The first thing I did was clean up, and then I made sure I stayed far away from Grandma!

Close to noon, the aroma of chicken frying wafted from the house making my stomach grumble. There on the table was a platter of fried chicken. It was the best chicken I had ever eaten!

Natalie Kim Rodriguez

The Gift of Good-bye

Silently, she stood in the hallway of her home of fifty years. Her face, worn and tired from lack of sleep.

"Niña, where's the bathroom?"

I looked up and stared into her hazel eyes filled with fear and perplexity. "Where it's always been, Grandma. Right there." I pointed to a door that was just a foot to her left.

"Oh," she replied.

Later, we sat, side-by-side, on the sofa. Grandma took my hand and said, "I think I'm losing my mind."

Nodding, knowing that two of her siblings had been diagnosed with Alzheimer's, I agreed. "Yes, I know, Grandma."

Lovingly she mustered a wry smile and said, "Let's say good-bye, now."

We embraced. She patted my back like she always did when hugging me good-bye from a visit. My eyes welled with tears as my heart knew this was her moment of control in circumstances. With head held high, she humbly embraced her present dignity and shared a meaningful moment with me, her niña linda. La Negrita liñda.

Years later, after disease had fully claimed her body and stripped the wise woman whom I loved, I saw her again dressed in blue. A casket was her new bed. Her eyes closed and warmth lost from her cheeks.

With head held high in pride, I gently held her ice cold hands and said, "Grandma, let's say our last good-bye, now." I closed my eyes to remember the day she held me in remembrance of us side-by-side, face-to-face.

There is a gift in partings when used in power to release what is inevitable.

The loss of a loved one to death.

The break of a dysfunctional relationship.

The removal of a bad habit.

The letting go of negative emotions.

Replacing old things with new.

A bitter sweetness is found in the heart that lets go when love and life meet distance and choice. Yet, the savoring of new things to come stave off the sorrow before it has time to set in when choosing to depart is embraced with hope.

I learned from my grandmother that a gift given in strength and dignity frees others to live. She released me from blame by acknowledging the inevitable. By her example, I have learned to be a giver of good-bye.

June Carter Powell

Doctor Granny

Granny could cure the common cold, asthma, or an earache with one remedy.

"A good dose of castor oil," she said, "will fix you up!" It appeared that the thought of taking a dose of castor oil cured as many ailments as actually taking it.

In addition to castor oil, Granny smeared goose grease on the feet for a headache, applied mud on bee stings, and mixed up mustard plasters for a chest cold. The only ailment Granny refused to treat was hay fever. Allergies had not yet been invented. That the malady always coincided with the haying season meant one thing to Granny: You did not want to pitch hay. Hay fever was cause for mirth by your fellow workers.

During the early '40s there was a shortage of manpower on the farm as all the strong young men had gone to war. Granny and Grandpa did as much as they could because farming was still an important source of food. It became necessary for the five grandchildren to dedicate two weeks during the summer to do the haying. Both Granny and Grandpa worked hard, with Granny having the additional duties of housewife and mother.

My time to work on the farm always came at the same time as my allergy season. I loved and admired both Granny and Grandpa and, in fact, was Gramps' favorite grandchild. I think it had more to do with my stubborn chin, and the fact that I seldom complained about having headaches or a sore throat. I just stuck that chin out, grabbed the pitchfork, and got the job done so I could suffer in silence and escape the castor oil remedy.

A summer cold, as Granny called it, meant that you got the full treatment of castor oil, goose grease, and the mustard plaster all at once. The fact that you often climbed out of bed worse than when you went into it meant one thing: You were never really sick in the first place. The red nose and itchy eyes were the result of having too much fresh air at night so the cure had some things added to it. In spite of the temperature being 89 degrees all night, your window was closed tightly, so if your nose ever had a fighting chance at breathing, it was cancelled out immediately by the heat and stale air in your room.

That I got through several years of Granny's cures has a lot to do with having an amazing immune system today. It was a test of endurance to get through the day without an encounter with Granny's jar of goose grease, or the poultice of white bread boiled in milk. The latter was placed over all possible infections until the "pison" was drawn out of it. This could take a couple of days but you did not remove the poultice before the appointed time had lapsed. When it had dried out completely, it was safe to remove it and the danger of infection was over.

With the removal of the poultice came a feeling of relief. Granny would examine the area carefully just in case there was a red line running from it up your arm. If it looked like a possibility, she cocked her head to one side and announced that you could have the following day off from work, but that meant you had to lie still for twenty-four hours, while she put hot towels on the area every twenty minutes. She would soak the towels in boiling water, which she wrung out with incredible ingenuity to avoid being burned and placed on the offending area until it cooled and then she did it all over again.

* * *

The day I sat on a chicken in the outdoor biffy I learned that I was not just another grandchild, but Granny's favorite. It was getting dusky and I was in a rush. The sudden squawking of a startled chicken sent me running outside and straight into Grandpa with my clothing in disarray. I will never forget the expression in his voice as he suggested that "Your grandmother would never do a thing like that! Young ladies in my day did not behave in that fashion! What you need is a good dose of castor oil!"

"Yes, Grandpa," was all I said as I completed tidying up, secretly thanking my lucky stars I had not taken a dose of castor oil before this episode or I would not have been nearly as poised. I went into the house to find Granny.

"Lord o' mercy!" she cried, "I thinks you musta seen a ghost! What's wrong wit'ya, child? You're as white as a sheet!"

I told her what had happened.

"Castor oil won't fix that one!" she said with a twinkle, adding, "Don't worry about that old goat. Before I knew him he wasn't nearly as good a man as he thinks he was. Now come on and have some hot cocoa. It'll do ya lots more good than castor oil. You and me are gonna have a nice day tomorry," she promised. "After the milkin's done I'm gonna learn you how to make a mustard plaster and a bread poultice. Maybe we'll talk about castor oil too," she promised.

I nodded obediently, thinking that it might be interesting to learn about Granny's cures even if I had no intention of giving castor oil to anyone.

"Come," she said, "you are almost an adult now and that's why Grandpa was so gruff. So it's time you larned about babies and things. I ain't gonna live forever," she continued, "and someone has to carry on my doctoring know-how."

"Oh no!" I cried in dismay. "You can't go, Granny!"

"I ain't going tomorry," she said, "but I have to teach someone. I choose you."

"Wow!" I said. Would I be known someday as Dr. June? It was an honor that I vowed to deserve.

One thing was certain—if I could learn enough to treat hay fever as a real malady, I would willingly take doctoring lessons from the one and only Dr. Granny!

Doctor Granny's Home Remedies

Mustard Plaster

½ cup of white flour
2 Tbsp. mustard powder
3/4 cup cold water

Mix cold water and flour together well. Add mustard and stir. Heat on stove—a woodstove is best for this. Carefully stir while heating just so it thickens but does not get lumpy. Cool and spread on clean flannel. Place on sick person's chest to clear the congestion.

For a child, reduce the amount of mustard to make the plaster milder.

Bread and Milk Poultice

1 cup whole milk
1 slice white bread, with crusts removed.

Heat milk to boiling, stirring to keep from burning.

Break up bread and stir crumbs into hot milk. Cook for about 7 minutes, then remove from stove. When cool, spread thickly on clean flannel. Place over sores that look as though they are going septic, like where a sliver has just been pulled out. Leave until completely dried out before removing. Guaranteed to draw out poisons.

Tammy Pfaff

Time Is Precious

Grandma was a unique woman. Hazel LaRue Stewart never yelled a day in her life that I can remember. She developed a case of multiple sclerosis in her late thirties from which she was miraculously healed. She no longer needed her leg brace; all her symptoms had disappeared. The doctors had seen only one other such case before. It was recorded in medical history.

Grandma and Grandpa moved around quite a bit over the years. One particular move was to a small motor inn in Glen Mills, Pennsylvania—in the middle of nowhere. Here they had the opportunity to manage the motel and live in the house with office quarters. They had a few regular tenants, some quite colourful in personality.

One strange occurrence that happened at the motor inn during their stay was when a maintenance man caught a large white owl, and convinced my grandparents to put the animal in his own room at the inn, free of charge. The only furniture the owl owned was a large tree branch that took up most of the motel room. It was something to see through the large plate glass window.

It was an exciting time to spend the weekend at my grandparents. They let me help fill out cards for new customers. My favorite pastime was after Grandpa would retire to bed. Grandma would let me stay up past ten and tell me stories of her childhood. Part of the fun was roasting hot dogs in the fireplace.

Grandma once told me a story of how she and her eight brothers and sisters would make homemade root beer. Another story was how their father would set up a tire in the middle of the living room during thunderstorms, assuring them that they wouldn't be struck down by lightning.

They had peculiar superstitions. One particular story I remember took place after her father had suddenly passed away during the Great Depression. Grandma Stewart would have been about twelve years old when he died. A young man who lived on a potato farm a good distance away would bring potatoes from his father's farm to share with Grandma's family. They were desperate times. This young man ended up marrying my grandmother in 1937.

My grandma has since passed on, but she taught me many things. She taught me how to pray when I was just a little girl, and never to use the word "hate" toward anyone. She taught me how important storytelling is. She cooked for a living and taught my family some of her famous recipes such as tomato soup meatloaf and peanut butter fudge. She loved to cook all the holiday meals and never sat down to rest.

When Grandma passed away I inherited three very precious items: a beautiful portrait of her, a broken ceramic clock her sister had made, and a broken necklace watch. The strange thing is, a few days after wearing the necklace watch, it began to keep time. I figured it was a God thing and Grandma was somehow saying, "Time is precious, use it wisely." The items are still very dear to me. They will always remind me of the time spent with my grandmother and how precious that time was.

Tomato Soup Meatloaf

Hazel LaRue Stewart

1½ lb. hamburger
½ cup Italian breadcrumbs
¼ can tomato soup
dash of Worcestershire
2 Tbsp. ketchup
1 egg
1 Tbsp. milk

Mix well. Mould into oval shape and place into 9x13 pan. Cover and cook 1 hour at 350 degrees.

Mix ¼ cup of milk with remaining tomato soup. Pour over meatloaf and cook an additional 15 minutes.

Brian Mullally

Alice in My Bedroom

In the beginning I hated sharing my bedroom with Alice. I'd had a room all to myself in our last house—before Dad lost his job. And I resented Alice poking her nose in my stuff and telling my mother whenever I jumped on my bed.

It couldn't have been much fun for Alice either—this had been her house once. But after her sons left home, she couldn't afford the rent. So my parents took over the house, and my grandmother shared the back bedroom with me— her nine-year-old grandson.

Tiny two-story, terraced cottages lined both sides of Fawcett Road when I was a kid, and their black slate roofs shone like sealskin after a summer rain. Two rooms up and two rooms down, with a utility room attached to the rear. A water closet was tacked on the end like an afterthought that my dad called a lavatory, and my mother referred to as the toilet.

The old houses were still there the last time I went back to England and visited Croydon. In the 1930s they were all painted a uniform dark green; now they're decorated in all the colours of the rainbow and the owners speak a dozen different languages. They all have proper bathrooms and people park their cars on both sides of the street.

Cars were a rare sight when I was a boy, and bread and milk were delivered by horse and cart. We called the utility room the "scullery." It had a shallow clay sink with a single cold water faucet in one corner. A mass of concrete in the opposite corner encased a large copper bowl with a fireplace beneath it.

Mother boiled our laundry in the great pot, and on bath nights she used it to heat water and scoop it into a zinc bathtub. The door connecting the scullery to the living room was locked whenever the females of the house were bathing. If we males were caught short, we had to walk around the whole block and enter the toilet via a narrow alley running behind the backyards. It was a constant source of complaint, and as my father remarked on more than one occasion, "It's a hell of a long way to walk for a widdle."

My mother believed in everything modern so she banished old-fashioned chamber pots from the bedrooms. Alice and I were not to be trusted with candles because of the danger of fire. If we wanted to relieve ourselves in the middle of the night, we had to grope our way downstairs. It wasn't a problem for a surefooted boy, but Alice had a stiff leg and it took her ages to climb up and down the narrow staircase. When I tried to squeeze by her, she would tap me gently on the backside with her walking stick and say, "Hold your horses, you young rip!"

To a child of the 1930s, old people looked the part, and elderly widows wore black. Alice's three daughters tried to persuade their mother to add a little colour to her dress, but she steadfastly ignored their suggestions. "After all," they would say, "Father has been dead more than fifteen years now."

Grandfather William had died of his wounds soon after he returned from Mesopotamia at the end of World War I. Granny had dressed in black ever since. She wore a piece of shiny black silk below her neck, which she called her "front." It was kept in place with a brooch with a Royal Air Force crest, given to her by her youngest son, Ernie, on the day he left to help keep peace in Iraq—the new name for Mesopotamia in 1936.

Alice's clothes smelt of lavender, and she kept little bags of lavender seeds in her dresser drawers. A silver-framed photo of her husband, resplendent in army uniform, stood on a wicker table beside her bed, next to the glass for her false teeth, her smelling salts in a bottle with a glass stopper, and the button hook she used to fasten her old-fashioned high boots.

On long summer evenings, it was still daylight when I was sent to bed. I lay listening to the sounds of the radio seeping through the floorboards, and picturing my mother's dark head leaning close to the radio, enjoying her favourite shows as her knitting needles clicked and clacked.

Alice didn't approve of the radio; she called it "an instrument of the devil." On hot summer nights she would bid her daughter an early good-night, slowly climb the stairs, and then sit by the open bedroom window, enjoying the cool breeze and waiting for nightfall to provide her with the privacy to undress.

On nights such as these, she would lean back in the long shadows and relate scenes of her girlhood. Alice left home at the age of twelve to become nursemaid to a wealthy family, crying herself to sleep at night because she missed her mother.

Her father was John Mock, a stonemason and a strong supporter of the Church of England, who believed all the stories in the Old Testament. During his long life, John had two wives and eighteen children. Alice was the third daughter of his second wife.

The stories of my grandmother growing up in a North Devon village during the 1870s fired my imagination as a child, leading to a lifelong interest in storytelling. Most of her sisters married farmers and fishermen. One sister ran away with a warden from the dreaded Dartmoor Prison and reared her children in a windswept cottage high on that lonely moor. Alice's brothers followed in their father's footsteps and became stonemasons.

Alice fell for a piano salesman who sang popular songs in a furniture store to demonstrate his wares. On Saturday afternoons Alice would don her best frock to go and watch William perform. "He stole my heart away with his big brown eyes and lovely deep voice," she would say, shaking her grey head.

Alice ran home to her parents following the birth of her first child. But her mother sent her away. "You made your bed, my girl. Now you must lie in it." The newly married couple finally settled in Dartmouth, and over the years Alice gave birth to seven more children. Through it all she took in other people's washing and worked as a housemaid for Lady Devonshire. After her husband died, she brought her two unmarried sons and my fifteen-year-old mother to Croydon to find work.

"Are you still awake, boy?" she would say at last, loosening her iron grey hair and allowing it to fall free on her bent shoulders. Sighing softly to herself, she massaged her thigh and stretched out her stiff leg, before fumbling under her long skirt to release the leather belt and let the iron brace fall to the floor.

In my grandmother's time, all meals had been cooked on the black metal stove that sat in an alcove in the living room. My mother had a gas cooker; however, the old metal stove still served as our primary source of heat in winter. Electric light was still in the distant future. The kitchen table was used for everything—daily meals, rolling pastry, cutting out dress patterns, and ironing. In later years I struggled to complete my homework on the scrubbed surface.

The remaining room on the ground floor contained the rarely used front door. The parlour was the keeper of family photographs. It was kept closed and

I was allowed to sit on the furniture only on Christmas Day or for funerals. Climbing up the steep stairs you came to a tiny landing that separated the two bedrooms. The front bedroom belonged to my parents, where my mum and dad slept on Grandmother's feather bed, old but cozy. Granny and I slept in tiny twin cots in the back room.

I always tried to wake up before Granny and go downstairs. If she awoke first, she'd make me hide my head under the bedclothes until she was dressed. Sometimes I would peek at her trying to hook her stocking with the crook of her walking stick, drag it up her poor withered leg, and connect it to her suspender belt.

Just when I thought it would never get done, she would tell me to come out from under the covers and fasten the buttons on her boots. I liked using her buttonhook, slipping it through the eyeholes, and pulling the buttons into place until Granny patted my head.

"You're a good boy, Brian," she would say. "I'm leaving you all my money when I'm gone."

Mum told me that Granny's savings were all spent. But I didn't care. Alice Priscilla Quambra Mock left me a legacy that I've treasured forever.

Alice Klies

Grandma's Crepes

Caroline was a small woman with a big heart. She came to the United States in 1911 from Switzerland. Sitting by the large window in her home, she reflected on her journey and her life in Arizona, while waiting for her granddaughter, Alice, to arrive for her weekly visit. Grandma Caroline looked forward to these visits with fondness.

Caroline was the kind of grandmother every child dreams of having in their life. As she watched for Alice, her flawless complexion and soft brown eyes were reflected in the windowpane. Looking the picture of a refined Swiss lady, she was attired in her powder blue dress with tiny yellow daisies running through the print. She would never, ever wear those things called slacks! Her long blonde hair, turning white, was braided and drawn back into a knot at the nape of her neck. Caroline's eyes smiled, even when her mouth did not.

Skipping along the sidewalk, Alice bounded toward the front door. "Schatzi, Schatzi," Grandma called out. "Come, come, we make the crepes now."

Alice burst through the door, threw her backpack on the couch, and ran ahead of Grandma to the kitchen. Grandma, close behind, yelled after her, "What, no kiss and hug for your grandmother?"

Alice stopped short, turned around, and opened her arms wide. "Aw, Grandma, I love you." Alice thought her grandma talked a little funny but Daddy explained to her that Grandma was from another country and was still getting used to English.

Grandma motioned her to the old kitchen table where the crepe making was about to begin. Alice squealed with delight when she saw all the ingredients laid out before her. There were bowls and utensils and a large cast iron skillet sitting on the stove waiting for the yummy substance coming its way.

With a trembling hand, Grandma pointed to the bowl already containing all the dry ingredients—flour, sugar, baking powder, and salt. Alice rushed to the table with an eagerness to please. "Schatzi, quick, pour the milk," Grandma urged. She hoped Alice's hand was steadier than hers. Smiling, she thought, *If she spills it, so what. She is only seven.*

Alice carefully, oh so carefully, poured the milk, watching it swirl through the mixture. Grandma then nudged her to add the butter, eggs, and vanilla. Alice knew exactly what came next. After all, she had been doing this since she was five! She diligently grabbed the whisk, bringing it back and forth through the dough, and then making quick little circles, turning her wrist.

Grandma was already at the stove heating the butter. "Quickly, Schatzi, come with the bowl." Alice picked up the bowl and stood next to Grandma. She didn't stand too close, because Grandma always warned her how hot the skillet was. Grandma smiled sweetly at Alice and tweaked her nose, leaving a slight flour smudge on the tip.

Slowly, Grandma then took a ladle and scooped just enough of the mixture. When it hit the pan, she rotated the pan this way and that until a thin film coated the iron skillet. Within minutes, Alice watched as her grandma gingerly loosened the edges before flipping the crepe to the other side. As each crepe was finished to a golden brown, it was placed in a stack separated by waxed paper. Alice could hardly contain her excitement and anticipation of gobbling them all up.

Caroline now placed them on a flowery china platter and carried them to the table where two settings were already in place. In the centre of the table sat a bowl of homemade applesauce, sweetened strawberries, and Grandma's old shaker full of powdered sugar. Alice started to reach for a crepe, but Grandma Caroline touched her hand softly and nodded her head toward her folded hands. "Schatzi," she said quietly, "you remember, we must thank the Lord first." Folding her little hands, Alice bowed her head and Caroline squeezed her knee. "Here we are again, Lord, thanking you for these delicious crepes and for my delicious granddaughter. Amen."

Grandma Caroline's Crepe Recipe

1½ cups flour (Grandma never measured)
1 Tbsp. sugar (Grandma would tell me she would put in 2 tablespoons
when she made them for me)
½ tsp. baking powder
½ tsp. salt
2 cups milk (batter should be rather thin)
1 Tbsp. butter (If Grandma was still in the "old" country,
the butter would come from Gabby, the family cow)
1 tsp. vanilla
2 eggs

Put all the dry ingredients together. Stir in all the other ingredients and mix until very smooth. Heat butter in iron skillet and when bubbles start to form, pour scant amount of batter into pan. Right away, you must tilt skillet this way and that until a thin film covers the bottom of the skillet.

Watch carefully and begin to loosen the edges and flip till both sides are a golden brown.

You may stack them individually between waxed paper until ready to eat and then serve them with fresh sweetened strawberries, homemade applesauce, and powdered sugar out of an old can with holes in it! Enjoy!

Connie Kinnell-McKinney

The Heart of the Matter

All together, I had only a few days with my maternal grandmother when I was growing up, but needless to say, the time I enjoyed with her was definitely quality time. My mother was the baby in a family of seven living children. By the time my two sisters and I came along, my grandparents were well into their sixties.

My grandmother, Helen Miller, had been born and raised in the Horseheads, New York, area near Elmira and had married my grandfather, George Loren Ellis II, from the Arkport area. They raised their children on a dairy farm from the heights of one of the Allegheny hills outside Arkport.

Actually, dairy farming was one of the few occupations that such hill country was good for. For me, as a child growing up, it was a slice of heaven on earth. I loved the Ellis Hill Road leading up to the farm. It was long and steep, rising at what seemed like a 45-degree angle, but it led to Grandpa and Grandma's house and that was all that mattered. At the base of the hill was a small creek where we would go wading or exploring for unusual "fossil" rocks that held the imprints of small creatures and shells. Grandma and Grandpa's farm was midway up the long hill. The old family farm was a child's paradise in which to roam and explore. When Grandpa retired, and the cows were gone, there still remained a few remnants of the years past waiting to be discovered. It only took finding an old milking stool, or a bottle of Sloan's liniment, to start the questions stirring in our inquisitive minds—questions we'd find the answers to during a checker game with Grandpa or, at Grandma's side, as she crocheted a winter hat or mittens for her granddaughters.

My grandparents were the salt of the earth; honest, caring, forthright, nurturing people who believed in God and lived out their values without hypocrisy. They were a shining example to my young mind and heart. My younger sister, Valerie, was more Grandpa's buddy, who shadowed him almost constantly and kept him busy with game after game of checkers or Chinese checkers, played with marbles. My twin sister, Holly, and I spread ourselves out a bit more between Grandpa and Grandma. It was especially fascinating to me to watch Grandma cook with her old-time wood stovetop and oven. I could never exactly figure out how she was able to adjust the oven's temperature. The oven part of the stove was separated with a metal wall from the wood burning part. Grandma used this stove for years and cooked such wonders as bread pudding for Christmas, pot roast for Sunday dinner, and especially her chocolate chip and molasses cookies, the latter for which she was the most famous.

For every church dinner or missions fund-raiser, it was expected that Grandma would bring her molasses cookies. For Grandpa's hearty farm breakfast, it was expected that her molasses cookies would be the crowning finish to fill Grandpa with the energy he needed for the morning chores or errands. Finally, for bright-eyed, hungry grandchildren, those cookies could always be found in the little pantry off the kitchen, neatly stored in old, round, Kodak movie film tins. Grandma's pantry was like a trove of buried treasure and the highest prize were those cookies.

Grandma's molasses cookies were not only delicious, but also fun to watch in the making. Grandma would get down her largest pottery bowl, with the faded pink ring around the top. It was her cookie bowl; the taking down of which heralded the beginning of a fresh batch of her special recipe. If the three of us girls were not out exploring for frogs from the creek or fossil rocks, we would be quarreling over who would help stir the flour into the brown concoction, usually getting half of the flour on ourselves or the counter. Grandma would just laugh and help us get the dough finished to roll out (on the now pre-floured counter).

The next thing her granddaughters would argue over would be who would be the favored one to roll out the dough, but "not too thin," she would say. This was an art in itself. Too thin and the cookies would be too hard after baking. Too fat and the cookies would end up tasting too dry. Grandma had found the perfect balance. We were never disappointed. As soon as the first handful of dough was rolled out just so, Grandma would pull out a metal, wide-mouth jar rim (otherwise used for holding down a canning lid) and dip it in a little flour and start making those magic circles. Like Pavlov's dogs, our mouths would begin to water. Carefully, she would use a metal spatula to scrape up the circles, one by one, and place a dozen of them on her cookie sheet.

Then, the real magic would begin. For just a moment, Grandma would disappear into her pantry and retrieve a jar of her homemade jelly (usually grape, strawberry, or plum) and begin scooping a rounded teaspoon full of the yummy sweet stuff. She would then gently press the contents into the indentation, made from the spoon, in the centre of each cookie.

Finally, she would lightly sprinkle a little sugar over the total of each cookie and slide the cookie sheet into her oven with confident ease, just like she had done hundreds of time before, and set her timer for ten to twelve minutes, all the while being careful that the cookies would not get too brown or over baked.

In my young mind, the hardest part of all came next—the wait! Soon, after a checker game with Grandpa, the cookies were out and cool enough to eat. Grandma would call us to the table for milk and a cookie. It was then that the drooling ceased and the real fun began.

How was a kid to attack the jelly in the middle? Ah, so many choices. Should one plow right through to the middle or nibble around the jelly centre and save the jelly for last? Or, would it be better to take a little of the jelly with each scrumptious bite? Decisions. Decisions. The only way to know for sure would be to try each tactic on another cookie! Somehow, Grandma Ellis seemed to understand our childhood dilemma and did what grandmas do best. With a twinkle in her eyes, she creatively looked the other way, as we experimented with the vanishing cookies. I began to wonder, when I was older, whether or not she had watched the same scenario enacted when she was raising her own children.

Grandma Ellis passed away when I was sixteen, but her cookies remain with us to this day. I now make them with my own grandchildren.

Sometimes, I plow right through with sheer joy when I think of the memories Grandma left to me. Other times, I nibble around the edges and slowly savor those same memories with a thankful heart. Either way, just like her cookies, Grandma was the sweetness in the centre of her home and, forever will be the same, in the centre of my heart.

Grandma's Molasses Cookies

Helen Miller-Ellis

1 cup sugar
1¼ cup shortening
1¼ cup molasses
2 eggs
½ cup hot water
3 tsp. soda—level
1 tsp. cinnamon-scant
½ tsp. ginger
1 tsp. salt
½ to 1 tsp. jam or tart jelly
6 cups flour (more or less)

Mix well, adding the flour last, a little at a time, until the dough is soft and easily handled. Take a portion of the dough and place on a floured mat or countertop. Roll out to about 3/8-inch thickness. Cut with a large, round 3½-4-inch cutter. Be careful not to roll the dough out too thin.

Place ½ to 1 teaspoon jelly in the centre of each cookie, according to the amount of jelly preferred. The jelly will spread out some during baking.

Sprinkle each cookie with sugar and bake. If preferred, the sugar may be sprinkled on first before the jelly is placed.

Bake at 400 degrees for about 10-12 minutes on lightly greased cookie sheet. Be careful not to overbake.

Enjoy!

Deb Kemper

Naomi's Eyes

A tall, angular Indian woman
plain, dark, and gentle
who strode cross a reservation
to harvest wild berries for pies.

The char swept porch, yard, and house
with homemade brooms.
Shelled corn from the cob
to feed chickens each day

The seamstress measured bodies
with wide palms and yardstick.
Cut patterns, drawn on flour
Sacks, from bridal silk.

Young ladies became princesses
hiding virtue behind veils
of lace and sequins
spun by Naomi's large hands.

Many nights she'd comfort
me, a sickly grandchild.
Rocked and prayed through tears
of exhaustion and grief.

Years after she'd passed,
strangers who knew her welcomed
me to their home exclaiming,
"You have Naomi's eyes!"

Now my grandson studies
pictures of me at five.
"Nana, I gots your eyes,
don't I?"

"Nick, we have a special gift
from a saintly woman.
We are blessed
with my grandmother's eyes."

Every passing year
my mirrored glances
reveal more of Naomi,
looking back at me.

Shane Joseph

Nanna was my Guardian Angel, and I didn't know it

My grandmother (Nanna) was a frail woman, devoted to her religion and her family. When I was six and was boarded with her for several months during my mother's temporary incapacitation, she took me from church to church, and allowed me to discover the differences between novenas, benedictions, and block rosaries. The smell of incense meant that Nanna was nearby.

When I was eight and caught the mumps, she came to care for me, while Mum kept my other siblings isolated. To heal my swollen jowls, she daubed my face with an old wife's remedy, a mixture of lime and Royal Blue laundry powder, the combination of which smelled like FART. I was subjected to this twice-daily application of the blue smelly goop which put me into a foul temper and kept me on the brink of throwing up. To distract me, she read me Bible stories and often talked about guardian angels. I had one, Nanna said, but I was not supposed to see her.

When I awoke to my stink each morning, I would see Nanna lying on a mat on the floor beside my bed. She would jerk into life the moment I moved, and from her bloodshot eyes I could see that she had done that several times during the night when my fever had risen and ebbed and I had tossed and turned in my sleep. I longed for the smell of incense instead of fart, and complained to her. "Don't quit," she would say. "It will all get better soon." And it did.

When I was nineteen, things had gotten pretty rough in the old country; an insurrection in the south had been tragically quelled and another one was brewing in the north. I was struggling to complete a degree despite government restrictions, needing extra tuition in a subject I detested—statistics. After a tiring day at a brainless full-time job, I would ride in a hot and smelly bus, packed with homebound office workers, to my statistics class, to spend three hours computing formulae that I did not understand.

One day I thought of quitting. Nanna lived not far from the tuition class, so I dragged myself to her home, looking for a cup of sympathy, and validation for my decision to give up. Instead, I received a cup of tea, cookies, and a stern look from her. "Don't quit. You are special, not like those others. You have to show them the way out of this sorry land." She had begun coughing then—weak lungs, she said. I finished my degree five years later and left the "sorry land" and went to the Middle East in search of better employment.

When I was thirty, flush with petro-dollars and about to become a father for the second time, but still not having found my promised land (for the old country was well into its civil war by now), Nanna died suddenly—her lungs finally gave out. I read the telegram in Dubai and realized that I could not travel for her funeral as my passport had expired and the consul wouldn't be visiting for two weeks to renew expatriate travel documents. As I sat down to send a message to the family, announcing that I was unable to travel, a voice said to me, "Don't quit." Ashamed of taking the easy way out, I left the office, got into a taxi and sped across the desert to the consul's office in Abu Dhabi, and did not leave until he renewed my passport. The following morning, I was on a plane bound for the old country.

I arrived at Nanna's home just as they were closing the coffin (in the old country, corteges left from the deceased's home not the funeral parlour) and I got a final glimpse of her. She looked even smaller than when I had last seen her, but there was serenity in her face, something that I had never seen before. Then I realized that her whole life had been one of struggle; her peace had come with death. Someone was lighting incense, and my tears that had been stifled—since "big boys don't cry" had been instilled into us at school—started to flow freely again.

The following morning, while waiting for my flight back to Dubai, I read a local newspaper article that said, "Canada opens its doors to immigrants from Asia." I had never considered Canada before because I had heard that it was a very cold place and that you needed to speak French to get by. "Don't quit" came that voice again. I wrote a letter to the Canadian High Commission requesting an application form, mailed it, and boarded my return flight.

My Canadian application sailed through, while countless others to Australia and America had been stuck in backlogs for years. Within eighteen months of Nanna's death, I arrived in Canada, accompanied by my wife and our two young children—landed immigrants. That was just the beginning, for my entire extended family followed soon after. For a while our home in Scarborough was like a halfway house, with family members arriving, finding jobs, buying houses, and moving on until everyone had left the sorry land and settled in this new land, which wasn't so cold after all, and where you could get by quite well with English only.

It has been twenty-five years since I arrived in Canada, and they have been good years; a few ups and downs, but years of personal growth and enlightenment. And with enlightenment has come the realization that my old Nanna was my guardian angel all along, only I hadn't known it at the time.

I know that she is still around me for I make Post-it notes and cartoons that typify "Don't Quit" for the moments when I am down on myself. When I receive rejections from publishers, up comes the "Don't Quit" sign by my PC, I am pretty sure that seeing me self-medicating on optimism this way must give the old lady a chuckle, wherever she is now.

And when I get the smell of incense, I look around...

Sally Jadlow

Nell's Dresses

If a brother or sister be naked and destitute for daily food, and one of you say to them, "Depart in peace, be ye warmed and filled," notwithstanding ye give them not those things which are needful to the body; what doth it profit? Even so faith if it hath not works, is dead, being alone (James 2:15-17 KJV).

After Grandma's passing I inherited her walnut chest, contents and all. In the bottom drawer, I found a large mayonnaise jar of buttons. Green buttons. Red buttons. Black buttons. White buttons. Ones with rhinestones. Mother-of-pearl. Even one that looked like a large fang drilled through. This jar sat on the floor next to Grandmother's treadle sewing machine. Her "sewing room," located off the kitchen, was an empty nook under the staircase of my grandparent's farm home. The sewing machine fit the width of the stairs overhead, with a bare lightbulb and pull chain to illumine her work space. Grandma cut the buttons off of garments too threadbare to patch anymore and deposited them into this jar.

I carefully unscrewed the lid and dumped a few into my hand. How many garments had these buttons adorned?

In my mind's eye, I remembered her leaning over the contents dumped on the old wooden kitchen table hunting for "just one more" to match the five she held in her hand. She needed the sixth one for the dress in progress. For the past couple of days, Grandma spent every spare minute between garden chores, being the wife of a busy farmer, and canning, to work on this project. I visited their home every year for two weeks during the height of polio season as Mom thought it best to keep me away from as many people as possible to lower the risk of infection. She decided her parents' place in southwest Missouri had "less germs."

"What are you sewing, Grandma?" I asked.

"It's a dress for the hired hand's daughter."

"Why? Can't her mom sew for her?" I said as I joined in the hunt.

"Nell's mother is blind. If I don't make Nell some dresses, she'll have to go to first grade in overalls. No little girl should have to go to school in overalls. Don't you agree?"

I hadn't really thought of going to school without dresses. Every summer my mom made me new ones. Even the boys in my class didn't wear overalls. Schools must be different here in the country, I reasoned.

"How did her mom get blind?" I asked.

"Syphilis."

"What's syphilis?"

"A bad disease people get when they sleep with someone not their husband or wife."

"Oh."

I remember thinking, *Do some moms and dads sleep with other people? I wonder if anyone I know sleeps with someone else? Do they have syphilis?* These were new thoughts to my nine-year-old brain.

Near the end of my visit, we took the dresses Grandma made to Nell's house. She lived down a dirt road back in the woods. The shack, surrounded by dirt worn slick of grass, had several hound dogs tied in the yard. Little Nell bounced off the porch to greet us at the car. She wore a pair of overalls cut off at the knees that looked about two sizes too small.

"Mom! Miz Edmiston's here!" She ran into the house to fetch her mother.

Presently Nell appeared at the screened door with her mother on her arm. Her mother's long blonde hair fell softly around her shoulders.

I'd never been to a blind person's house before. Despite the sad state of the yard, the house appeared to be neat and in order, in spite of the unpainted boards on the outside. I wondered how a blind person could keep a place so clean.

"Come in, Miz Edmiston," Nell's mother said.

She led us into the small, dimly-lit kitchen filled with a woodstove, an icebox, and a simple table with mismatched chairs.

"Please sit down." Nell's mother felt for the chair and sat. "What can I do for you, Miz Edmiston?" She looked past us as if she were looking far away.

We sat, and Grandma drew out the three dresses from a grocery sack. She placed them on the worn table. Nell's eyes lit up and a grin spread across her face.

"We've brought some dresses for Nell to wear to school."

Nell ran her hand over the cotton dresses. "Oh, Mama! They're beautiful!" she whispered. She picked one and held it up to her chest, dancing around the room on one foot and then the other.

Her mama's eyes filled with tears. "Thank you, Miz Edmiston. That was so kind of you."

Silence reigned in the car on the way home. I had a lot to think about.

* * *

I scooped the buttons back into the jar and replaced it in the bottom drawer. Over fifty-five years later the lessons learned from that visit remain with me.

Lord, help me to remember that children learn what they observe more than what they are told. May my actions speak as clear as my words.

Gay Ingram

Sunday Dinner at Meme's

Sundays used to be the special day of the week—a respite from the daily routine. Every other day, you woke up knowing what to expect. One day merged into the other. Saturdays were a preparation for Sundays, a day spent getting chores and duties completed so you would be free the next day. Even waking up on Sundays was different, slow and leisurely, stretching and releasing a sigh that came from your toes. Only on Sundays could you sleep a little later.

Not that there wasn't a routine to our Sundays, but the routine was special. Even breakfast was different. Instead of the usual bowl of cold cereal, we drank icy cold orange juice with floating slivers of pulp, ate sizzling bacon and fried eggs along with stovetop-toasted bread and real butter spread quickly so it melted. Breakfast was a leisurely affair with everyone seated at the table together. Having my father sitting at the head of the table made this meal special. Every other day of the week, long before shafts of sunlight pierced our sleep, he left for work, most nights not returning until our bedtime.

With breakfast over, we older sisters cleared the table and washed the dishes. Then, off to change into our Sunday clothes for church. Headed out the door for Mass, the tantalizing fragrance of a pot roast simmering on the back burner sent us on our way. Home from church, we changed to play clothes and rushed to the front porch, eager for the first arrivals of aunts, uncles, and cousins.

My family shared a duplex with my mother's parents, Meme and Pepe, as they were called. Mom had two sisters and four brothers, all with families of assorted sizes and living within a forty-mile radius. For as long as I can remember, everyone tried to make the trip each Sunday to have dinner at Meme's and spend the afternoon together. As each car pulled into the yard, doors would fly open and excited cousins would pour out. Kids were corralled and made to help carry an assortment of bowls and dishes.

Entering by the familiar back door, the arrivals crowded into Meme's old-fashioned kitchen. Aunts and uncles greeted each other as if years had passed instead of just a week, the room reverberating with multiple conversations. Men folks would sneak a surreptitious look at the warming shelf of Meme's capacious wood-burning stove. Eyes lit up when they saw the loaves of homemade bread or Meme's specialty, made-from-scratch pies. Children darted between adults, growing rowdy until they drew ultimatums to go outside and play or else.

Pepe usually tried to tap Uncle Albert's bald pate to make him jump. This always produced spontaneous yells and body jerks, much to the amusement of those watching, but not the victim. Then, Uncle Albert would retaliate. When the responses got so exuberant that innocent bystanders were in danger, Meme firmly called a halt to the shenanigans.

Once the "girls" arrived, Meme retired to her favorite rocker where, like a queen, she directed her subjects. Her work completed, now she would be waited upon. Hands got busy opening the table, adding leaves to its fullest extension. Another daughter dug in the bottom drawer of the buffet for the largest tablecloth while others found plates, utensils, and serving dishes in the pantry. No matter how many turned up, the old pedestal base table always stretched wide enough for all. Cramped positions and bumped elbows were a part of this family's togetherness experience.

Once the meal ended, adults remained seated as conversations continued in full momentum. We children were urged to return out-of-doors to amuse ourselves, the eldest given responsibility for the younger. Bored with adult chatter, we lost no time escaping. Free to devise our own entertainment, the youngest soon settled in an enormous sand pile. Occasionally, a mother lifted the curtain aside, checking on a little one. The more active set claimed the tree-shaded side yard, reserved for vigorous games attracting kids from the neighborhood. Kick-the-Can, Simon Says, and Red Rover produced yells and screams of joy for hours. I chose to tag behind the "young ladies" who spent their time strolling up and down the sidewalk, giggling and teasing one another like teenagers the world over.

While the children played, the ladies cleared the remains and shared duties in the pantry until all the food was stored and every dish returned to its shelf. The men, meanwhile, moved outside and settled in a collection of chairs under the shade of a spreading maple tree. Here they were allowed to share the more "male-like" news. The afternoon drowsed along and in time conversations dried up.

As if on cue, someone asked Pepe to play some music. Always ready to oblige, he reentered the house and found his instruments. Settling in his easy chair, he began to blow his harmonica. As sweet notes filled the air, bodies drifted inside. Soon every chair was occupied. Kids sprawled on the floor or used Daddy's legs as a backrest.

When Pepe's breath ran out, he traded the harmonica for the fiddle. As one after another called out requests, his fingers coaxed old-fashioned melodies from the instrument. A magic blend of voices sang the familiar songs. Pepe kept ignoring Meme's request. Each repeat grew in irritation. At a certain point...and only Pepe knew how far he could goad her...he gave an enigmatic smile. Then, the notes of her favorite hymn, "Amazing Grace," would begin and she'd settle back in satisfaction.

The darkening room signaled time to leave. Mothers began packing up bundles and gathering sleepy children, little ones were carried to the car without waking from their naps. As cars backed out the yard, last minute reminders came flying out open windows. With a sense of anticlimax, we made our way back indoors. But we weren't disappointed. We knew the week would pass quickly and next Sunday would find us gathered again for another Sunday dinner at Meme's.

Linda Hutsell-Manning

My Grandmother Laura Douglas Hutsell

Born in Churubusco Indiana 1880
older sister, Myrtie never ever splashed
in puddles, climbed up trees while younger
Laura fudged her Bible verses, left her shoes
unlaced, had that saucy sparkle in her eye.

Excelled at Whitely School grade after
grade top marks in reading, recitation
math and music, a songbird staying
after school to help the slower ones
who stumbled over words and sums.

By 1896, the Whitley School had grown
and Laura, now sixteen, became a teacher
sixty-three second and third graders, kept
in line with steely glare and just reward
her choir a gem throughout the countryside.

Where she met the dashing Floyd remains
unknown, he a music student in Fort Wayne
sent packing by his father once their secret
marriage was exposed, he organist and
choir master, she teacher till her baby showed.

1909 in Minneapolis Floyd, now Episcopal
church choir director, wrote a football song
for U of Minnesota, won a hundred bucks
a windfall for these two struggling to get by
Laura at church each Sunday with two sons.

First daughter died at three, another buried
shortly after birth. Floyd's fortune soured
they fled to Winnipeg, he a theatre manager
enlisted in the great war 1916, AWOL'd 1917
left his Laura to find work and raise their sons.

They lived in rooming houses, hotel rooms, her
twelve hour days, Hudson's Bay bookkeeper
nurses' house mom, Eaton's clerk, the elder son
kept order and a watchful eye, the younger threw
his caution to the wind, dreamed wealth and fame.

In 1945, no income or stability, she came to live with
us, the family of her younger wilder son, there to
give a helping hand, steady the storm-filled days
nurture her only grandchild, fill my childhood years
a cornucopia of love and possibility and hope.

Helen L. Hoover

Mud Pie Memories

"Look, at the potholder I made," I announced to my parents when they picked me up at my grandmother's home. During my grade school years, I was allowed to stay with her for a few hours or overnight. She lived in a modest house with few personal possessions. Her lack of stuff, though, did not limit her kindness to others and enjoyment of life.

She kept old tin muffin pans, pie plates, and chipped bowls at her house for my use of making mud pies. What fun I had mixing the dirt and water and then pretending this was special baked goods for her and me. I decorated the "pies and muffins" with grass, leaves, and seeds. She delighted in my culinary creations.

While we waited for my mud masterpieces to bake in the sun, she taught me to sew. Her box of quilt scraps provided material for making potholders. I'm sure I made mistakes, but she commented, "You've made a very nice potholder." Throughout the following sixty years, sewing continues to provide an enjoyable pastime for me and that ability started at my grandmother's house, using her foot-powered treadle machine.

In the evening, we played Chinese checkers. When it was my turn, she said, "Now, don't jump yet, look at all of your options." She showed me jumps that were to my advantage and insisted I think my way through the game. Playing games with family and friends is still a fun time and Chinese checkers is one of my favorites.

Mud pies, sewing, and Chinese checkers are great memories from visits with my grandmother. Even more important, though, she exhibited complete acceptance of me through her actions and words. I didn't have to perform a certain way to receive love from her. She loved me just for me. That memory has sustained me through rejection by others as they expected a certain performance from me. In the years since, I realize she exemplified God's unconditional love. Extending unconditional love to others reflects God's love to us: "We love because he first loved us" (*1 John 4:19*).

Londa Hayden

Almost Heaven
(Dedicated to my grandmother, Mary Estelle Van Vorst)

I could hardly wait to see Grandma and Grandpa again. All summer long, just me with my own bedroom and my own bathroom. Not having to share with my sister or brother was the best part of all. Grandma spoiled me and made me feel special. We went everywhere together. In El Paso, Texas, the hot summers stretched on for months. Grandma often stopped for ice cream on the way home from running errands. On one such stop, her wrinkled lips encircled a straw to welcome a refreshing strawberry milkshake. Unfortunately, all my licking efforts were not fast enough to keep the ice cream in my cone from dripping onto my bare legs. My knees squeezed together as I watched the goose bumps surround a Neapolitan splatter. The side view mirror reflected an image of me with ice cream dripping from my chin. "You look like a billy goat," Grandma said. She laughed and handed me a napkin.

Everything was fun at Grandma's house. We ate dinner on TV trays in the living room and watched "Mash" with Grandpa, who'd served in the military for many years. Grandma taught me how to sew a dress, and how to knit a scarf. I helped her make doll furniture for her many paying customers. I even made a round bed for my doll, which made me the envy of all my friends back home. We picked peaches and figs from the trees in the backyard, and Grandma taught me how to can them. Of course, I ate some too.

Grandma always showed kindness and compassion to me and to others. When Nasha, her Spanish-speaking housekeeper of many years, came to clean house, Grandma often gathered canned goods and placed them in a grocery sack for her to take home.

"I never had nothin' growing up," she said, "but I always swore if God blessed me with my own house that I'd share whatever I had with anyone who needed it." She kept true to her word, and I never forgot to follow in her footsteps.

Even when I did something wrong like dumping the peas on my plate in the garbage when her back was turned and lying about it (of course, she spotted them in the trash), I knew she still loved me. Forgiveness was never far away. At home, my parents were always too busy to spend much time with me. Grandma kept me by her side. I used to dream about running away to her house, but I'd hear her common sense inside my head telling me otherwise. Besides, how was I supposed to get there? If I got caught, my parents would just bring me back home, and I'd get in a heap of trouble.

Spending the summer at Grandma's house was almost like heaven to me. She welcomed my desire to go to church. My family wasn't much in the way of religious, but Grandma nourished my desire to know God better. We went to church all the time, and she gave me my first Bible. When I asked questions about God, she answered them. I dreamed about having a family that went to church together. She accepted me no matter what I did or what I said. She corrected me and taught me right from wrong. I felt I could be myself around her. That summer I grew up a lot, both physically and spiritually.

As our time drew to a close, we went on a fun trip to play in the dunes at White Sands, New Mexico. Grandma taught me how to bargain with the merchants at the marketplace in Juarez, just across the border. I purchased a white blouse with embroidered flowers. When it was time for me to return home, my grandparents gave me a good-bye party at the church. For this festive event, I decided to wear my new blouse with yellow, bell bottom, hip huggers that snuggled against my hips, evidence of the few pounds I'd gained over the summer. A large safety pin provided the needed extra width, as I struggled to secure one side to the other. Picking up my suede leather belt, I sucked in my tummy and pinched the leather end tight as I worked it through each pant loop. This allowed the beaded fringe to hang down the side.

That looks cool! I thought.

When it was time to leave for the party, my grandparents scanned me up and down, and then looked at each other. I thought Grandma was going to tell me to change clothes, but she didn't say a word. Instead, she gave me the gift of unconditional love by accepting me in this awkward stage of my life. That one special summer was the last time I spent with my grandmother. I think fondly of my time with her. And when I do, I remember it like it was almost heaven.

Lisa Harris

Grandmother's Springerle Cookies

Every Christmas season I make several batches of springerle cookies from my grandmother's handed-down recipe, and give them as gifts. To my family, these hard anise-seed cookies, embossed with a raised design, are known as "Grandmother's Cookies." Each time I press one of her three wooden molds into silky-textured dough, I think of my grandmother doing the same, as well as her mother, and her mother's mother. It's as if my soul travels through time and communicates with my female forebears. Our hands have touched the same piece of wood—carvings passed from one cook to another—and over a century they have produced a symbol of love and family.

About the size of a billfold, the molds tell me where I come from. They're made from a light-coloured wood, probably pear, and each contains pictures that conjure up an "Old World" image—dainty swans paddling through still-mountain lakes; stone castles strategically built on a bluff; plump apples, pears, currants, and a cluster of cherries, ready for harvest; antlered-stags bounding through fields; a carousel slowly turning to tinkling festival tunes.

As I recreate her recipe, I imagine her in her kitchen, a smiling matronly woman with grey hair piled high on her head, standing among her well-used pots and pans. She presses the molds into the rolled-out dough, leaning into them, so they leave a perfect scene behind. Her cookies are difficult to make. The dough must be supple enough to take the mould's imprint: too dry, and there will be no picture of a flower basket or leaping trout; too wet and the dough will stick to the cherry clusters and the sailing ship's riggings. After imprinting, she would cut the dough into rectangles and set it out to dry overnight. The next day, she would painstakingly remove each cookie with the blade of a sharp knife, the back wet with water, and place the cookie on a baking sheet sprinkled with anise seed. Again, the conditions must be just so: dough that is too moist will stick to the rolling surface, dough that is too dry will crumble and break, and the stag's antlers mangled and the carnival carousel's flag snapped in two.

After almost three decades of baking results, I've concluded that a perfect cookie either requires a certain alignment of the moon and the stars, or my grandmother's special touch.

Springerle cookies are German, specifically from Swabia, and date to medieval times. They were given at festive occasions: births, weddings, and holidays. In my family tradition, they were made only at Christmas. But my grandmother wasn't German. She was British, born in Dorset County. So where did the recipe and molds come from?

At first glance, she probably either borrowed the recipe from a friend or clipped it from a magazine. And the molds I inherited, along with the words "these have been in the family for years," were probably purchased from a mail-order catalogue—so much for family tradition.

I had so wanted to believe that the recipe had been passed down from generations of family cooks that I investigated further. While her recipe might not divulge my grandmother's secret about how to replicate perfect cookies, I suspected it might render more information on my heritage. Through old church ledgers I searched for a Germanic wanderer who left behind a cookie legacy in Dorset.

I didn't have far to look. My grandmother's father-in-law was of German descent. Both of my great-great-grandparents were born in Germany, both in the southwestern region, both in what was then the grand Duchy of Baden, in the heart of Swabia and springerle cookie country.

On a recent trip to the region, I found similar cookie molds in a museum. Many were made with elaborate carvings, and would produce a far fancier cookie than my molds. But one was simple, made from a similar type wood as mine, and approximately the same size. Looking at the cookie mould in its case, I knew I had followed the right track in my family history quest.

In all probability my Grandmother's Cookies were my grandfather's grandmother's cookies—I had been baking a cookie whose recipe spanned five generations.

As for the pear-wood molds, who knows? Perhaps they were Fredrika Schneider's, my German great-grandmother, born almost two hundred years ago.

She would have passed them down to her son, who gave them to his son's wife (my grandmother), who handed them to my mother, who entrusted them to me. And, one day I will pass them to my grandchildren, who will continue to make Grandmother's Cookies—a creamy-white rectangular treat embossed with scenes from a faraway land, a continued symbol of love and family.

Grandmother's Springerle Cookies

2 eggs
1¼ cup sugar
1 grated lemon rind
1 tsp. plus extra anise seed
1 tsp. anise extract
2¼ cup cake flour
½ tsp. baking powder
1 tsp. salt

Springerle molds (sold in specialty shops or through the Internet)

Beat eggs until thick and lemon-coloured. Add sugar gradually then beat with a handheld electric mixer for 10 minutes (the duration of beating is important). Add flavorings (lemon rind, anise seed, anise extract), stir in to blend. In separate bowl combine dry ingredients (cake flour, baking powder, salt). Add dry ingredients to the egg/sugar mixture very slowly. Beat by hand until a silky texture results.

Gather dough in ball. It should be slightly sticky. Flour rolling sheet and rolling pin. Roll dough to ¼-inch thickness. Immediately impose designs onto dough. Repeat until all the rolled dough has been impressed. Cut along edges of stamped cookies with a sharp knife (but do not remove). Make sure all cookies' edges are cut; otherwise they will break when it's time to remove them from the rolling sheet.

Cover sheet with impressed dough with light cloth or paper towel. Let stand in a cool place for 24 hours.

Following day: Preheat oven to 300 degrees. Grease cookie sheet with butter. Sprinkle buttered cookie sheet with anise seeds.

With back of a sharp knife, carefully remove one cookie at a time from the rolling pan. Wet finger with water. Wet back of cookie with wet finger. Place onto prepared cookie sheet, embossed side up. Place cookies an inch apart.

Bake for 25 to 30 minutes, until firm on top, and slightly golden around edges. Do not overcook.

Let cool. Remove from sheets. Store in tight container at room temperature for several weeks before serving. Cookies should be hard; best eaten when dunked in coffee or other liquid.

Gram's Wisdom

When my boyfriend, Bill, invited me to his family cookout, I nervously agreed to go. I would be meeting his large family for the first time. I was shy and the thought of meeting that many people at one time scared me.

The ten-mile drive from my house to his passed quickly as he filled me in on the various relatives I would encounter. The closer we got, the more apprehensive I became.

Pulling up in front of his parents' two-story, country, brick home sent butterflies fluttering in my stomach. As Bill led me to the backyard where the cookout was being held, my palms became sweaty and a lump formed in my throat.

Rounding the house, I saw a sea of people: some sitting in lawn chairs, others throwing horseshoes, a couple of men at the grills flipping burgers and hotdogs. Kids were playing tag, tossing a Frisbee, and squealing as they ran around the vast yard. Women were putting tons of food on a long table.

Bill introduced me to his parents, sister, and brother as well as aunts, uncles, and cousins, and my head swam, trying to keep faces attached to names. Each one greeted me with a handshake, a smile, or a hug, making me feel welcome.

"Bill, how in the world did a rascal like you find a pretty, petite flower like this?" Bill's uncle Floyd teasingly asked.

My face turned three shades of red.

"Just lucky, I guess," Bill said.

"Well, ya better hang on to her 'cause one of these other young whipper-snappers will be trying to make a move." Uncle Floyd guffawed at his own wit.

As we made the rounds, I caught a glimpse of a robust figure emerging from the house. The woman lumbered in our direction, wiping her hands on the apron that covered her colourful summer dress. She was a tall, big-boned woman with salt and pepper hair pulled into a bun at the nape of her neck; her skin tanned and leathery.

"Well, Billy, this must be the lassie you have been telling us about," she said, clapping Bill on the back.

"Suzy, this is my Gram Clara, the best grandma in the world," Bill introduced her, with a boyish grin on his handsome face.

"He always was a charmer and trying to get his way with flattery," she said, beaming.

"Nice to meet you." I stuck a trembling hand out to shake hers.

"Don't be so formal," she bellowed and grabbed me, pulling me to her ample bosom in a bear hug.

I became more comfortable as the evening wore on. Bill's sister, Judy, and I hit it off instantly.

The whole bunch joked and kidded each other with snide remarks, but I could tell they were a close knit family. This was so refreshing for me to see. My own relatives were not close.

By the end of the evening, I felt as if I had known his family forever, especially Gram. She treated me like a part of the clan.

What a grand lady, I said to myself. I wish I could have had a grandma like this growing up. Dad's parents died before I was born and Mom's were old and passed away when I was young. I missed out on the joys of grandparents. I know this woman will become an important part of my life.

Bill's family was so loving and made me feel right at home. As we were preparing to leave, Gram invited me to spend an afternoon with her. I eagerly accepted.

Over the next few months, I visited her often. Gram became the grandmother I never had. She told me the struggles of growing up in a family of twelve and her being the oldest and only girl. I saw the love shining in her hazel eyes as she told me about raising six kids of her own. Swelling with pride she talked about all the grandkids.

Even though she had several grandchildren, she embraced me into the family—always willing to teach me a new talent or give me a word of wisdom. But my favorite time was when she would hustle me into the warm, inviting kitchen and teach me to make her famous chicken and noodles, dressing, and peach cobbler.

She would start dumping flour, eggs, salt, and milk into a bowl, never using measuring devices.

"Gram, how much of each ingredient do you use?" I would ask her.

With a shrug of her broad shoulders she would reply, "Just a pinch of this and dash of that, a palm full of something else."

I would watch her nimble fingers put ingredients together and try to figure out the amounts for each recipe. "How am I ever going to be able to figure out all the right measurements?"

"You'll just have to keep making the dishes until you get it right," she would say with a chuckle.

As we talked and worked I was amazed at the wisdom of this gentle woman that towered over me.

"Suzy, you know the way to a man's heart is through his stomach," she would say with a twinkle in her eyes.

"Maybe so, but the smell of that peach cobbler sure is making mine growl."

On one of my visits we sat in her comfortable, worn living room and Gram taught me to quilt. With wrinkled hands she showed me how to make the intricate stitches.

Her face lighting with a smile that reached to her heart, she told me, "Well, girl, I know you and my grandson will be getting married soon, so let me tell you the secret to a happy marriage. Always look your best when your man comes home from work. Meet him at the door with a hug and kiss. Show him you missed him while he was gone. Keep his tummy full of good cooking, the love alive and let him know he is the most important thing in your life and you won't have to ever worry about him straying."

I assured her I would do my best to adhere to this advice.

Two years after the wedding Bill and I started our own family, and again, Gram was there for any questions I had. Since my parents had moved to Florida and Bill's had taken a job in Indiana, I don't know what I would have done without Gram's support and help with my three children when they were babies.

A few years after my youngest child was born, Gram's health started to fail and she went home to be with the Lord. My heart was broken. I missed her so much. Even though I had only a few years with her, I will treasure the tremendous impact she had on my life. The wisdom of some of the best advice I could ever have gotten will stay with me forever. I'm sorry my kids didn't get to experience her as they grew up.

I now have grandchildren of my own. And just knowing this wise, loving, and caring woman has helped me to be a better grandmother. I can still hear Gram say, "Suzy, put God first, always love with an open heart, and everything else will fall into place."

John J. Han

A Perpetual Guiding Light: Memories of Korean Grandmother

As an immigrant, I have led a hectic life in the United States for more than two decades. During busy times, I rarely think about my home country, South Korea, where I lived thirty-one years of my life. Similar to other first-generation immigrants, however, I occasionally recall the country I left behind. Sights and sounds from the Old World flood my memory when I see images of Korea on TV or online. The most memorable image is not a place or sound, though; it is an undying image of my paternal grandmother, Hwa-dong Kim. As the eldest son within my clan, I was blessed with her unreserved love. She passed away more than three decades ago, but she still remains in my heart.

In my early years, Grandmother served as my virtual mother. Although my mother was an angelic person, a mild intellectual disability prevented her from developing mothering skills. Grandmother never went to school (almost all girls didn't go to school in her day) and didn't even know how to spell her name, but she was a woman of wisdom and discipline. She did everything within her means to nurture me—both physically and emotionally—and help me get ahead in life. According to her, I was her "first and foremost grandson" among a dozen others. It was a great morale booster for me, because I was not that loved by my father, a man of unpredictable rage. She protected me from my father's barrage of verbal abuse and from his sharp punches that fell on my young cheeks. He hated me because I reminded him of my mother—his lawful wife, from whom he distanced himself a couple of years after their arranged marriage. Grandmother represents some of the good things that happened to my largely unhappy childhood and adolescence.

The most striking feature of my grandmother was her bent back. It reminds me of that of her own mother, who lived in the same village. I remember seeing my maternal great-grandmother once in my very early childhood. She scurried toward our house with a stooped back across the rice fields; it was amazing to see an old woman with her back ninety degrees bent walk fast. My grandmother's back was not as severely bent as Great-grandmother's. Grandmother kept her posture somewhat straight by walking with a bamboo cane. When we were walking together, she would regularly stop to stretch her back and to let out a long breath.

Like most Korean women, she had a petite stature of about 5'3". She also had small but sharp, black eyes that glistened. She was proud of her small eyes; she used to say, "My eyes are small, but I can see much better than those who have big eyes. The sight counts, not the size, right?" Her cheekbones were prominent, and she always had grey hair. In those days, hair-dying was unheard of, and elderly people were not ashamed of their grey hair—it represented wisdom and seniority. Her hair was neatly combed and tied into a ball at the lower back of her head, and a binyeo—a Korean traditional hairpin—adorned the ball.

My earliest memory of Grandmother comes from a day when I was about two or three years old. We walked around the irrigation canal behind our house and then went beyond the big embankment to the mudflats. The purpose of our trip was to gather withered plants for heating and cooking. The flats were divided into two by a shallow salt river that ran to the Yellow Sea about two miles away. Because there were more dried plants on the other side of the knee-deep river, we rolled up our clothes and crossed it. Then, Grandmother began to collect plants by using a scythe, and I played in warm sunlight, chasing land crabs as well as ugly-looking, index-finger-sized grey mudskippers. I don't know how much time we had spent there when Grandmother pointed to the approaching waves from the sea. It was time for the seawater to refill the shallow river. The waves were about two feet high and only a hundred yards away. To a young boy's eye, they looked menacingly huge. They kept rushing toward us, and I panicked. Grandmother appeared to be panicky as well, but she regained her composure, crossing the river safely with me in her arms and the firewood on her back. Shortly afterwards, the spot we had crossed became covered with raging currents. That particular incident left a deep impression on me. It was the first among many incidents that made me turn to Grandmother—rather than my parents— in a crisis situation.

While Grandmother dearly loved me, she was also a disciplinarian. An embarrassing episode stands out in my memory that involved me, my aunt, and a young boy next door. In my childhood, I used to play with Young-nim, an aunt from Wolsan village. She was my father's cousin but only one year older than I, so we were friends from early childhood. We visited each other's house a dozen times a year; she came to my house for errands, and I went to her house with my family to attend overnight ancestral rites. We sometimes fought but generally got along well. We were also unified in our hatred toward the young boy next door, Chang-ryeol, who was about three years old. He sometimes walked over to my house, because Grandmother gave him free food. (He was being raised by his poor grandmother who had lost her husband in her twenties.)

One day, the boy again invited himself over to my house when Grandmother was cooking. My aunt and I hated to see him again. As expected, Grandmother gave him a bowl of rice gruel boiled with red beans, and he gladly accepted it. We didn't like his presumptuous attitude, so spitefully we soiled the porridge with dirt. Unfortunately, Grandmother saw it and became very angry at us. Saying that our action was sinister enough to be punished by the will of heaven, she chased us with a stick in hand. We ran away toward the fields but in different directions. One moment Grandmother chased me, next moment she chased my aunt, and then she decided to chase only me; I was her own grandson! Fearing for my life, I sprinted along the bumpy rice fields for about ten minutes. By that time, Grandmother had lost her energy and stopped pursuing me. I don't know what happened that night. I remember being very scared about returning home, and I am sure I was punished in due time. In the meantime, my aunt conveniently had gone back to her home three miles away, thereby escaping Grandmother's wrath. I thought it was unfair, but I couldn't do anything about it.

Other than this episode from the early 1960s, I cannot recall any moment when I feared Grandmother. Actually, she was the biggest nurturer for me during the years when many of my fellow schoolmates suffered from malnutrition and starvation. Her primary passion was to do all things that would help me escape the life of a poor peasant. When I was in junior high, she made soy milk for me by breaking soy into pieces with a stone grounder. Although it tasted funny, I also knew that it would do my body good. When I attended high school, she broke her arm while attempting to retrieve chicken eggs atop the rice sacks. She wanted to feed me with those eggs before anyone else in the family could take them, but unfortunately, she slipped and fell to the ground.

She even looked after me during my college years in Seoul. She planted a few vegetables on a narrow strip of land along the back alley so that I could eat fresh, pollution-free food. She made sure that I drank a carton of milk delivered every morning. Feeling selfish about monopolizing the milk, I sometimes insisted on sharing it with her. However, feigning lack of appetite, she told me to drink the whole carton.

Near the end of my senior year of college, Grandmother developed severe stomach problems, which turned out to be terminal stomach cancer. In March 1979, after suffering for several months, she breathed her last. As her lean body lay in repose, she looked peaceful and wrinkle-free; all the ravages of illness had departed from it. Her death came as a huge shock to me, and I wept for many days. I had lost the primary protector and caretaker in my life, and I would never be able to see her again in this world. Even today, tears sometimes well up in my eyes when I remember her.

Grandmother taught me that I am a valuable person who can do something important in life. My father, who passed away in 2009, used to tell me that children can never repay their parents and grandparents for their love, because by the time they are ready to do something good for them, those parents and grandparents are not alive anymore. Then, what do you do? You pay back your ancestors' love by giving unconditional love to your own children, who will then repay your love by giving unconditional love to their own children. In other words, love does not ascend but descend. My two daughters remind me of the love I received from Grandmother; I love them unconditionally because Grandmother loved me so. She was and still is my guiding light which provides directions and wisdom for life's journey.

Kimberley Sherman Grove

Grandma's Visit

The odds were in our favour. There were five of us. There was only one of her. My grandmother had agreed to manage the household while my parents went on a well-deserved vacation to Mexico.

Grandpa didn't join her in her volunteer mission. He'd probably heard the family stories.

On one occasion the mailman had carried home the twins while on his route. At their roly-poly age of three they were like two squirming, squealing piglets under each arm. His mail sack was around his neck and he was almost bent backwards with all the extra weight. James and Bruce had wandered off and he had managed to round them up to return them home. The rest of us hadn't noticed their absence.

I was too busy stepping in wet cement sidewalks that had just been paved by the city workers, sitting on fences that had just been painted, or plucking the tops off tulips from the neighbour's garden. Once my best friend, Terry, and I skipped off to the shopping mall which we knew in our five-year-old hearts we shouldn't do, but the thought of Popsicles on an overheated summer day was stronger than our guilt. I was punished for that one. It was in the days of spankings. I got to choose my torture. I opted for staying in my room all day. Terry got both the slap and the solitary confinement.

My older brother and sister did their share of upsetting the family circle of harmony by punishing each other. One night when Joan came home from skating, Robert locked her out. She sat on the porch in below zero freezing weather waiting for my parents to return from their dinner out. My mom still chills up when she remembers the story.

Although Grandpa wasn't willing to submit himself to the unknown mischief we might get into, Grandma was a fearless lady. She had helped keep her home during the Depression by earning money babysitting.

She carried a frail frame, but she tended to tame us with her tender touch. I, for one, expected little change in my life with her arrival. There was a routine. She would need to follow it. While walking home with Grandma returning from our walk to the grocery store, I asked the usual question.

"Can Terry stay for lunch?" I expected no resistance.

"No, dear, we have to get lunch for enough mouths. Terry can come another day."

"But Mommy always lets him," I said.

"Well, Mommy's not here."

This wasn't the way it was supposed to be. I decided I couldn't tolerate such ungrandmotherly behaviour. I ran off, hearing my grandma's voice disappear behind me.

"Kim, come back," she cried.

I had the advantage. I wasn't carrying bags full of groceries like Joan and Rob, or pushing a stroller like Grandma. I arrived home enough ahead of everyone that I was able to hide. I chose my brothers' closet behind all the clothes. I even put on my older brother's shoes so if anyone looked in they wouldn't see my sandals.

I could hear Terry's little voice talking to my grandmother.

"If anything happens to Kimmy, I don't know what I'll do."

My twin brothers started giggling.

"It's not funny," said my grandmother.

"Do you think she could have fallen down a well?" Terry asked.

"I think it's time you went home for your lunch. We'll let you know when we find her."

She opened the front door, then recruited Rob and Joan to help. Rob took his bike to return to the store looking for me.

Grandma's voice went up an octave as she called my name. She and Joan looked under every bed, behind the couch, and in the bathtub.

James and Bruce got up from playing with their toys on the floor. I don't recall if it was the tone of alarm coming from their throats or their investigative skills that found me, but I wasn't lost for long.

My grandma was not the kind of person to stay angry. Instead of scolding me, she hugged me. "Please don't do that again," she said.

And I didn't. I decided that maybe it was more important to get to know her than include Terry at the lunch table. It's my only recollection of Grandma looking after us.

Sandi Greene

Sky-diving Is for Grandmas, Too

My grandma rocks.

Being likened to a rock is not a negative connotation—us Gen-xers know it's a compliment to be associated with this slang term. My grandma still tells the story of when, as a child, I walked up to my grandpa and told him he was "bad." He looked perplexed, wondering what he did wrong until my grandma explained that to a kid being "bad" means you're "cool" (and being "cool" means you're a neat person, not literally cold).

As I've grown up, my grandma has been like most loving grandmothers, teaching me to bake cookies, taking me to Disneyland, and buying me gifts. What has impressed me the most, however, is my grandma's passion for life. Since she retired, she has accomplished some interesting activities. Those that have stuck with me:

My grandma has skydived—twice (no one believes me until I show them the pictures).

She, with my grandpa, turned their favorite hobby—photography—into a full-time business.

She taught high schoolers at a church.

She went to college and got certified to become a volunteer EMT at the local firehouse.

She danced with a ladies dancing group for years.

Every summer she traveled to a different location.

She embroidered dozens of blankets for grandchildren and great-grandchildren.

She has taken my daughter to her summer house every year and entertained her for a week.

When she celebrated her fiftieth wedding anniversary, instead of your typical celebration, she and my grandpa held a party where everyone came dressed in 1950's attire and danced for hours to all the classic hits.

She bought a cat that cost more money than my first car.

While admirable, it should be noted that these activities haven't been easy. My grandpa had quadruple-heart bypass surgery and a follow-up heart attack, and my grandma has dealt with constant pain in her hips and legs from osteoarthritis and also had a heart attack. Still, no matter what obstacles come, she manages to overcome, carrying on and checking off unique to-do-before-I-die tasks along the way. She has never lectured me about loving life or reaching my dreams—I can clearly soak up that message from watching her in the act.

My observation doesn't lead me to believe, of course, that every senior has to jump out of an airplane in order to enjoy life. What I do value, however, is my grandma's ability to grasp that getting older doesn't mean having to slow down or give up all your hopes and dreams because you're too "old." If anything, growing older means doing more and living every precious moment to the fullest, given that the sunset is drawing nigh.

My grandma's value of enjoying life is one I admire and hope to practice throughout my own life. Grandmothers can leave a lot of different legacies to their grandchildren—mine has chosen to leave the virtue that life begins every day if you want it to and nothing can stand in your way—not even your age. All you have to do is put your fears aside and rock.

Mary Gordon

My Grandmother Wore Army Boots

My father and mother were entwined long before they "entwined" (outside wedlock, as it turns out, but we didn't know that till they were both long gone). My dad's parents, Robert and Annie Byers, were a lot older than my mom's parents, Martin and Glady Reid. Dad was a dashing nineteen-year-old man of the world, the big guy around town on his visits home, and Mom was just three when she announced to her parents that she would marry Clyde Byers when she grew up. And she did.

The two families were starkly different. The Byers were early arrivals in Massey, on the north shore of Georgian Bay. Granddad Robert John Byers (known as R.J.) was a travelling salesman, peddling supplies up and down the Ottawa Valley from his father's livery in Eganville. She was Annie Greer, a pretty Irish girl with a glass eye, born to Christy and Joanna Greer in Merivale, near Ottawa, in 1868. Hers was a large, hard-working farm family, one of the lucky ones to land on rich productive soil in the new country. This branch of the Greers arrived in Canada in 1848. The loss of her eye—when, where, and how—remains a mystery.

R.J. must have scooped up the comely Irish lass on one of his sales trips, and hied off to the northern frontier around 1890. When the town incorporated in 1904, he was elected their first mayor. Hard living—and we suspect, hard drinking—ended his life in 1916, leaving Grandma Byers to eke out a living and raise her remaining children on her own. To make ends meet, she grew strawberries, baked the best soda biscuits in town, "clipped coupons" (the erstwhile term for collecting interest from bonds) once a year, and delivered babies.

My mother's parents, on the other hand, arrived nearly thirty years later, in search of a living. Martin Reid came from an upwardly mobile middle-class family, one that continued to climb the financial and social ladders in the new country. Martin chose another route, one of ideology, war, and poverty. He married his third cousin, Kathleen Gladys Wabb, the daughter of a pioneer in the French River area and his Aboriginal wife.

The entwining of the families began with the babies. Grandma Byers bore eight children before R.J. died in 1916. From then on, she delivered nearly all of Grandma Reid's eleven children. She was the reliable midwife—dour, but able— for most of the families in town.

One of the surviving stories came from my uncles Art and Fred. My mom was born in 1916, following one of Grandpa's furloughs from the army. He was then gone for well over two years, leaving a gap in the every-second-year birth pattern. When the next baby came along, Mother was nearly four. She watched Mrs. Byers clumping down the stairs after the delivery in her big heavy boots, wiping her hands, shaking her head, and muttering tersely, "That child's got no neck. No neck at all." Mom's older brothers couldn't find her for dinner later that day. They finally spotted her crouched behind the barn, sobbing inconsolably. She had taken Mrs. Byers at her word and figured she had a deformed and ruined sister.

I was terrified of my Grandma Byers. She was short and stout, with thick, tough hands. Conscious of her glass eye, she was in the habit of never looking directly at anyone. Her long white aprons were stiff with bleach and starch. She spoke only in short, gruff monosyllables. Her back was stooped from years of work. She also wore army-type boots, really. I walked carefully around this frightening old woman.

She died in 1951 when I was five, so I had to learn about her "real self" from others. My dad revered her. She was the formidable model he held up, the model of perfection for my mother. Mom would never become the cook he wanted her to be. Early in their marriage, he presented her with a little red recipe box he had made at work, with this recipe inside:

Maw's Salad Dressing

1 cup vinegar
1 cup water
1 cup white sugar
Put in top of double boiler.
Then 4 Tbsp. flour
2 good tsp. mustard
little salt & 2 eggs

Beat up, and mix into flour and mustard making a paste.

Stir that into vinegar and water and stir good while pouring it in, cook until it thickens.

She must have been a most complex woman: there was a polished piano in the parlour, but nobody ever played it. There were no physical displays of affection, ever, but she kept a cot ready downstairs for anyone from the Sagamok reserve caught in a snowstorm on the way home; she filled the house filled with the aromas of baking, but had no appetite for pleasure; the beautiful family silver was bagged up and hidden in the attic, not to be used; and though she delivered babies, she never delighted in them. So many contradictions.

Her eldest daughter, Charlotte, ended up on the streets in Toronto. Every once in a long while, she'd turn up at her mother's door, sick, dirty, and broken. Grandma always took her in, cleaned her up, fed her, healed her, and sent her on her way. After Grandma died, there was no one left to help Charlotte, and she ended her days in a provincial psychiatric hospital.

Grandma Byers delivered her own grandchildren as well. When finally one daughter produced the first male, this indomitable old woman named him after her dead husband, then took him home to live with her for the first ten years of his life. He remembers those years well. "She was a hard, hard woman," he says. There was no laughter in the house, and no loving. It was a shock to land at the age of ten into a boisterous family of six sisters. He barely knew them, and never understood why he had been separated from them in the first place.

I fantasize that she regretted leaving her family behind and that she felt trapped in an unhappy marriage to a domineering drunk. She lost two daughters to diphtheria just after the turn of the century, and a grown son to septicemia from an infected tooth some years later. I look at the contrast in images: Grandma as a small pretty woman married to the town mayor, and Grandma fifty years later, a formidable old battle-ax. I imagine my grandmother, and begin to build some romance into her early life. Soon I begin to feel her contradictions within my own life. I don't want to inherit that meanness of spirit, but I sure crave that endurance.

In 1951, Grandma slipped from the stoop as she was hanging out the wash. Days later, a passerby stopped in and found her on the cot downstairs, unable to move. My father was called. It took cajoling and then coercion, but Grandma finally agreed to a doctor's visit. However, when the doctor said she would need hospitalization, she dug in her heels. Dad said she thought hospitals were where you go to die. When even Grandma realized she wasn't going to make it through the inevitable pneumonia, she asked to be taken home to her family. Dad went with her on the long train ride, Grandma on a stretcher, and she died in her family home.

Donna Clark Goodrich

Grandma's Organ

There was nothing unusual about the pump organ. It was old, but not antique.

It wasn't beautiful. Specks of green paint dotted the finish. The pedals were worn and glue held the stool together in several places.

And it didn't play well. As soon as one began to pump the pedals, three discordant notes vibrated. The bellows leaked, and a low F-sharp sounded like a foghorn.

But I wanted it! When word came that Grandma had died, I asked if I could have the organ—and soon after, the moment I longed for arrived. I sat down to play. This was my organ now.

I was disappointed, however. The instrument didn't sound the same in this two-story, nine-room house on a noisy city street. It belonged out in the country, in the corner of a "patchwork" house my step-grandpa built one room at a time.

That was this organ's home. Over in the corner of the living room. Near the library table holding a recent copy of the *Farm Journal.*

Grandma had a set routine whenever she played the organ. First she lifted the top gently and pushed it back. Next she removed her "spectacles" and wiped them with a corner of her ever-present apron. Then she placed the songbook on the bookrack. Now she was ready to sing: "Shall We Gather at the River?" ("That was your grandpa's favorite song," she never failed to tell me. "He'd sing bass and I'd sing alto.")

In my home the organ just didn't sound the same. It seemed to have a personality all its own—the same as the original owner. As my fingers softly touched the keys, memories of my childhood flooded my mind.

* * *

After "supper" at my grandparents' farmhouse was the signal to go out and sit on the workbench on the back porch and smell the hollyhocks and the lilacs. Time to listen to the buzz of mosquitoes, the hum of a bumblebee. Time for one last check for eggs from the henhouse.

Or time to listen to the "Farm Roundup" or Gabriel Heatter's news or "Hymntime" on WCKY, Cincinnati.

Or time to lift the top of the organ and sing.

* * *

Grandma's organ changed our lives. Oh, not right away but gradually. Her personality began to weave itself around us and, as I played, I could almost hear Grandma's voice.

When dust collected on it, I heard her say, "If something needs to be done, do it now."

When I piled books or letters on the top, her voice echoed, "A place for everything and everything in its place."

When Christmas rolled around, I heard her familiar, "Me? I don't want nuthin'. I've got everything I want."

And I found myself talking back:

"We thought you'd outlive us all, Grandma, as healthy as you were. Seventy-five years old and you still walked over a mile to the store almost every day. Still chopped wood for that old potbellied stove in the front room, still worked in your strawberry patch.

"Guess it must have been when you went into the hospital—for the first time in your life. I can almost hear you telling the maids how to clean your room. The store-bought bread must have tasted funny to you, the canned vegetables, the frozen desserts.

"The doctor said it was the 'flu,' but we knew it must be something more. Later he said your heart gave out. All the years of working on the farm, chasing the chickens when the fence broke, scrubbing floors on your hands and knees, doing the laundry on the washboard. Years of raising children—losing three out of six, one baby dying in your arms. Of watching your husband killed instantly after he was hit by a car on the way home from church.

"Your Sunday school teacher came to visit you in the hospital. You were feeling fine, you told her. A little tired perhaps. She walked down to the end of your bed and as she turned to say 'good-bye,' there was no answer. You had already said your last good-bye.

"But it wasn't really good-bye, was it, Grandma? You always told us, 'Not good-bye, just so long.' You just went up to play on a better organ, didn't you? One where the bellows didn't leak and there were no green paint spots. One where the cloth on the pedals wasn't worn through and the F-sharp didn't sound like a foghorn. You just went up to sing with Grandpa, didn't you? 'Shall We Gather At the River?' You in your alto and he in his bass."

I miss you, Grandma. It was the memories I really wanted, not the organ.

Linda Gillis

Love—Chocolate Style

Perhaps it was one of those Sunday afternoon visits to Grandma Twedt's house that caused my earliest addiction—chocolate. Grandma made the BEST chocolate cake in my world. It was made the old-fashioned way—wooden spoon and big pottery bowl, carefully creaming sugar and butter together; adding eggs, cocoa, and buttermilk before mixing in the dry ingredients—not by opening a box, cutting open the bag, and dumping it into a mixing bowl. Grandma's cake was a shade lighter than dark brown and formed a slight bulge running end to end in a 9x13 cake pan. Each bite held firm until it melted in my mouth. However, it was the ICING that gave me a chocolate fix.

When I was a kid, I'd get away from my three brothers by spending time on Grandpa and Grandma Twedt's farm. I especially liked the times I helped Grandma get ready for Sunday company. As the sun began to peek through the lace curtains of the kitchen window, Grandma would tie on a flour-sack apron with rickrack trim around the neckline and already have sacks of flour and sugar on the counter. I'd drag a two-step stool across the floor to the counter to watch Grandma toss together sugar, yeast, salt, and flour and then add some water to make bread dough. She'd dump it onto a clean dish towel, ball up the dough, and knead the sticky glob until it looked like half of a white basketball. An hour or so later she'd say, "Wash your hands and punch her down," so it could rise again.

The table on the back porch became the resting place for white and wheat dough "a'rising." Then Grandma whipped up a batch of cookies (oatmeal or molasses crisps), rolled out piecrusts for whatever fruit was in season, and last, but not least, stirred up the chocolate cake.

When the bread came out of the oven, it was my job to rub a square of waxed paper over a stick of butter and smear butter on top of the hot loaves—

not too hard or they'd collapse in the middle, sort of like finger painting with waxed paper. Then, I'd help Grandma clean up the mess—she'd wash, I'd dry. Sometimes it took two or three tea towels before we'd get the stacks of bread pans, cooling racks, spatulas, and greasy measuring cups and spoons dried and put away. Grandma always left the dishwater in the sink to wash one more pan and spoon after making the icing for the cake.

To the best of my recollection, Grandma always used a fork instead of a spoon to stir the sugar and cocoa together in a saucepan. Then she added butter, a dash of salt, capful of vanilla, milk, and the secret ingredient—a splash of cold black coffee. She'd stand at the stove and stir the boiling ingredients until it thickened enough to stick to a spoon. Then she'd set the pan of molten liquid to chill in a bowl filled with ice water. Every now and then she would drop a half teaspoon of icing into a cup of cold water and if it formed a soft marble, it was ready to beat.

At the right moment, Grandma sat down at the kitchen table with a wooden spoon to stir the liquid. I'd pull my chair up close and watch her strong hands cut through the icing, and we'd talk. "Grandma, you make the best bread in the whole world." She'd chuckle and say, "Oh, Linda, your mom makes the best bread!" Every now and then, she'd stop beating and check the icing to make sure it didn't get too hard to pour onto the cake.

"It's ready!" Grandma would finally announce and poured the icing over the cake, filling in all the holes and crevices. Then she'd hand me the pan and spoon and say, "It's all yours, Linda. Be careful for the cuff on the sleeve of your blouse." I'd lick the wooden spoon first, and then start on the pan. When the spoon failed, my whole hand went in and came out looking like a chocolate lollipop.

Within a half hour, the icing set up and looked like a chocolate ice skating rink—perfectly smooth and almost shiny enough to see reflections of the chocolate smudges on my face. The baking now completed and the goodies covered with plastic wrap or tea towels, I would declare, "Grandma, you have the best bakery in the county!"

On most Sunday afternoons, the back door to Grandpa and Grandma's house swung open to any of their eight children and over two dozen grandchildren. The men sat in the living room to talk farm stuff, and the women hovered around the dining room chatting and keeping one eye on their kids. About four o'clock, Grandma would say, "It's time to put the coffee on," and head to the kitchen with a couple of helpers to make beef or hot chicken sandwiches and get "lunch" ready (noon meal was called "dinner" and evening meal "supper").

I always showed up in time to watch Grandma cut the cake. She'd dip the tip of a long sharp knife into a glass of water (to keep the fudge from shattering into small pieces) and cut eighteen perfect pieces that could have qualified for a photo shoot for the front cover of *Good Housekeeping* magazine.

By Sunday evening, the baked goods were reduced to just enough to satisfy Grandpa's sweet tooth during his morning coffee breaks during the next week. Everyone went home with full tummies, and I guess Grandma went to bed early.

I tried to make Grandma's cake for my own family, but the good old Duncan Hines chocolate cake mix made a better hit with the kids than my attempt to reproduce Grandma's cake. Today, when I get a whiff of chocolate cake baking, I'm instantly transported back to Grandma's kitchen. I can almost taste the fudge icing still warm in the pan.

Sour Cream Chocolate Cake

by Grandma Gertie Twedt

1963 Bergen Lutheran Cookbook, Roland, Iowa

1½ cups sour cream
2 eggs
1¼ cups sugar
1¾ cup cake flour
3 Tbsp. cocoa
½ tsp. salt
1 tsp. vanilla
4 Tbsp. hot water
2 level tsp. soda

Beat cream and begin to add eggs one at a time. Beat until well mixed.
Sift sugar, flour, salt, and cocoa together and add to cream and egg mixture.
Add vanilla.
Add soda dissolved in hot water.
Bake at 350 degrees for 40 minutes or until a toothpick comes out clean.

Chocolate Fudge Icing

2 cups sugar
½ cup cocoa
½ cup milk (or ¼ cup coffee and ¼ cup milk)
½ cup butter
1 tsp. vanilla
Pinch of salt

Mix sugar and cocoa together in saucepan. Stir in milk. Add butter. Cook over low heat and stir until butter melts. Continue to cook over low heat until mixture comes to a rapid boil. Cook 3 minutes more. Remove from heat. Add vanilla. Place pan in cold water and continue to stir until it begins to thicken. Pour over cake and allow icing to firm before cutting it into pieces.

Joy P. Gage

My Grandmother's Home

Without giving it much thought, I came early to believe that adults were put on earth to make life smooth for kids. If there was a problem, Mother handled it. Whatever she couldn't handle, my father took care of and if he couldn't handle it, there was always Grandma.

My maternal grandmother was our go-to person during the first decade of my life. We moved a lot—seven houses in ten years—and lived with Grandma in between. If my father was out of work, if he was working out of state, if someone was ill, we sought refuge at her cabin. I grew up thinking, "Other people move, grandmothers stay put."

I loved her house—a three-room log cabin with a sleeping loft, holding treasures no one else had. Potted geraniums bloomed in the kitchen window. A huge red flour barrel stood in one corner, and in the corner nearest the door a glass shelf stretched across one wall. A real bathroom sink was tucked into that corner. Everyone else in the community made do with wooden shelves and a metal washbasin on a table. But at Grandma's cabin, we washed up in a sink just like town people used. Of course, not even Grandma had indoor plumbing so a five-gallon lard can stood beneath the sink to catch the water.

Subconsciously, I learned a lot about creating a home from my grandmother and her cabin. My grandparents had been city people before Grandfather decided to buy (sight unseen) a new home in the country. Family lore has it that my mother (thirteen at the time) burst into tears at the sight of the log cabin with newspaper-covered walls. But Grandma never cried over problems. If it could be fixed, crying was a waste of time. If it couldn't be fixed, crying wouldn't help. She went to work turning the sixty-year-old cabin into the bright and cheery home I knew as a child. By then, the country was in the midst of the Great Depression and my grandfather and my father were often out of work. But Grandma brought stability to her family through her determination to always make the best of things and she softened the edge of poverty through touches of beauty.

Three months after I married, I began life as a pastor's wife in a three-room pine-paneled cabin in a logging camp. We had very little furniture and nothing with which to decorate the house. But my mother made white organdy curtains for the windows, giving us something of beauty. I gazed at them often each day.

In the years that followed, we lived in a variety of houses, some more challenging than others. With each move I would remember the lesson I learned from my grandmother's cabin. No matter how old or how worn, any house can be turned into a home through touches of beauty.

Corinne D. Furtney

A Gift that Lasts

My grandmother passed away September 2008. She was ninety-five years old and had an incredible life. She lived through the wars, had seven children, and when the youngest two were still at home, her husband passed away. To provide for her family, she had to work outside the home at a time when women didn't. She lived every day to its fullest: babysitting at the church until age seventy-five, bowling in a league well into her eighties, visiting the "old" people, and finally giving up driving at ninety.

She loved to bake, my mother loves to bake, and I think I inherited my love of baking from both of them. Every time we visited, my grandmother baked something special for each of her grandchildren and then sent us home with goodies to eat. When we stayed with her for a week during the summer, she would give us some cookie dough so we could make our own tray of cookies. Now when I make peanut butter cookies or doughnuts, the smells remind me of my grandmother's kitchen and her love for her grandchildren.

We also had special games we played. She would hide homemade butterflies in the living room and we would try to find them. Then we would get a chance to hide the butterflies and she would look for them. She had so much energy I didn't think I would be able to keep up with her.

Out of all of my wonderful memories of my grandmother, the thing that stands out the most in my mind about her was her faith which she lived every day. She raised her children in the church, and when her grandchildren visited her she took us to church as well. When I visited, I would often find her in the morning with her Bible open and kneeling for prayer. She would also play songs and hymns on the piano for us to sing along with her.

As she got older she would say that she didn't have much to give to her grandchildren and great-grandchildren but she could pray for all of us and I'm sure she did! Her strong faith and trust in God could be witnessed daily. Her example is a gift that I will always have.

Linda Rose Etter

Handyman Grandma

When people ask, "Who are you most like, your mom or dad?" my answer is, "I am like my Grandma Baker." That woman could fix anything and was "Miss Independence." I loved helping her fix and improve her home. It was the 1950s and she didn't have running water so I pulled her red wagon to the neighbour's and filled the two pails from their outside water faucet. When it was time to mow I used the push reel mower, not a gas one. In the summer I would find her chopping wood with an axe and stacking it for the wood burner next winter.

As a little girl the one thing that I didn't like was going to the "outhouse," especially at night with a flashlight as the spiders and insects worried me. I wonder why she built a two-seater. She lived alone and the extra hole added to the aroma of the small surroundings. Since I didn't want to be in there very long, I learned to go quickly.

Grandma had to defend her property from kids stealing her plums. After firing a round or two of rock salt, they left with amazing speed. It stung enough to make them think twice about robbing her.

It wasn't all work and no play. She made the best sugar cookies and homemade bread in the world. In my little hands those cookies seemed as large as saucers. The smell of the bread baking couldn't be missed as you approached her door.

For entertainment Grandma had an African grey parrot named Polly. She got her when Polly was eleven years old and had her for thirty-three years. During that time she taught Polly not only how to talk but also to carry on a conversation. Polly would identify every food on our plates as we walked through the room with her huge cage. As Grandma and I ate in front of the black-and-white television with three stations, Polly would call out what food she would like from our plates. It was so much fun feeding and talking to Polly. She was a lot of company for Grandma when we weren't visiting.

Now that I am in my sixties, I am just as independent as Grandma. I do as many of my home repairs as I can. The big difference is that I use power tools! I also have a parakeet that keeps me company and reminds me of how important Polly was to Grandma.

I can still see Grandma on her roof in her sixties, putting on her own shingles. Now I realize how amazing she was. I miss calling her and stopping by to see what adventure she is tackling. But what she taught me about life, hard work, and taking care of yourself is priceless! And the smell of those cookies and bread baking will stay with me forever.

Handyman Grandma's Favorite Sour Cream Sugar Cookies

Mabel Baker

2 cups sugar
1 cup butter
1 cup thick sour cream
3 eggs
1½ tsp. baking soda
4-5 cups of flour
1/8 tsp. nutmeg

Cream butter and sugar. Add eggs and sour cream and mix. Sift in 4 cups of flour, baking soda, and nutmeg. Mix well. Add additional flour until dough is thick enough to roll out on floured countertop and not too sticky. Roll dough to about ¼ - 3/8-inch thick, then sprinkle sugar on top of dough. Cut out cookies with a large round cookie cutter or the mouth of a glass about 4 inches in diameter. Place cookies on a lightly greased and floured cookie sheet. Bake in preheated 375 degree oven for 12–15 minutes

Graham Ducker

Grannie's Sky

I was thinking of Grandma as the headlights illuminated my Assistant Director nameplate in the observatory parking lot.

I stepped out into a cold clear sky, as innumerable stars and galaxies spread across the infinity of a black prairie-type night.

It was a Grannie Sky, and I became mesmerized in time and space—and memories.

"I just love nights like this," Grandma had said. "It's like looking back into eternity."

I agreed. "Let's call it a Grannie Sky."

It was on such an evening that I climbed the hill on Grandma's farm where I spent the summer holidays.

After barely passing grade eleven, I had agreed to Dad's suggestion to give Grandma a hand on her small isolated farm in Saskatchewan.

The bus ride to Estevan went well enough, but by the time the local bus dropped me off at the end of Drapo (shortened from Drapovitz) Lane, I was positive the whole venture was a bad idea.

Grandma must have been watching, for I no sooner began walking down her road than she, wiping her hands on her apron, came hustling out of the house.

I noticed she was limping so I jogged towards her.

Grandma smelled of fresh homemade bread when we hugged.

"Oh, it's so good to see you, Henry," she said in the wonderful Ukrainian lilt I grew to love. "My, how you've grown!"

"Good to see you too, Grannie."

"Come in. Come in. You must be tired. I vill show you to your room and then ve vill have some fresh bread and strawberry jam."

About a third of a loaf remained by the time I put down my knife and leaned back in the chair. Life was looking a whole lot better.

There was always a lot to do around the farm. I helped with the weeding once I learned to tell one from something Grandma had planted.

She also put me in charge of the chickens, while she looked after the two cows. We cleaned the stalls together. I forked out the soiled straw, and then we laid down fresh bedding.

Each evening after the chores were done, we made a campfire, roasted marshmallows, and talked, often staying up long after we—especially Grandma—should have.

I knew Mom had spoken with her. I kept waiting for Grandma to ask a bunch of dumb questions such as: How is school going? Why vasn't I studying harder? What vas I planning to do with my life? But she never did! Somehow I wound up doing most of the talking.

Even while working alone, Grandma's counsel was there. "Life does not happen all at once. It is like a long chain. You must make each link strong, because you vill not know its relationship until much later."

With the new school year approaching, I was not looking forward to returning to the city. Even with all the work, it was going to be really difficult leaving Grandma.

And so it was, under one of those Grannie-Sky nights, we were sitting around the dying fire. I was tending the coals while she knitted. (It was amazing how she could knit with just the firelight.)

I was edgy. I began poking at the coals with a long dry stick and making fiery drawings in the air.

Suddenly she said, "Henry, did you know that people are like different types of vood? Some are like that dry stick you're vaving around. They attract attention but don't leave much behind. A few are like those hardwood pieces: It takes a long time for them to start, but once they do, the impression they leave on society lasts a long time."

I stopped. "What kind of wood am I, Grandma?"

She did not answer right away. Finally she plopped her knitting in her lap and looked right at me.

"Vell," she began, "let me put it this vay: You are certainly a better quality vood now than ven you first arrived…if you know vat I mean." She resumed knitting.

"I think so," I said, but I knew exactly what she meant. "Um, would you mind very much if I went for a walk, just up the hill there?"

She smiled. "Mind you valk slowly so that you don't sprain your ankle."

I gave her a quick hug and headed for the knoll. With her latest piece of philosophy playing in my head, I lay down and stared up at the stars.

The only part of school I had liked was astronomy, so I soon located the constellations. When I remembered the left toe of Orion was the white giant star Rigel, I compared it to the dim North Star on the tail of the Little Dipper.

"You'd think that an important star like Polaris would be brighter." Grandma's gentle words filtered in. "Often a small significant contribution to mankind lasts longer than some exciting invention that benefits very few."

As I headed downhill, I resolved to study harder. "Maybe I can become an astronomer. Maybe I could find a new star; a new star for Grandma."

* * *

The rumble of the observatory doors opening shattered my musings. Once again the telescope would peer into my Grannie's Sky.

A tear slid down my cheek.

With memories of fresh-baked bread wafting through my mind I waved at the stars.

"Good night, Grandma."

Peggy J. Cunningham

In My Grandmother's Eyes

She was my grandmother, but more than that she was my "mom." What a unique and wonderful combination! She was a remarkable lady who rescued a motherless, eight-month-old baby girl—me.

This self-sacrificing grandmother stepped up to the challenge of caring for me, a helpless baby, when my mother abandoned my dad and me to start a new life thousands of miles away. The divorce devastated my dad, and I doubt he ever got over the pain of losing the love of his life. He relinquished the care of his baby to his mother while he tried to begin a new life for himself, but he never seemed to find the happiness he was looking for to replace the hurt in his heart.

My grandmother never thought twice about caring for me, even though she was nearly fifty years old. She immediately swooped me up to be my protector and provider; I was safe under her wings. I became her baby and she became my mother. In some ways my grandmother was a grandma to me, in other ways a mother. She nurtured and loved me with a mother's love, compared to nothing else except a grandma's love. I had them both rolled into one. I became her little princess; she curled my hair every day and dressed me royally. I looked like the Shirley Temple of our small town.

Life was glorious. My clothes were delivered to my closet as though from a laundry service, my bed was made seemly by my fairy godmother, and meals were always on time in our house and fit for a king, or should I say princess. This virtuous woman never had an unkind word to say about anyone, and she always praised my real mother. That must say something about the lady—she praised the daughter-in-law who disappeared, leaving her mother-in-law with a baby who needed much attention.

Like any grandmother, me included, we want to embrace the role and lavish the grandchild with love and we don't necessarily want the responsibility of disciplinarian. She didn't want that role either, and I enjoyed the benefits of that part of the union. I was the princess of the house, never required to do ordinary chores. My grandmother did all the work, while I got all the blessings. Oh yes, she had a housekeeper once a week, but since her requirements for cleanliness far exceeded other people's standards, she would clean her house before the cleaning lady arrived. No one could enter her doors unless the house was spotless, not even the cleaning lady.

I will always be grateful for my grandma's influence that led me to a life of helping children; she was an exemplary role model. She also is the reason I grew up with no animosity towards my biological mother whom I met for the first time when I was twenty-three years old. We quickly formed a friendship and love for each other and we keep in touch even now, although thousands of miles apart.

People often ask what that meeting was like emotionally. I respond by saying, "If you were to meet a stranger today, what would be your emotional response?" That is how it was, no emotion for me, and surprisingly, I had no desire to hug this lady I resembled in many ways. However, the emotional roller coaster ride leading up to the encounter was another story. Planning for the event made me more nervous than the actual meeting itself. We had a two-year old son, her grandson. How would I choose to handle that situation? If this woman never wanted to see her daughter in all those years, why would she want to see her grandson? It was a decision I had to make, would I take him with me or wait for her to ask to see him? I chose to let her request the meeting, which she eventually did. The emotions were in high gear as I entered the funeral home where my mother's mother was being viewed; my husband by my side. It was ironic that my maternal grandmother had always wanted the two of us to meet, and now she lay in a casket close to the scene where the meeting would finally take place.

Princess Peggy finally met her real mother, but the example I had daily growing up was still the one I desired to emulate every day of my life. My grandmother may not have been my biological mother, but she was my real mother in every sense of the word. She worked hard, especially for me, and gave generously of all she had, and served others always. When I married my high school sweetheart I didn't know much about cooking or cleaning, but I knew I wanted to be like the woman I loved and admired all of my life. I wanted to have a clean house, be a fantastic cook, and serve others as she did daily. Maybe Grandma didn't make me do things a wife, mother, or grandmother would do, but better yet, she showed me how to be that woman by her example. I learned those things almost by osmosis. After I was married I spent more memorable hours watching and learning from her as she continued working well into her eighties, serving others and cooking for the family restaurant.

All through my childhood Grandma worked in the restaurant, making her special dishes and overseeing the business. Every time she left our beautiful house I worried she wouldn't come back because of an accident. I wanted to go everywhere with her so I could protect her from harm which, of course, wasn't possible. I am sure psychologists would say I feared being abandoned again. There may be some truth in that, but I would disagree with that theory in my case. Contrary to what any mental health professional would say, I never feared being abandoned by my grandmother. My greatest fear was that through uncontrollable circumstances, not of her choosing, she would be taken out of my life. I knew she would never leave me willingly.

Some may think it was a tragic childhood, but I would disagree because I was blessed to have been a princess in my grandmother's eyes. She's in heaven now and I miss her; but she didn't leave me. She is in my heart forever.

Joanne Culley

Child Prodigy

Bold and daring, my grandmother smoked, drank, played cards, and wore pants at a time when such behaviour by a woman was frowned upon. She got away with it because of her talent, charm, and beauty. She was a professional pianist who was the centre of attention wherever she went.

When I was young, she was a role model for me of a self-confident woman who had lived a fulfilling life. As I got older, and realized the limitations that some women had to face, I came to know how special she was.

Born in 1897, Ida Fernley forged a life for herself, getting paid for doing what came naturally to her. At the age of four, she went to a parade with her mother on Yonge Street in Toronto to welcome the troops back from the Boer War. The band was playing "Soldiers of the Queen," a marching song. When she ran home and played it by ear perfectly on the piano, her family realized she was a child prodigy. At eight years old she was demonstrating pianos at the Canadian National Exhibition. In a flyer produced for the event, she was described as "the most wonderful child pianist ever heard in Canada." She had "a phenomenal memory, no less than 78 different selections are included in her repertoire."

When she was twelve, Ida played in the storefront theatres that showed silent movies and presented vaudeville acts. She watched what was on the screen or stage and played accordingly: suspenseful music for a dramatic scene or something cheerful for a happy one. With no music in front of her, she said she was "faking it." Her future husband, Harry Culley, played piano in the theatre across the street.

When the two married, Ida at seventeen and Harry at eighteen, they both returned to their respective parents' homes, not knowing any differently. Their first son arrived seven months later, a scandal they tried to hide by moving up their anniversary date after the fact. She took a few years off from performing and had a second son.

When her husband realized he needed the allure of her presence on the stage, they developed their career together as duo pianists—two pianos, four hands—playing on the stage and radio. She adopted the stage name "Claudette" and they called themselves the "Black and White Spotters" after the black and white keys, playing live on two grand pianos in the studio. They had their own radio show called "Hot Spots" on CKCL, a station in Toronto that broadcast popular songs of the day. A reviewer in the *Telegram* wrote, "For consistently fine work, the two-piano team of Claudette and Harry Culley are hard to beat. Any night of the week you can be assured of an interesting 15 minutes." The duo also appeared on CBC and CFRB and as guests on Kate Smith's CBS variety radio show in New York City.

Then, they felt the full force of the Great Depression. When advertising dropped and their radio work evaporated, they lost their house and their livelihoods. They had to look for work beyond North America and found it touring in the British Isles and South Africa from 1936 to 1938. They sent money back home to support their two sons, who were living with their grandparents.

Their audiences in South Africa were mostly white, and Ida didn't think this was fair. So, she insisted that they play in the theatres for the blacks also, even though they weren't paid for it. However, they received many bouquets and presents in return.

While performing at the Paramount Astoria in London, their gas masks within easy reach, the duo began to take the rumblings in Europe seriously. Upon their return to Canada, they found a country that was gearing up for war, with the economy on the upswing. Building on their international fame, they soon found enough radio and stage work to keep them busy.

Ida wanted to stay blonde and attractive forever and so took her beauty regime seriously even after retirement. Accustomed to applying her own makeup for the stage, she kept it up. She would not emerge from her bedroom without her "face" on, which involved applying powder, mascara, and fire-engine red lipstick. I envied her perfectly manicured nails, painted to match her lips—my own were always stubby and short because I bit them. She never let her hands touch dishwater without rubber gloves.

One of my earliest memories is when I would accompany her by streetcar to the salon where she went every week for forty years. Located in a brownstone apartment downtown, it was a mysterious realm of female transformations where women sat contentedly reading beauty magazines under humming steel dryers, their hair screwed up in curlers. Then we would go back to her house where she entertained me by playing songs such as "Tenderly," "The Man I Love," and "Stardust." Her hands flying over the keys, she'd look over at me smiling and ask what I'd like to hear next.

Fascinated by her beauty rituals, my cousin Barbara and I loved to sit in front of the three-way mirror of her vanity. We'd spray ourselves with perfume from her atomizer, spread Italian balm all over our hands and faces, curl our eyelashes, and try on her earrings, all the while imagining ourselves in her glamorous life.

We begged her to bring out her leather-bound South Africa album. She'd open it up on the dining room table where we gazed at the photos of her and my grandfather relaxing on the deck of the Stirling Castle ship, being surrounded by dignitaries in Johannesburg, or playing with the wild monkeys in Durban.

Then she opened her old trunk, stamped with labels from around the world, to show us her haute couture gowns designed by Norman Hartnell. "He's the designer for the Queen you know," she would say proudly. And we would imagine her strolling onto the stage from one side while my handsome grandfather came from the other, meeting her in the middle to each sit down at a grand piano and play Gershwin's "Rhapsody in Blue." With her wavy hair and pencil-thin dark eyebrows, she would be wearing a sparkly, one shoulder dress, while Grandpa would be in his white tie and tails.

When people complimented her on her talent, Grandma took no credit herself; she simply deflected it by saying that she was making the best use of the talent God gave her. This was a remarkable statement, considering she wasn't otherwise religious and never went to church.

A rebellious teen myself, I confided in her my problems with my parents and boyfriends. She commiserated with me, pushed my hair back, told me how beautiful I was, and that everything would all work out.

I think she was a better grandmother than she had been a mother. She said children held you down and she complained about changing diapers when she wanted to be out at the movies. She advised me not to have children (counsel which I eventually ignored). Her life was not without heartbreak. Her younger son, also a musician, took to drink and died of lung cancer in his fifties. I think she blamed herself for being away from home during his formative years.

Grandma's resilience in the face of adversity and her positive attitude have helped me face challenges in my own life. And she also showed me that being charming and beautiful doesn't hurt.

Faye Braley

I Remember Nana

My mother's mother, whom I remember as "Nana," was affectionately known as "Fritz" by her husband. If that conjures up an image in your mind of a stoic German, you would be only half right. German she was. Stoic she was not.

Our family bounced in and out of my grandparents' home so often when I was a child that I have more memories of their home than I do of any other place where we lived. Sometimes we were there because my father was out of work. Sometimes we were there while my father helped them care for their small farm. Sometimes my father was working in another state and our family needed shelter.

Nana had raised three sons and a daughter, but seemed perfectly willing to take on two more girls and a boy if the situation warranted. Though she held the family together with an iron will, what I remember was a sense of comradeship between my grandparents, and a comfortable feeling of "belonging" when I was with them.

Nana's house had a screened-in front porch, where there would be either a crock of sauerkraut aging, or a bushel basket of produce waiting to be cooked or canned. I had free access to either of these food sources, and my favorite treat was to pluck a turnip from the basket and eat it raw. I still prefer almost all vegetables raw.

I also made friends with the baby animals on the farm, and sometimes napped in the yard with my head resting on the flank of a sleeping calf.

Some of my earliest memories of Nana are of her laughter. When I hear the expression "belly laugh" I think of Nana. She didn't just laugh—she laughed all over!

Nana and I had great fun making things together, especially at Christmas when I as a little girl became interested in the giving process. We spent hours weaving our secret plans and crafting small gifts that made a huge difference in my life. At one point when our family was living in another state at Christmas, and I was missing Nana's happy scheming, I received a letter from her. In it was a drawing of her head, with over-large ears, to remind me she too was aware that this was usually "secret time" for us.

When my grandfather died, Nana took it in stride as she had taken other hard times throughout her life. Only after the funeral was over did her armor crack. As we walked into her house she sobbed, "Who's going to wake me up every morning saying 'Good morning, Fritz!'?" I realized then that though I thought I knew her so well, I had no idea how deep were her emotions. It was a side of her I had never before experienced.

In later years when I was married and had two children of my own, Nana would come and stay with us for a month or so. It didn't take my children long to learn that if they sang "nana, nana, fo-fanna, nana" she would laugh so hard we would all be forced to join in. In the evenings we would play games that the children enjoyed. One of Nana's favorites was "Aggravation," which she consistently called "dirty marbles." Despite any frustration over having her marbles sent home one evening, the next evening we were right back at it.

During those visits I gave Nana free rein in my kitchen. One of her pleasures in life was trying out recipes she dreamed up or saw in newspapers or magazines. I always thought "green gravy" (made from asparagus) was her invention, until my husband was served green gravy at a small college in Canada.

Usually Nana would try a recipe, freely substituting or omitting any ingredient called for if we didn't have it on hand. At tasting time she would give a disgruntled "humph! I don't know what was so special about that!"

One day Nana told me she had read that rolling a roast in ice-cream salt would keep it from drying out in the oven. Nothing ventured, nothing gained! We tried it on the next roast. Indeed the roast was moist, but the gravy made from the drippings would curl your tongue! We found it hilarious and with a mental shrug went on to the next idea.

When Nana was eighty-three she took her first plane ride. She was living in Phoenix, Arizona, with her youngest son, but each summer she would take a long Greyhound bus ride to St. Louis, Missouri, to visit her oldest son. That summer my uncles talked her into taking a plane, using the reasoning that she would arrive sooner and have longer to visit. Wouldn't you know it? The plan was hijacked! It was the beginning of the era when hijacking became a threat, and the plane spent many hours in the air, circling airports until a landing could be negotiated. Except for irritation with persistent reporters, Nana took it with aplomb, only commenting that she had torn her hose when she had to exit the plane off the wing. I thought that would be the end of her flying experience, but the next summer she traveled to St. Louis on her new favorite means of transportation—an airplane.

When she was in her nineties, Nana lost her eyesight. Though her activities were curtailed, she found new enjoyment sitting in the backyard of her son's home, listening to the birds. One day my aunt sent one of her girls out to get Nana and bring her in for lunch. But Nana was no longer there. Only the body remained. She died as she had always lived—enjoying life.

Elynne Chaplik-Aleskow

Her First Grandchild

She is one of the great loves of my life. I lost her in a plane crash February 12, 1963; however, the memory of my maternal grandmother Fannie Lebedow inspires me every day of my life.

I was my grandma's first grandchild. The bond between us was magical. One of my greatest treats as a little girl was sleeping over at her apartment. The room I slept in had twin beds, very high and fluffy. I always needed help getting in at night.

One morning my grandma came in to check on me and I was not in bed. The window next to the bed was halfway open. Her apartment being on the third floor, she panicked, thinking that I might have fallen out the window until she realized that I fell out of bed and in my sleep rolled under the bed. Years later we always shared a good laugh about that morning's discovery.

My grandmother was a tall woman with striking silver hair. She was handsome and stately in her carriage with a soft smooth skin that always smelled like fresh Palmolive soap. People's heads turned toward her when she entered a room.

She was my grandma, a woman whose love for me was unconditional and giving. Loving her was natural and easy because she loved me back with such genuine joy and caring. It always felt good to be around her. I looked forward to seeing her, touching her, and smelling her scent. With her I shared many of the happiest moments of my childhood.

One of the greatest legacies my grandmother left me was showing me how to love. She passed this natural gift on to my mother as well.

One of my treasures is a picture I have of Grandma in her housedress. My mother tells me that she remembers her mother always stunningly dressed. That is not the childhood memory of her that I cherish, however. In her housedress she would take me grocery shopping and would tell me to pick out any candy I wanted. I always got the pretzel stick. I would hold her hand as we walked doing errands, returning home in time for the delicious lunch she would prepare for me. Her kitchen pantry filled with desserts was like Disneyland to me.

As I grew older, my grandmother became a friend with whom I could share my feelings. One day my mother and I had the worst argument we had ever had. I was twelve years old. I packed my belongings, willed my precious board games to my sister Linda, and ran away from home. Of course the place I ran to was my grandmother's new apartment that was fortunately a few miles from my home.

When I arrived, she fed me and waited until I was ready to talk. My grandmother never pressured me or forced me. Our relating was easy and empathic. Her legacy of listening without judging is one I have tried to implement in my relationships.

A few years after losing my grandfather, my family convinced my grandmother to take a vacation in Florida. She was with my mother and youngest sister Ivy at the beginning of her holiday. Before they left for home, my mother found a small hotel for seniors and my grandmother stayed on for twelve more days.

My beloved grandmother never made it home. The commercial plane she was on hit a squall during the first ten minutes it was in the air and crashed in the Florida Everglades. Everyone on board was killed. My grandmother was sixty-seven.

I can touch the raw agony of that day when we found out that we lost her like it was yesterday. I was seventeen and about to graduate from high school and head to college in the fall.

In losing Grandma Lebedow I lost one of the great loves and friends of my life. I hope she would be proud of the woman I have become. I smile at her picture every day. Frozen in time in her housedress, she smiles back at me.

Linda Carlblom

Would the Real Grandma Please Stand Up?

Mom and Dad walked quietly past Grandma Olean's casket on a cold and windy March day. Mom gently pulled a lavender rose from the spray of flowers that adorned its top. Grandma would never see her grandchildren grow up. Worse yet, we would never remember her. My brother was only two, my sister two weeks old, and I was not even born.

Grandma Olean, my mother's mother, died at the young age of forty-eight, a victim of breast cancer. Five lonely years later, Grandpa left rural Indiana and moved to the wild west of Arizona in hopes of building a new life. A year later he fell in love and married, and Grandma Roselin gracefully "stepped" into our lives.

That was fifty-five years ago. Grandpa passed away in 1995 and Grandma followed three years later. They were married thirty-three years. Looking back, I feel incredibly blessed to have had a step-grandma who made me feel she wasn't a "step" at all, but the real thing. From my experiences as a child and my observations as an adult, I see many things Grandma consistently did right to make us feel whole.

Grandma wasn't afraid to love us. She didn't hold back hugs, smiles, or kisses just because she entered the family late. She took on the role of grandma without reserve. She didn't wait for us to give her the O.K. to love us. She just did. We could always count on an enthusiastic greeting when we bounded through her door and her arms flung open wide to give us warm hugs. She even kept a small trunk of toys in the extra bedroom just for us, and a full apple-shaped cookie jar on the kitchen counter. We always knew we were wanted and welcome.

Grandma never tried to replace anyone. Grandma Olean was not a taboo subject, even if Grandma Roselin was around. Often Grandma Roselin would bring her up herself, and always in a positive light. "I understand your Grandma Olean loved flowers," Grandma would say while cutting flowers from her own garden. If she ever felt threatened by the memory of Grandma Olean, it never showed. She didn't pretend Grandma Olean never existed, but rather, she accepted her as our grandma too, and carved her own place in our hearts simply as another loving grandma.

Grandma loved our grandpa. There was no doubt they loved each other. That didn't mean they never uttered words of frustration to each other. Even so, an undercurrent of love always flowed beneath the exasperation. We knew the love would return as quickly as the frustration had come.

Grandma and Grandpa enjoyed each other's company and had fun together. They loved to camp and fish. They rode bikes together. They went on cruises. They were involved in church activities. They picked fruit off their backyard trees and gave the excess to family and friends. They did all these things right up to Grandpa's death at the age of eighty-eight, and often included us in their activities. They enjoyed a full life and their abundant love was never hidden from the grandkids. Their marriage served as a positive model for us to follow in our own lives.

Grandma taught us things. While Grandma showed us how to knead the dough for homemade bread, she taught us a Swedish childhood rhyme she'd learned from her mother who emigrated with her family from Sweden. She taught my sister and me to crochet blankets for our dolls and to paint by number. As we watched birds fly in her backyard, Grandma told us what kind they were and pointed out their distinctive songs and features. We had fun, and we kept busy at Grandma's house, learning all the while.

Grandma supported and encouraged our interests. Seldom did Grandma miss one of our school concerts or church programs. She and Grandpa often came to encourage and support us in our activities. It didn't matter if we were any good. They were proud we were involved in something worthwhile. As a child, I took their presence for granted. But as an adult, I can see the lasting impact it had on my life. I was valued. I had an extended family that cared enough to take a night out of their busy lives to show their support for my interests. This built up my confidence and self-esteem without my realizing it at the time. I was as proud to have them at my programs as they were proud of my participation.

Grandma never used the word "step." "This is my granddaughter, Linda," Grandma said, eyes beaming with pride. She always introduced me as her granddaughter. Not her step-granddaughter or Don's granddaughter, but her granddaughter. In her heart, that's who I was. And in my heart, she was my real grandma. Had she inserted the word "step" into the introduction, it would have held me at arm's length, somehow implying that I wasn't as accepted or loved as much as I would have been had I been her blood grandchild. Wisely, she chose to omit the "step," silently saying, "I couldn't love you more even if you were my own."

You may feel that since she was the only grandma I ever knew, this disqualifies me from understanding the complexity of blended families. Not so. I grew up knowing this was a blended family. We thrived in it regardless of the lack of blood ties. My children also live in a blended family now, due to divorce. Thankfully, they, too, have step-grandparents who make them feel just as loved as mine did. Loving children and grandchildren who aren't your own doesn't come easy. But it is possible, and when you do, you make a tremendous and lasting impact on your family's harmony and well-being.

You see, when a grandparent's love abounds, steps aren't needed to reach from one heart to another.

Karen L. Cole

Grandma's Braid

Nellie opens her underwear drawer, lifts the serviceable snuggies and large-cup bras which are her staples these days. Warm undershirts, piled on the other side, help to fight the chill when she's working in the barn or outside. Even in the winter, the chores must be done: the chickens fed, the eggs gathered, the hay and straw pushed down the chutes to the main part of the barn for bedding and food. Not to mention the milking, though the boys, especially Donald, usually take care of that.

No one else sees her underwear anymore. Jim's been dead ten years and none of the kids sleeps with her now. They're teenagers and young adults. Nellie frets at the thought of the day when they'll all go off and get married, though Bonnie is only fourteen, so hopefully, it will be awhile.

Ah! That's what she was looking for, the thick braid of auburn hair—her hair—cut off in one fell swoop shortly after Jim's death in '22. She knew then she would have to sell the farm or keep running it with the help of the kids, maybe the occasional hired man. Donald was ten then, and already doing the work of a man. He was even driving their Model T, though not very far.

* * *

Nellie kept the farm but that long hair had to go, so when her sister Mae and husband Ben drove up to show off their new Ford, she asked Mae to chop off the braid.

"But Nellie, your hair, it's so beautiful."

"I don't have time or need for beauty now, Mae. I've got to keep this farm running and take care of my family."

"Have you thought of going back to teaching?"

"Teaching is fine for single women, but I've got my own kids to worry about now. No, I'm going to be the best farmer in Pierce County."

As Mae sawed through the thick braid with the largest scissors from Nellie's sewing box, she wept, swiping away a tear or two so she could see what she was doing. But Nellie merely gritted her teeth and said, "Don't be sentimental, Mae. It's only hair."

Only hair. Nothing like the value of this farm where all but one of their six children were born. Marcella had died as a baby in Colourado, so Wisconsin—where she and Jim had grown up and fallen in love—was a refuge after that loss. How could she leave it?

* * *

A smile creeps across her face when she thinks of how pleased Jim was to present her with the oak china cabinet four years ago for her birthday. It holds a place of honour in their dining room, along with the best dishes and, unfortunately, too much junk, so easy to stash in those drawers. Life as a farmer is so busy especially with kids underfoot. Lamoine was only a baby, still crawling around when Jim brought the china cabinet through the door, and Nellie yelled at Rochelle to pull her out of harm's way. A fine piece of furniture. She was sure it would last a long time.

Willard arrived a few months after the china closet on the first day of a sunny October. He seemed to have a weak heart, the doctor warned her. Yet by the time Bonnie made her entrance into the world in March two-and-a-half years later, Willard was thriving.

Then her world exploded in chaos. In early November of '22, Donald and Rochelle came home from school, victims of the scarlet fever epidemic sweeping through the county and mowing down young and old alike. Nellie had survived an earlier bout of the disease before her marriage, and believed she was immune. But Jim had never experienced it, so he avoided the sick children. With Nellie's patient care, her two oldest rallied and recovered. But little Lamoine, now five, fell deathly ill. Nellie insisted Jim move to the barn to avoid contracting it, but when Lamoine died, he re-entered his home, and became the fever's next victim, nine days after his young daughter.

* * *

Nellie crushes the hair to her chest, walks over to the bed, bows her head, and weeps. How she has managed to raise those four children and keep the farm running for the past ten years is a wonder. But her heart longs for the days when Jim would twirl her around the dance floor, her auburn hair flowing behind her. Her days as a young teacher seemed charmed and so much easier than keeping a farm going. She glances at the wedding picture on the wall, where her hair was pulled up in the fashion of the day. Looking at Jim, so tall and handsome, brought more tears. She is startled out of her reverie by someone at the door: "Yoo, hoo, Nellie, can I come in?" It is her neighbour, Maggie, no doubt in search of coffee and a chat.

Nellie wipes her eyes, leaps up, stuffs the braid beneath the undershirts, and heads for the kitchen.

* * *

Nellie hung on to that acreage for another sixty years, running a profitable farm, till her once-brilliant mind filled with confusion and she couldn't manage alone in the country. Her china closet went to Edith, Donald's widow, who kept it another twenty-two years until she died in '04. Then I became the proud owner of Grandma's gift from Grandpa, a grandpa I never met.

No one knows what became of Grandma's braid.

Gary Boutin

Canadian Maple Taffy

French Canadian holidays in my childhood included Réveillon where family enjoyed fun, feasting, and mouthwatering desserts. At Christmastime Grandmama and Mom placed maple candies in my stocking and shared them during our holiday meals. Christmas at my grandparents' home in West Montreal, Quebec, brought me an abundance of food and love.

On Christmas Eve Grandmama and the women of the family prepared Réveillon, the late evening meal. After Midnight Mass at the Notre-Dame De Montreal cathedral, we savored Réveillon, where a little maple treat appeared magically near my plate from Père Noël, our Santa Claus. This meal included French meat pies and holiday dishes to delight my eyes. Grandmama and Grandpapa shared the bounty of maple taffy and candy all evening.

One year, I asked, "Grandmama, how is maple taffy made?"

"Gary, you need maple syrup, time, and snow," she replied.

"Where do we get the maple syrup?" I asked.

"We purchase maple syrup from the maple camps, but we must wait for spring."

This is my family's story of maple taffy, also known as *tire d'erable* in Quebec, and how it gave me an appreciation for all Canadian traditions.

Later in the year, when the days became warmer, but the nights were still cold, the maple sap started moving up the trees. This signaled the time to drive to the camps north of Montreal in the Laurentian Mountains. Though it was spring, we still needed to dress for the cold weather.

"Gary, wear your long underwear and snowsuit, and meet me at the front door."

"Grandmama, I am ready!"

"Where are your boots, hat, and the gloves knitted for you by your mother?"

Well, I was almost ready. I had to dig out my boots from the front closet, put them on, and go into my room and find my gloves. One was on my bed and the other was under it. Wow, I was lucky to find them, I thought to myself. Now, where is my knitted hat?

My grandfather peered around the doorway of my room. "Come to the front door, I have your hat."

The adults wore flannel shirts, waterproof pants, long parkas, and boots. Once we were ready, we dove into Grandpapa's 1964, white-roof with turquoise body, Chevrolet Bel Air four-door sedan. The two-lane roads were still covered in grey ice slush, but some were cleared so visitors could purchase supplies from the camps.

The rutted driveway caused our car to bottom out. We seemed to drive endlessly until finally we reached the maple shed. The log cabin had an attached souvenir store, with a dozen tables outside cut from half logs. As we all got out of the car, each door opening into the green vegetation, Mom said, "You can go and play but stay close. We will be inside. Don't get into trouble!"

I peered inside the cabin where the walls were adorned with all kinds of handcrafts, doilies, paintings, sketches, quilts, blankets, lumberjack red shirts, socks, and shoes. The best part was the refrigerated glass cases containing several shelves laden with different kinds of candy all placed in neat rows. The most popular among Canadians was maple leaf candy. I also saw sugared candy, maple cookies, and maple syrup.

For me, the camp had its own adventures. While my grandparents were buying gallons of maple syrup, I ran around the log tables and into the forest, making believe I was a lumberjack like Grandpapa. I climbed a birch pretending to cut the top off for daylight to pop in. I hopped in and out between the shadows playing with imaginary foes. Though it was not even noon, my enemies surrounded me, and I would try to foil them into giving me their secrets. The adventure was endless and after the purchases had been negotiated, Grandmama called, "Gary, come to the car, it's time to go home."

Usually it would take a bit of yelling for me to leave the green woods and my rivals behind, but a bribe of a maple treat opened my ears. Grandpapa reached for the wooden box of treats and winked his eye, dispensing one soft maple sugar bear candy to each family member. The rest of the treats were saved for Christmas.

When the holiday arrived Grandmama gathered the family together. At first the grown-ups would meet in the living room near the woodstove and trade stories. I, being the oldest cousin, led the way to the backyard to skate on our little ice rink until dinner was ready. After dinner, Grandmama gave me instructions for our annual treat. "Gary, take your cousins and find the cleanest snow in our backyard, near the maple trees at the edge of our woods."

A blizzard had blanketed the backyard filling it with fresh clean white snow. As I was leaving, Grandmama gave me a new aluminum pan and told me to fill it up. My job was to scoop up the snow with the help of my cousins and place it into the pan.

While that was happening, my grandmother was in the kitchen preparing the maple syrup taffy. She poured the syrup into a metal saucepan, then boiled it to condense it. She would occasionally test the taffy by taking a teaspoon of it and dropping the liquid into cold water. If it turned into a hard substance, the mixture was ready. Next Mom took the aluminum pan to a shelf outside the kitchen back door.

The last step is what my dreams were made of: Grandmama scooped up the saucepan from the stove and poured the liquid over the snow. The maple mixture immediately turned into taffy. Voilà, all that was left was to take the hardened taffy from the snow and eat it.

Réveillon in our family formed the centre of the holiday, and my memories of this Christmas taffy reminds me of my Canadian home, even though now most Christmas days I spend basking under the California sun.

Maple Taffy Treats

Obtain Canadian maple syrup of good quality.
Range stove, equipped with a saucepan.
Candy thermometer ready to read 256 degrees Fahrenheit.
Large aluminum tray for the clean snow.
Snow shovel to scoop with.
Pour the taffy liquid maple mixture on top of the snow.
Pull out the hardened taffy and enjoy with your loved ones.

Phyllis Ciarametaro

Nana's Garden

"Cake and ice cream in fifteen minutes," Aunt Millie called to everyone in the garden, as she and Aunt Sally stood on the back porch of my Nana's house. Everyone in the family had assembled for Nana's ninetieth birthday, and my aunts had cooked up quite a spread.

Upon arriving, I parked in the cul-de-sac behind the house. Hundreds of lilacs could be seen from the street hanging over the old weathered fence. I entered through the garden gate, and stepped into paradise. The yard was ablaze with colour. Standing at the entrance of this floral wonderland, I took a deep breath as the scents enveloped me.

Nana's prize roses were my favorite. She had a variety of sizes and colours, from white to burgundy, with and without thorns. I wandered around admiring the snowballs, lilies, tulips, irises, and all the other flourishing flowers, trees, and bushes. I stopped often to admire an unusual colour and to smell some of the blooms.

Being in Nana's garden brought back wonderful childhood memories of working with her. I remembered turning the soil, digging the holes for her prize bulbs, and misting the yard with the garden hose. I loved wiggling my toes in the warm, fine earth, but it was hard work. Sometimes I stayed overnight so we could get an early start in the morning. My Nana was not a strong woman, but between the two of us, we would drag bags of soil around the yard and spread them with our hands, or pull a child's red wagon full of rocks up from the beach near her house. She used these stones to separate and outline the areas for each species. Her garden was a haven of beauty, and the envy of her neighbors. Throughout her life she had won many awards and ribbons. Nana had a wonderful gift.

She was in her glory today, celebrating her birthday with her family around her. An air of contentment, peace, love, and happiness surrounded the house. My mother Rose, and aunts Millie, Sally, and Anna, had placed vases of beautiful flowers in each room, creating an intoxicating fragrance.

Nana had designed narrow paths, and placed cement garden furniture throughout the area. Walking around the beautiful surroundings, I could stop and sit in comfort to enjoy the beauty. In the darkest corner of the garden was a small fountain surrounded by white twinkle lights, which hung from the lilac trees and illuminated the entire area. In another dark section of the yard, Nana had designed and built a grotto where she placed a statue of the Blessed Mother; here she had planted many of her award-winning roses.

My aunts had gardens of their own, but not as grand as Nana's. No matter how hard they tried, their efforts could not compare with their mother's, but they kept trying.

My mother was the oldest of Nana's daughters, but unlike her mother's and her sisters', her garden was small. Much of our yard was devoted to playthings for me and my sister. We didn't have the variety of flora that Nana had, but we did have roses. Mom's favorites were American Beauty.

Today I asked Nana a question that I had wanted to ask for a long time. "Nana, what is your secret for growing such a beautiful garden?"

She smiled, put her finger to her lips, and whispered in my ear. "I pick a bouquet of flowers at the beginning of the season, and again at the end. I take them to church, and I place them at the feet of the Blessed Mother, Mary. I say a little prayer of thanks to her, and the next year my flowers are more beautiful than the year before."

I had always admired Nana's faith, and smiled when I remembered Nana's first name is Mary.

Kathryn MacDonald

Grandma's Soup

With bristle brush she scrubs root vegetables
before chopping and tossing them
into hot olive oil to soften in the pot.
Onions, carrots, and slivers of cabbage
perfume the kitchen with autumn's garden.
As the veggies sweat, she adds beans,
broth, a splash of red wine,
bay leaves, rosemary, salt and pepper
before covering the pot to simmer.

Time passes and she stirs,
sees vegetables and spices rise and fall
like soups in another kitchen
where her husband strode
from door to stove, vibrant,
his youthful exuberance and energy
filling the room with hungers.

Snow falls steadily against windowpanes
she smiles remembering Grandma
holding another wooden spoon to her lips,
her cheeks cool from the frosty walk
across the path between their homes,
separated by the large garden
separated now by time and passages.

Recipes collect in cupboards
and she wonders if one day her grandchild
will stand and stir a pot of soup
with garden vegetables
to share with a young partner
eager for life to unfold.

A cane tapping the floor takes her out of reverie.
Its sound moves close
until wood-shavings clinging to his flannel shirt
mix with the kitchen's soupy scents.
Scooping a spoonful of broth, she turns,
raises it to lips shadowed by grey beard
and he sips,
his voice murmuring praise
for Grandma's soup.

Maggie Brackley

How Sweet It Was

Black felt hat set firmly on her head and further secured by a large faux pearl hat pin, the funeral hat my father called it, Grandma would step out towards the bus stop, her bearing indicating a firm sense of purpose. She was headed for one of her favourite social outings, a funeral. Her generation had a fairly prosaic attitude to death: We all have to go sometime, accept it. The funerals were always those of elderly people, sometimes just passing acquaintances, but it was a good chance for the surviving friends to meet up, sing a few hymns, then enjoy a genteel afternoon tea. Not a bad afternoon's outing. She would then return home to an evening of nonstop television played at full volume. Television to her represented a miracle, the world in her living room. She watched everything from quiz shows to documentaries featuring the great figures of the twentieth century—Winston Churchill being a huge favourite, along with ballroom dancing contests, sitcoms, and of course Coronation Street.

Grandma came to live with us when I was about ten years old. While this new living arrangement called for some adjustments on the part of the adults in the family, my sister and I found the new order of things entirely beneficial. One of my fondest memories, perversely, was being home sick in bed with one of the usual array of childhood ailments: measles, chickenpox, mumps, or just common old flu, and Grandma would appear in my bedroom and light a coal fire in the fireplace. In Scotland in the fifties each room in our house still had a working fireplace and coal delivery was commonplace. The flames would play on the walls and the ceiling as I lay there feeling utterly cosseted. A further touch of Grandma's was some refreshing lavender water sprinkled on my pillow. Oh, the joy of being sick in Grandma's household.

Birthdays brought ritual gifts of food and sweets, usually Lindt dark chocolate cigarettes, honeydew melon, and Tunisian dates in a wooden box—in those days regarded as expensive fruits for special occasions.

However, where Grandma really excelled was in her tablet making. On grey, wet, miserable days, numerous in Scotland's disagreeable climate, Grandma would quietly make a batch of tablet—a traditional Scottish sweet, similar to North American fudge, but not so creamy. It tends to be dry, sugary, crumbly stuff with an overtone of caramel flavour. So many grey days, so much tablet, it's a wonder our teeth survived the sugar onslaught.

While recipes for tablet appear simple, it can be frustratingly difficult to get it just right. Apparently it's all in the manner of the stirring, the exact number of minutes to keep it at a rolling boil, the colour when ready, properly scraping down the crystallized sugar clinging to the sides of the pot, and heaven knows what other sleights of hand.

It took me many tries to master the art and I must have used a small boat full of sugar in my efforts over the years, although my mother and sister seemed to inherit the knack with ease. Once upon a time there was an actual recipe on blue, lined notepaper, handwritten in the fine copperplate of my grandmother's generation, stained and spilled on with frequent use, as all good recipes are. Our twenty-first-century version is a typed copy, written from memory of the original.

In today's world of over-anxious parenting, making children sugar-laden candy to cheer them up on a grey day would no doubt be regarded as utterly reprehensible. How fortunate we were to grow up when it was merely a grandmother's innocent act of love.

Scottish Tablet

5½ cups white granulated sugar
1 can (approx 400 gms.) sweetened condensed milk
½ cup unsalted butter (do NOT substitute margarine)
1 cup fresh milk to dampen the sugar
1 tsp. vanilla essence

Essential equipment:

A heavy bottom cooking pot, deep enough to contain all the ingredients and still leave room for vigorous stirring.

A long-handled wooden spoon
9x11 cookie tray

WARNING: Be careful in handling the mixture. It will eventually reach a temperature of around 115 degrees C and any splashes on the skin will cause a painful burn.

Pour sugar into pan and dampen with cold milk. Add butter and condensed milk, keep stirring, and bring to boil on medium-high. This usually takes about ten minutes.

Continue to stir; white colour will gradually turn to golden, then caramel colour. Be wary of dark streaks—that means it's burning. This process will take about 20 to 30 minutes of continual stirring (you will note this recipe requires strong wrists). Drop teaspoonful of mixture into cup of cold water. If it forms soft, sticky ball, it's ready. At this point, stir in vanilla.

Remove pot from heat and scrape crystallized sugar from sides of the pan down into mix to help with setting process.

Pour mixture into buttered cookie sheet to set. After about ten minutes when it's just starting to set, score mix into squares. When it hardens, it's ready to eat.

Leah Murray

Distaff Trio, Plaited

"Come over to the light," said Gram. "I'll spin Rapunzel's legend from your hair."

My eyes still blurred from the stings inflicted by a brushing out of Mam's
I looked askance at Gram, already there.

"Tch! Win, the maid's all white eyes and wings!" cried Gram in mock dismay, all ham,

Then spoiled her mummery by winking in my face when Mam bent down to get a pin

She'd dropped when sudden in came Gram.

Gram gave me the mirror, shifted my place, snapped elastic onto her thin wrist. Into knobbly fingers took brush, and with surprising grace

She gently made my tresses straight and slim.

"Look you, Win," and Gram traps mane in place with fingers, brush, and band.

She tugs a tail up to my crown while Mam comes closer, better for to gauge
How Gram's ancient digits keep their pace.

"Now just split this cable into three—it's always three, you mark, with us—
One for the maiden she is, one for the mother you be, and one for the crone that I am,"

Sorting my horsetail into separate strands.

"Hook 'em through the fetching paw," Gram advised, wiggling her left hand in the air,

"Maiden left, mother middle, crone right—crone's always right," she said aside to me,

Dropping strands between each pair of fingers.

"Take up the crone and twist her doesil thrice." She twisted rightmost strand right.

"Then cross it left atop of maid and mam—who's boss, eh?" she cackled in my ear.

Mam smiled down at her Mam's busy fingers.

"Tuck it into the maiden spot—when a crone crosses over, she returns a maid."

Gram tucked the twisted strand away. "Just like in life they all three move along,"

Said she, shifting strands each a finger to the right.

"Now, look here," she told me. "You see what's happened? The crone's the maid
The maid's become a Mam, and the Mam's a crone at last. Vengeance, hey?"
The old woman winked at me in the mirror.

"You just go on like life, same old things again: crone twisted thrice
Crossed over, made maiden, maiden made Mam, and Mam made crone,
'Til you run out of hair to make your rope with."

All the while she suited action to words, and moments later my flying mane was tamed,

Trussed into an ordered, heavy rope, Rapunzelite in strength, and glowing gold
Well able to take Gram's tugs without Mam's stings.

Coleene D. VanTilburg

Doggy Treats from Gramma Joyce

Opening the door, a pack of giggly children strained to keep a "beast" of a dog in control on a short nylon rope. His wagging rear end knocked the children off balance, but with glee they quickly asked if this dog belonged to us. Resembling a polar bear, he looked at me, and I saw his drooling tongue and smiling grin that said, "Where's dinner?"

Coming to the door, my husband joined me and quickly told the children, to my surprise, that the dog did not belong to us, but he willingly volunteered to take him in and look for his owner. Over a hundred pounds of boundless energy, fifty I am sure his head weighed alone, bulldozed into our living room and into our hearts. A yellow lab no one claimed became ours after default. We named him "Chance."

We soon learned that Chance loved to eat. Insatiable, he gave back in love and our two boys adored him. The first Christmas with Chance found an additional stocking hung on the mantle next to the others for our family. My last purchase and wrapped gift, Chance's large meat-flavored chew bone, lay hidden and secured on top of the fridge. Santa's cookies and milk stayed safe inside those doors as well.

A favorite recipe for Christmas, Chocolate Chip Chewy Bars, came from my mother Joyce, who snipped this treat from the daily newspaper. Stapled 3x5 index cards, organised perfectly, filled a recipe box my sister and I remember fondly. Magazine cutouts and soup label finds made for some of the best meals at our dinner table. Pulling out this yellowed recipe card for the chewy bars became one of the joys of our holiday baking. I usually make several batches every year.

These bars are easy to make and give. Infused with honey, the amber gold liquid glues all the ingredients together and pure joy meets the palate.

As the years went by, Chance continued to love on us as much as we loved on him; and he never lost his appetite. Gramma Joyce, fragile in stature but tough in determination, kept her distance from Chance's wiggly rear end which with one close encounter might throw Gramma "for a loop." A mutual respect seemed to exist between these two. Never having a dog of her own, she showed her love for our dog by categorizing a section in her coupon box: "Chance." Then on her visits, the coupon envelope she brought with her came stuffed with discounts for a certain puppy's belly validating my practical mom and giving Chance a well-stocked section in the pantry. None of those doggy goodies, though, contained chocolate chips.

Gramma Joyce has now passed on. Recipe traditions made at Christmas time remind me of days gone by when as a little girl I waited for the opportunity to lick the beaters or enjoy the cinnamon-sugared pie crust cookies. Not as disciplined as my mother, many nights I let my young son stay up late, punching cookie cutter stars and bells into the sugar cookie dough and yes, licking the beaters. Timmy and I produced dozens of bars and decorated cookies, piling them high in different groupings ready to deliver around the neighborhood or to special friends. My son, not always in the best health, visited the local E.R. one year many times.

"Mom, this year I want to take a plate over to the hospital…can we do that?" he asked.

"Sure," I said. "It will be fun to go there for a different reason. The nurses and doctors will love your cookies, Tim, and be happy to see you feeling better. That is thoughtful of you."

So, we did just that.

Christmas baking began and my son and I started with our favorite of course, the CCCBs. Two batches rested on the rack on top of the stove, shoved to the back. For some reason, all of us left the house at different times for different reasons, leaving the cookie bars to waft their scrumptiousness to Chance's nose.

Pulling the jelly roll pans off the stove, Chance scarfed up every last chocolate chip bar. Walking into the house, I looked at him sprawled on the floor, paws outstretched, his head down and his eyebrows alternately shifting up and down, avoiding eye contact with me. Like a child, guilt was crumbled across his jowls and soon his rumbly tummy told me the bad news.

Every Christmas, the tradition continues. I bake the bars, but they have a different name now. We call them "Chance Chewy Bars." Our memory of our "extraordinary" Lab and the Christmas treats made with yellow cake mix brings laughter and warms our tummies as we remember all of these precious family members: Grandma Joyce who first plopped those beaters into the sticky honey batter and added the sweet morsels of chocolate chips; Chance, our lovable canine with an iron stomach who blessed us with his big paw hugs and his chocolate kisses of unconditional love; and Timmy, my baking partner in crime, who now sweetens heaven with sparkly cookie sprinkles and takes a plate of CCCBs to God.

Chocolate Chip Chewy Bars aka Chance Chewy Bars

Cut coupons and then purchase:

1 9½-oz. package of yellow cake mix
1 cup packed brown sugar
2 Tbsp. soft butter
2 Tbsp. honey
2 eggs
1 16-oz. package semi-sweet chocolate chip morsels

Combine all ingredients in large bowl. Stir until blended. Spread into well-greased 9x13 baking dish. Spread mixture with spatula dipped in water. Bake at 350 degrees for 25-30 minutes. Cut into squares when cooled. Keep out of reach of big dogs. Enjoy.

Janet Piedmont Kivisto

Laundry and Love

Grandpa's white "union suits" hung on the clothesline like three limp scarecrows. Grandma and I had just hung them up to dry. Actually, Grandma had hung them up and I had the key job of handing her the clothes pegs. This division of labour made sense at the time because my head barely reached the belt on her pink gingham dress.

I knew that the union suits were Grandpa's long underwear, but they were different from my brother's long-johns. These had long-sleeved shirts attached to the pants. And why were they called union suits? Grandpa was pretty old and I independently deduced that he had probably worn them in the American Civil War while fighting on the side of the Union. I never shared this deduction with people of more advanced mathematical skills or they would likely have pointed out that he was nowhere near 120 years old.

My grandparents lived in western New York State, a painful seven-hour drive away from my home in Quebecup. Because of my parents' anxieties associated with winter travel, our first visit of the year was at Easter and the last was at Thanksgiving. For me, Easter was the best holiday of the year. Thanksgiving always held a tinge of sorrow, but summer was the season of greatest promise. It meant longer visits, sunshine, and time alone with Grandma.

As our car approached their village, I would shake off the last dregs of my Gravol-induced drowsiness and watch for each significant landmark: the cemetery, the high school, the soup factory, and the Italian corner store. When we rounded the corner of East Park Street and the giant maple tree in front of their house came into view, my hands would move into position. The left would sit just over the lock and the right would rest lightly on the door handle. Into the driveway we would pull, then make a slight turn behind the cellar door, and I was free—free to hurtle from the car, knees pumping, straight to Grandma Sylvia's arms. No one in the world could have run that stretch faster than I did and no one could have been happier.

Grandma's clotheslines were out in her second backyard or, as I called it, the back-backyard. The first backyard was closest to the house. It had a huge walnut tree, chairs for grown-ups, and a neat hobby horse for children that Grandpa had made out of some kind of tractor spring. This first backyard was also used for extra parking when we had parties with all of the aunts and uncles and cousins who came to see us.

Behind the drive shed was the back-backyard. Two sets of clotheslines were stretched between the arms of tall poles and these lines did not move on pulleys like the one we had at home. It was necessary to walk along the lines to hang your laundry. If the load got to be too heavy, you would have to prop up the lines with long poles that had notches cut in one end. Grandma told me that, with five children, you would need lots of space to dry your laundry. She said she didn't mind the extra walk to the back-backyard because she preferred a more private place to hang her clothes, "My laundry is no one else's business." Once I grew to know one particular neighbour, I could understand her preference for privacy.

I loved the back-backyard. It was long and narrow and enclosed by trees and hedges. The grass there did not get trimmed as often as the lawn close to the house and so there were buttercups and daisies and a few dandelions. These made a wondrous carpet for a young princess dancing through her kingdom. White billowy sheets hanging from the clotheslines were passageways of marble lit by a golden sun and arching over all was a magnificent canopy of blue sky. What was the best part? The best part was knowing that Grandma was close at hand and that I could find her any time I wanted just by looking for her feet under the sheets.

The clothes pegs were quite intriguing. Real wooden pegs with long slits to hold the clothes to the line, they had no springs to pinch your fingers. They looked like little people with heads and legs and I was sure that I could see faces on some of them. I wondered if they talked to each other when they were alone in their woven basket. What kind of life could they have without arms or hands? Maybe they had been cursed by an evil fairy and they could only have arms when it was dark out. These thoughts were a little too scary for my golden kingdom and I returned the pegs gently to their basket. Sometimes my imagination took me places I didn't want to stay.

Besides, other jobs needed doing. The dandelion seeds had to be set free from their stalks and a bouquet of wildflowers had to be picked for Grandma. She taught me to hold a buttercup under my chin to see if I liked butter; a yellow glow was a positive test. The clover patches had to be explored; that was another one of Grandma's special skills. A master hunter of four-leaf clovers, she would swoop down onto even a small patch and emerge triumphantly with a trophy almost every time. I dreamed of developing such an eagle eye for one of those good luck charms.

Grandma's gifts to me never had a price sticker attached. She gave me her time and her attention, whether it was reading books or walking with her to town to pay her bills. And she taught me to sew and to bake. But her greatest bequest to me was a sense of being cherished, of being seen as a treasure. From her, I discovered that a child's spirit flourishes in a garden of unconditional love. Some people may think of heaven in terms of clouds and harp music. I wonder if it isn't a place of warm breezes, snowy sheets, and someone nearby who loves you beyond belief.

Dixie Phillips

Grandma's Faith

My grandmother had only a fifth grade education, but she graduated valedictorian from the University of Adversity. She was the firstborn child of alcoholic parents. Some of the trauma she endured left gaping holes in her soul. Her deep inner pain caused her to cry out to God as a young wife and mother, and she discovered the power in prayer.

As a young child, I realized God had given my grandma mountain-moving faith. When she prayed, God showed up. There is one memory etched in my mind's eye that I'll never forget.

My mother, Bonnie, was Grandma's second child. She suffered with bouts of severe depression and had to be hospitalized on numerous occasions. After another suicide attempt, our family was summoned to the emergency room. Grandma quickly found a place to pray. She wasn't gone very long and had an unusual bounce in her step when she returned. "The Lord spoke to me today. He told me Bonnie will live and not die. She is going to play her violin for Jesus in church one day."

I didn't say anything aloud, but thoughts were buzzing in my eleven-year-old head. *But Grandma, how will Mom ever play her violin in church when she doesn't even attend church?*

My thoughts were interrupted by the doctor's stern voice. "I think we saved her this time, but one of these times she will get the job done. You need to prepare yourselves for what's ahead."

Grandma, who was usually mild-mannered and polite, bolted from her chair. Pointing her crooked finger in his chest, she barked, "Now you listen to me, Doc. My girl is not going to die, but live and play her violin for Jesus in church."

An awkward silence enveloped the room. The doctor shook his head and made a hasty exit. "Religious nut! Mental illness must run in the family."

Mom's depression increased and there were more hospitalizations and suicide attempts. I often heard my grandmother reminding the Lord, "You promised I would see her play the violin for you."

When I was sixteen, my mother met a retired pastor's wife who had battled crippling depression. This woman took a keen interest in my mother and led her into a relationship with Jesus.

Mom became a faithful member of a Bible-believing church. One Saturday afternoon she announced, "I've been invited to play my violin for special music in church tomorrow."

Grandma let out a victory yelp and danced a jig. "I'm sitting on the front pew."

I have been in fulltime ministry for more than thirty years. I've learned much from Bible college and ministry experiences, but it was watching my grandmother's life that taught me the most about the power of prayer. She gave me a living example, of how an ordinary woman with a simple faith in an extraordinary God can move mountains.

Grandma resides in heaven now, but my precious mother is still living. She just celebrated her eightieth birthday, and on special occasions still plays her violin for Jesus.

Like a Mother to Me

Although you never gave me birth,
You were like my mother here on earth.

Theresa Elders

Special Yarn Blossoms

When our aunt and uncle had adopted us the year before, Mama (which is what I called my aunt) said we were special. Patti sure was. But just that afternoon the piano teacher grumbled that I was hopeless. Patti, of course, had paced through Tchaikovsky's First Piano Concerto without a metronome—and by ear.

As I dried the supper dishes, Mama thanked me for helping with dessert. I'd measured out the cookie ingredients. But even as she spoke, my eyes strayed to the icebox door where she'd taped Patti's drawings, delicate and droll as those in my beloved fairy tale books. My stiff fingers barely managed circle-snowmen and stick-people.

I sniffled, ashamed and afraid I'd never be special. When I'd learned at church that the Bible bans envy, I pretended to love my scraggly pigtails. Since Shirley Temple was beyond my ken, I tried to emulate Margaret O'Brien in "Lost Angel," squinting, scrunching up my forehead. At Woolworths, though, I noticed all the paper doll folders featured pretty, bubbly Shirley, not plain, earnest Margaret.

Mama took my towel, and then brushed my bangs back from my damp eyes. "You seem kind of sad. You know what? Tomorrow I'll talk to Mrs. McGee about getting you into Blue Birds."

My tears stopped right then. I knew that the troop met after school on Wednesdays, right while Patti's graceful fingers would be racing through "Fur Elise" on the living room upright, to the piano teacher's delight.

I loved Blue Birds! My early handiwork, a plaster of Paris palm print plaque, though undeniably lumpy, earned me badges for promptness and effort. Though I'd blotched some black paint on the bottom of my May basket, Mrs. McGee covered it with crepe paper grass, and took extra time to show me how to tie a ribbon to its handle.

Next we started to weave flowers to cluster into Mother's Day corsages. We'd dangle a six-inch length of yarn in the centre of a fork. Then we'd double a longer strand, hook it over the two tines on the left, and loop it back and forth, two tines at a time. We drew up the ends of the middle piece around the loops and tied a tight knot. When we slipped the yarn off the fork, we had a blossom.

I became a weaving demon. I begged yarn remnants from neighbors, toiled in secret at home, and cached my finished flowers behind a bookshelf. On the Wednesday morning before Mother's Day, I stuffed at least two dozen jewel-hued flowers into my lunch bag while Mama was occupied feeding the cat. That afternoon Mrs. McGee helped me assemble them into a bouquet and attached a safety pin.

On Sunday morning, during Patti's solo, I beamed at Mama from the front row of the choir. Her face was as radiant as the garland of yarn on her lapel. As we left the church, some women approached to chat. I decided that their rose and carnation corsages paled next to Mama's ruby, emerald, and sapphire nosegay. "Yes, Patti's voice is lovely," Mama said to my sister's admirers. "And Terri made my corsage. Isn't it special?"

Decades later, as a Peace Corps Volunteer I was assigned to the Belize Council of Churches, a settlement house in Mesopotamia, a poor neighborhood in Belize City. The Council worried about child abuse in that tiny Central American country. Local housewives, whose children came to the settlement house for the school lunch program, joined together, eager to help.

We decided we needed a simple way to get our message across to the public. The Council had boxes of old greeting cards sent by overseas congregations. We sorted out the best, cut them into bookmarks with pinking shears, and stamped them with the message, "Mark books, not kids."

We needed tassels, and I remembered Mama's yarn flowers. The women learned in minutes how to weave them on forks. Soon we had hundreds of bookmarks which we distributed at our positive parenting workshops and throughout the national library system.

After the bookmarks were featured on local TV, everybody wanted some. Flowered tassels swung from books everywhere. Our grassroots group grew in confidence, raising funds to send a delegation to a Caribbean conference in Trinidad. A few, though, had qualms that they'd be viewed as uneducated housewives from a poor underdeveloped nation.

The conference's keynote speaker emphasized in her address that life takes its value from its purpose. Our group discussed this as we set up our display, our bookmarks with tassels bright as the Trinidad sun. The surrounding booths featured the professionally produced materials of other delegations—brochures, slide sets, textbooks. We exchanged shy glances.

Then within seconds we were mobbed, our bookmarks snatched up, everybody asking how we made them, and more importantly, about Belize and its fledgling child abuse prevention program.

The keynoter herself plucked up a yarn flower bookmark and held it aloft. "Isn't this special!" she exclaimed. Our faces glowed in the tropical heat. I stroked the fleecy flower of the bookmark I clutched in my damp hand. The strains of a syncopated melody from a nearby steel drum wafted into the room.

Across thousands of miles and thousands of days, I flashed back to that moment in the church courtyard when Mama finally convinced me that I was special. I brushed away a tear.

"Yes," I agreed, nodding at my counterparts. "They're special because the women who made them are special."

We were. Mama'd said so.

Sharen Pearson

The Camping Cake

My mother-in-law was not a monster-in-law. She was the most precious, loving woman I could ever have imagined having in my life. From the beginning she treated me like her real daughter. She had four sons and if she would have had a daughter "she would have been named Sharen," she told me. How could I not feel part of the family?

Eileen was talented. She cooked, sewed, knitted, kept a great house, and was a woman of God. I never felt threatened by her skills because she was a great teacher and drew me into her arms with genuine love. With all of this domesticity, she also enjoyed the out-of-doors and camping. Four sons and camping made sense. Somehow she managed to gel the two sides of herself and so was born many favorite camping recipes. Her Oatmeal Chocolate Chip cake is a real winner. The faded, spilled on, crinkled copy of the recipe card she wrote years ago attests to my many renderings of it throughout the years. Happy camping (and eating)!

Oatmeal Chocolate Chip Cake

1¾ cup boiling water
1 cup uncooked oatmeal
1 cup brown sugar
1 cup granulated sugar
1 stick butter
2 lg. eggs
1¾ cups flour
1 tsp. soda
½ tsp. salt
1 tbsp. cocoa*
1 (12 oz.) package of chocolate chips
¾ cup chopped walnuts (optional)

Pour boiling water over oatmeal. Let stand 10 minutes. Add brown and white sugars and butter. Stir until butter melts. Add eggs and mix well.

Sift together flour, soda, salt, and cocoa. Add this flour mixture to the oatmeal mixture.

Mix well. Add ½ package of chocolate chips and stir. Pour batter into a greased and floured 9x13 pan. Sprinkle top with remaining chocolate chips and nuts.

Bake at 350 for about 40 minutes or until toothpick comes out clean.

*I like dark chocolate so I increased the cocoa powder to ¼ cup. Add an additional egg.

Cherry Pedrick

An Aunt's Legacy

This is about an aunt who was like a mother in my family.
She even got a "Mother of the Year" award from her lodge!

While going through Aunt Jeannette's things after her death, I found an interesting newspaper clipping tucked in with her photos. She was named "Mother of the Year" by her lodge. She had no live biological children, but she was a mother to many. It gladdened my heart to know others recognized this too.

Aunt Jeannette was born in Belgium in 1908. Aunt Margaret was born the following year and Uncle Al the next. It was because of him that I am here today.

I've heard the story many times: Grandma pinched Uncle Al's cheek and because he had a sore on his cheek, they wouldn't let him on the ship sailing for America. They missed the Titanic in 1912, so they sailed to America on the Lusitania the following year. I often wonder how Grandma felt when she heard the Titanic sank. I'm amazed that she crossed the Atlantic with three small children in third class. Steerage. The crowded smelly area down in the belly of the ship.

Grandma and her children made it to America and her beloved husband's arms. He had already emigrated and sent for his family. Grandma had only a year of happiness with her husband before he was killed in an industrial accident and she found herself alone in a foreign country with three children. People took care of each other then. Her husband's best friend married her and took care of her and the children. He tried anyway. He was an alcoholic. I think he was also abusive, but nobody talked about that. They didn't talk back then; they only whispered.

The new family moved west to Oregon and added two more children. My mother was the youngest. Aunt Jeannette became the head of the family. I think she was born that way. She quit high school to go to work and help care for the family. Grandma never spoke much English; her oldest child was her voice. Aunt Jeannette married in her early twenties, and within a year, she was pregnant with their first child. But life never turns out as we plan. Her husband was killed in a car accident. Soon after, she lost their baby. She went to secretarial school, then back to work.

* * *

My mother was wild. She married, divorced, married again, had my older sister, and divorced again. Then she married my dad who was an alcoholic, just like her father. Mom and Dad had a baby girl who lived just two years. I guess they were painful years. Charlene's little stomach blew up like a balloon with an enlarged liver and her skin turned bright yellow from the poisons that built up inside her, since she had no gall duct to take them to the liver. She was a brave little girl. The nurses marveled at her smiles and giggles, though she was gravely ill.

The local doctors couldn't help Charlene. She would have to go to Portland, 300 miles away, then down to California. That may as well have been the moon. My parents didn't have money to travel and couldn't afford a motel while the baby was in the hospital. But Aunt Jeannette could. She saved money for times like these, times when her family needed her. She sent my mom and dad and Charlene to Portland and California. The doctors there did all they could, but the baby couldn't be saved.

I was born soon after Charlene died. Aunt Jeannette looked at our small rented home and decided it wasn't big enough so she bought a big house for my family. My parents paid her back, of course, with interest. This interest went into a special savings account that Aunt Jeannette used to put my older sister and me through college. She also bought a car for my other sister who was born less than a year after me and never went to college. She paid for other things too: accordion lessons for my sister; art lessons for me; warm winter coats and who knows what else.

* * *

Aunt Jeannette was a nag. My mother complained about that, saying her gifts came with "strings attached." Years later I understood why. The "strings" were proper behaviors she expected out of the family. She gave, she provided, but we were expected to behave in return. My sisters and I were expected to have our rooms clean for her Sunday visits. She never yelled and screamed like my mother. She was kind, but stern. We dreaded her disapproval, and we put tremendous effort into earning her praise which was readily given when it was deserved. I grew up asking myself "What would Aunt Jeannette think?"

And my mom? Well she was expected to care for her children. My dad was expected to stay sober enough to at least go to work every day and bring home a paycheck. He did. Over the years the sober spells stretched from days to months to years.

Aunt Jeannette was never the domestic type. She was an independent working lady. My mother baked pies, cookies, and cakes from scratch and joked that Aunt Jeannette couldn't bake a meringue pie.

"She doesn't use enough eggs," my mother would say. "But she makes the best box cakes."

I waited for one of Aunt Jeannette's famous box cakes, but never saw one. As an adult, I found out a box cake is made from a mix that comes from a box. I was looking for a cake in a box. I bought Aunt Jeannette a bread maker for her eighty-ninth birthday. I thought she would never learn to use it, but she persisted until she was making perfect bread.

I didn't know the importance of making bread until she told me several months later, "You know my mother made good bread. I could never make bread."

Aunt Jeannette's was a predictable, disciplined life, except for the travel, especially after she retired. She went to Hawaii and brought back chocolate-covered ants and grasshoppers. I tasted them, and thought it must have been the most exciting thing to travel to exotic places like Hawaii. I dreamed of one day travelling and seeing the world. Then she traveled to Belgium and met relatives she didn't know, except from pictures and letters. My mother asked her to bring back some Belgian spinach seeds so she could once again make a Belgian dish made with mashed potatoes, bacon, and the special spinach. I had been accused of digging up the last of the Belgian spinach in my quest for fishing worms. I still don't think I did.

After explaining what she wanted, the Belgian relatives whispered together. A cousin left and came back with seeds. Aunt Jeannette brought them home in a small white envelope. We planted the precious seeds and watered them carefully. Two fine rows of trees sprouted, no Belgian spinach. We laughed.

Living to the age of ninety-five, discipline and structure contributed to Aunt

Jeannette's longevity. She ate balanced meals and walked at least a two miles a day until her mid-eighties. She discovered pizza in her late eighties. She had moved because her apartments were run down; not her apartment, for she painted it and carpeted it herself, but the other apartments. Her new neighbors went out for pizza. She hated tomatoes so she'd never tried pizza but she went anyway. To her own amazement, she learned to like this new dish.

Aunt Jeannette discovered pizza because of her desire for friendship. She had always been a sociable person and surrounded herself with friends. She loved doing things for others and spent hours feeding friends in nursing homes or just sitting and visiting with them, not just occasionally, but routinely, dependably. She took food to "the old lady" around the corner for years. I was surprised to learn that the old lady was ten years younger! And when people brought cake, candy, cookies, fruit, and other delicacies to Aunt Jeannette, much of it went right out the door to neighbors and friends.

Aunt Jeannette worried, but that's because she loved her family and friends. She turned her worries into prayers. Friends knew her prayers were answered and came to her with their needs.

One day, my teenage son was sitting on the couch by Aunt Jeannette. She reached into her purse for something. Smiling, she said, "I found them! I've been looking and praying for three days and here they are! They must have dropped into my purse from the edge of the couch."

My son had difficulty keeping his mouth firm and straight, trying not to laugh, as Aunt Jeannette pulled her false teeth out of her purse. This was one of the first indications that Aunt Jeannette was getting forgetful. Her speech slowed and she repeated things. Then the arthritis got worse. But still, Aunt Jeannette headed my family. Even though she's gone home to be with the Lord, she still influences my life. Every decision I make is based on God's will first, then Aunt Jeannette. Would Aunt Jeannette be proud?

Contributors Bios:

Sylvia Adams is the author of a novel, a children's book, a prize-winning poetry chapbook, *Mondrian's Elephant*, and the poetry collection *Sleeping on the Moon*, runner-up for the 2007 Lampman-Scott award. A poetry facilitator in Ottawa and Chile, as ADAR Press she publishes her groups' chapbooks.

Brenda Black is an author, inspirational speaker, and publicist from Deepwater, Missouri, with more than 1,500 published works to her credit. She is a pastor's wife, mother of two grown sons, and a high school Sunday school teacher who loves country living. Learn more about the author at www.thewordsout-brendablack.com.

A visual artist at heart, **Gary Boutin** paints with words memories of Canadian traditions. With a varied background he has worked in the US Air Force, hospital and school settings, and has tried his hands at computer work. All this gives him a unique perspective on life.

Maggie Brackley lives in Markham, Ontario. She has recently retired from the provincial government where she worked as a business analyst, and enjoys writing about her travels, as well as the occasional food memoir.

Faye Braley had her first work published when she was a sophomore in high school, and has in recent years been a contributor to several anthologies. Faye lives with her husband, Jim, in Cottonwood, Arizona and is now a grandmother herself.

Linda McQuinn Carlblom, Chandler, Arizona, is a wife, mom of three, and Grammy to five. She writes mainly for children and the adults in their lives. You can check out her books at www.wix.com/llcarlblom/Kids Believe and her blog, Parenting with a Smile at www.lindamcquinncarlblom.blogspot.com. Linda also blogs with other Christian children's authors at www.christianchildrensauthors.com.

Debbie Carpenter is retired from the children's ministry staff at her church in Tucson, Arizona. She enjoys writing and spending time with her husband, daughters, sons-in-law, and grandchildren.

Paige Carpenter is a Florida-based writer and illustrator. She graduated in 2008 from Florida State University with a degree in music, and she continues to pursue the magic of stories through art and fiction. Visit her blog at www.roguedoe.wordpress.com.

Elynne Chaplik-Aleskow is a Pushcart Prize nominated author and award-winning educator and broadcaster. She is Founding General Manager of WYCC-TV/PBS and Distinguished Professor Emeritus of Wright College in Chicago. Her stories and essays have been published in numerous anthologies including *Thin Threads, Chicken Soup for the Soul,* and *This I Believe.* Her husband Richard is her muse.

Karen S. Chow is an American-born Chinese and her mother emigrated from Taiwan. Karen likes to shadow her mom in the kitchen to learn Chinese recipes. She and her husband have one daughter and live in Arizona.

Theodore Christou is an assistant professor at the University of New Brunswick. Theodore completed his PhD at Queen's University in 2009. Prior to beginning his doctoral studies, he worked as a public school teacher in the Toronto District School Board. He is the author of two forthcoming books, one prose and one verse, titled *The Problem of Progressive* Education (University of Toronto Press), and *an overbearing eye* (Hidden Brook Press).

Phyllis Ciarametaro was born and brought up on the northern seacoast of Massachusetts where she and her husband, Joe, raised their four children. Retiring to Arizona, Phyllis has written several short stories. "The Day the Kids Bought the Tree" appeared in a 2011 Christmas anthology. She is working on her second mystery novel.

Judith Cleland has been writing poetry for a number of years. Her work has appeared in *Vox Feminarum, the Blue Planet,* and several self published volumes. Her inspiration is most often drawn from her love of nature and her childhood in Waterloo County.

Karen L. Cole is the author of *Lifting the Veil* (Hidden Brook Press, 2009), a memoir of life in the convent. Among other writings, her article "Quilts and Quirks" is included in *Wisdom of Old Souls* (HBP, 2008). She is hoping her novel *Southern Exposure* will find a publisher soon. htttp://karenlcole.wordpress.com

Dorothy Cox-Rothwell was previously involved in family business and now pursues interests in writing and art and is a Spiritualist minister with two grown children and five grandchildren. Married to John Rothwell, she is also a Reiki Master.

Joanne Culley is a writer and DVD producer whose articles have appeared in the *Globe and Mail.* Her documentaries include "Be My Baby," "Put the Brakes on Bullying," and "Breaking New Ground: Contemporary Canadian Architecture." She was the winner of the Media/Television Award for "In Celebration of Women" in 2001. Visit her at www.joanneculleymediaproductions.com.

Don Cunningham, Prescott Valley, Arizona, is the author of *Divorce and Remarriage Made Beautiful in His Time* (Tate Publishing), and several chapbooks of poetry, short stories, and essays. A retired social worker and licensed minister, he currently conducts a telephone pastoral care ministry at his local church.

Peggy Cunningham and her husband have served as missionaries in Bolivia, S.A. since 1981, where they have a children's ministry and two churches. She has written 13 children's books and contributes bi-monthly to *The Voice of Grace and Truth* and various other Christian publications. www.peggyjcunningham.com

Ardith Hird Davenport is a native of central Nebraska who learned the value of family from her parents and grandparents. Ardith and her husband have been public school educators since earning their bachelor degrees at Kearney State College in 1973. They have three adult children and three grandchildren.

Nell Davidson (nee Lowkeen) was born in Port Elizabeth, South Africa. She learned to cook by being her mom's prep person, observing her mother cooking, and listening to her mom's stories.

Linda Driscoll, Peterborough, Ontario, is a mother, grandmother, and great-grandmother. She still talks to her mum.

Graham Ducker is a retired Primary Methods Specialist who enjoys writing short stories. His favourite character is ten-year-old Jeremy. A major work (and screenplay) involves Jeremy riding a woolly bear caterpillar through his mom's garden, where he learns about insects.

Cheryl Edwards is a semi-retired administrator who now resides in Peterborough, Ontario. She has been interested in writing since an early age and is currently writing her memoirs for her grandchildren, Lucas and Alec.

Terri Elders, LCSW, lives near Colville, Washington. She's a frequent contributor to anthologies, including *Chicken Soup for the Soul, Thin Threads*, and *God Makes Lemonade*. A public member of the Washington State Medical Quality Assurance Commission, Terri received UCLA's 2006 Alumni Award for Community Service. She blogs at www.atouchoftarragon.blogspot.com.

Patricia Anne Elford, OCT, B.A., M.Div., is an educator, clergy person, and award-winning professional writer in various *genres,* published in literary publications, periodicals, anthologies, and on line. She is an editor of shorter pieces and books—recently, *Grandmothers' Necklace*, a fundraising anthology for *Grandmothers to Grandmothers*. When inspired, Patricia writes on anything "handy," her own hands included.

Linda Rose Etter taught school for 36 years. After finishing her Master of Arts in Biblical Studies, her first devotional book, *Listen To HIS Heartbeat,* was published in 2011. She lives in Adrian, Michigan, and continues to write devotionals and short stories. Visit Linda at www.etterlinda.com.

Raymond Fenech from Malta embarked on his writing career as a freelance journalist at 18 and worked for, among others, leading newspapers *The Times* and *Sunday Times*. He also edited two nationally distributed magazines, *The Globe Trotter* and *Living 2000*. His work has been featured in several publications in 12 countries.

Sandra Fischer taught high school English and owned a Christian bookstore in Indiana for several years. Much of her writing is devoted to stories from her experiences growing up in the Midwest. She has been published in *Guideposts*, anthologies, and online in *Faithwriters Magazine*. Sandra lives in South Carolina with her husband Craig.

Corinne Furtney is an elementary school teacher and volunteers with the youth in her church. She enjoys baking, travelling, and spending time with her family.

Joy P. Gage is the author of 17 books, president of Northern Arizona Word Weavers, and a mentor for The Jerry Jenkins Christian Writers Guild. She lives with her retired pastor-husband in Cottonwood, Arizona. Joy was born in her grandmother's cabin south of St. Louis in the Ozark foothills.

Joyce Gero, contributor to several Canadian anthologies, has taught creative writing at a federal correctional facility. A recent community college honours graduate in Office Administration, she is currently working to obtain certification in Supervisory Management through the Canadian Institute of Management.

Linda Gillis, Sun City, Arizona, is the author of three books. A 2006 winner of the Guideposts Magazine Writer Workshop, you can visit her at www.incidentsfrom.com.

Donna Clark Goodrich is a freelance writer, editor, proofreader, and conference instructor. The author of 23 books and over 700 published manuscripts, she lives with her husband of 52 years in Mesa, Arizona. Visit her at www.thewritersfriend.net or www.donna-goodrich.blogspot.com.

Mary Gordon is a wife, mother, and grandmother who has lived her whole life knowing there's a memoir or two at the end. She is retired, and lives on the banks of the Indian River in Warsaw, Ontario.

Janice D. Green is a retired elementary school librarian. She enjoys writing slice-of-life stories about growing up and—with the help of her family and cousins—wrote two books filled with pictures and memories for her parents when they turned 90 (see www.lulu.com/spotlight/janice_green). Her book, *The Creation*, was published in 2011. Visit her blog at www.honeycombadventures.com.

Sandi Greene is an online college English teacher and writes for teens and adults. She lives in Anthem, Arizona, with her husband Bob, daughter Justice, and son Micah. Visit her at www.sandigreene.com.

Alice King Greenwood, mother and grandmother of many children, has been writing poetry since her retirement from teaching school more than 25 years ago. She delights in teaching a Sunday school class of senior adults and in memorizing the Scriptures. Her hobbies include playing the piano and composing music.

Rita Grimaldi is an early childhood educator. She is also a fibre artist specializing in weaving handspun naturally dyed fibers into pictorial tapestries.

Kimberly Sherman Grove teaches writing at Loyalist College and Colborne's Community Care. She has also taught at the Trenton Military Family Resource Centre. She is a freelance writer and editor, and has been published in several major newspapers in Canada and USA, including the *Globe and Mail*, *The Toronto Sun*, and *The Boston Globe*. Her book, *Stories Inked,* will be released in 2012.

John J. Han, Ph.D., is professor of English and creative writing at Missouri Baptist University. An award-winning poet and nonfiction, he is the author of three volumes of poetry. His poems and personal essays have also appeared in the *Mainichi Daily News, Kansas English, Simply Haiku, Prune Juice, The Laurel Review, Wild Violets,* and numerous other periodicals and anthologies in the United States, Japan, Korea, and India.

Sue Hardesty grew up in Illinois and now resides in Northwest Arkansas. She is the mother of three grown children and has several grandchildren and two great-grandkids. She has had articles published and won several contest awards. The co-founder of a writer's group at her church, she has a book in the works.

Elaine Hardt is a retired educator, now devoted to Christian writing. The author of eight books, she posts poems, stories, and articles on her blog www.EncouragingU.blogspot.com, and has been teaching the Writers' Networking Group since 2003. She's married to Don, and they have two sons.

Lindsay Harrel is a writer and editor with a B.A. in journalism from Arizona State University and an M.A. in English from Northern Arizona University. She lives in Phoenix with her husband, cat, and dog, and serves in her church's music ministry as a singer.

Lisa Harris writes about family, outdoor adventure, travel, and food. Her articles and stories have appeared in a variety of publications, including the *Boston Globe* and the *Christian Science Monitor*. She lives in Tucson with her two daughters and a multitude of four-footed friends.

Londa Hayden is a freelance writer and native Texan living in Memphis, Tennessee, with her husband and three sons. She is a staff writer for *Southern Writers Magazine*, maintains a column at the *Memphis Christian Writing Examiner*, and is founding president of Bartlett Christian Writers. Visit her website at www.londahayden.com.

Helen Hoover enjoys sewing, knitting, and travelling. She and her husband volunteer with the Sower Ministry for retired Christian RV'ers. They enjoy their four grandchildren and three great-grandchildren.

Linda Hutsell-Manning's publications span 30 years and include 12 juvenile books, short fiction and poetry in literary mags, and, in 2011, her first literary novel, *That Summer in Franklin*, Second Story Press, TO. She had two poems in the fall 2011 issue of *The Prairie Journal*, Calgary, AB. Visit her at www.lindahutsellmanning.ca.

Multi-published **Gay Ingram** enjoys writing from the piney woods of East Texas. *Twist of Fate,* her latest novel, was released in 2010. Recently she published *Some Write Thoughts*, a book for writers seeking to perfect their craft. Visit her Web site at www.gayingram.com.

Sally Jadlow serves as a chaplain to corporations in the greater Kansas City area. She also teaches creative writing. Sally is the author of *The Late Sooner* and *God's Little Miracle Book I* and *II*—both available in hard copy and e-book version. Visit her Web site at www.SallyJadlow.com.

Linda Jett, a member of Oregon Christian Writers, freelances from her home in Newberg, Oregon, where she also massages clients and plays with three grandchildren. Her works have appeared in several anthologies; her poetry often appears in OCW newsletters.

Shane Joseph is the author of three novels and a collection of short stories. His latest novel *The Ulysses Man* (Blue Denim Press) was released in October 2011. For details, visit his Web site at www.shanejoseph.com.

Deb Kemper, freelance writer and poet, hails from northwest Florida. She now lives in Kansas City, Missouri, with her husband and three dogs.

Connie Kinnell-McKinney was born in Hornell, New York, and raised in different areas of New York and Massachusetts before attending Cottey College in Nevada, Missouri. She now resides with her husband in Carthage, Missouri, where she enjoys spending time with her four grown children and five grandchildren.

Janet Kivisto practiced nursing for several years and, during that time, wrote many articles on well-being. Presently she is exploring the fascinating and occasionally frightening worlds of creating fiction and quilts. She is thrilled in her new role as a grandmother and lives with her husband in Brighton, Ontario.

Glenn Kletke lives and writes in Kanata, Ontario. His latest work appears in a recently published collection by Bookland Press. It contains poems by the Field Stone Poets and is titled "Whistle For Jellyfish."

Alice Klies is a member of Northern Arizona Word Weavers in Cottonwood, Arizona. Now sixty-eight years old, she has been writing since she was a child, mostly memoirs of her family and friends. She has worked as a tennis pro, marketing director, teacher, and public speaker.

Donna Langevin is the author of *The Second Language of Birds* and *In the Café du Monde*, Hidden Brook Press, *2005* and *2008*. Winner of the Cyclamens and Swords poetry contest in 2009, "In Lieu of an Obit" was short-listed for the Descant Best Poem of the Year 2010 Winston Collins prize, and for the GritLIT Poetry Competition in 2011. Her short play, "Man with a Butterfly Hat," will be performed at the Alumnae Theatre in Toronto in 2012.

Peggy Levesque has written for and/or edited several publications in and outside of Arizona and has contributed to three anthologies. A member of two local Christian writers groups, she is currently marketing her first novel and is working on the second. She has served on her church advisory board and has been involved in "reading theatre." Contact her at www.peggy.levesque@cox.net.

Donna Lee Shane Loomis is a wife, mother, grandmother, and grateful child of God. A third generation Colouradan, she cherishes her role as grandmother to nine beautiful children. She says, "The greatest gift I can give future generations is to pass on the legacy of the past generations and the love of the Lord."

Kathryn MacDonald published *A Breeze You Whisper* (poems, 2011) and *Calla & Édourd* (novel, 2009), both with Hidden Brook Press, as well as *The Farm & City Cookbook* (essays and recipes, co-authored with Mary Lou Morgan, Second Story Press, 1995). She teaches literature and writing online in Ontario's college system.

Kathleen Martin believes she inherited her mother's most influential trait of 'Keeping the Peace.' Published works include: *Martha McKay Brown 1875-1947* (grandmothers' anthology); *Time of Trial: Beyond the Terror of 9/11; Signatures* (anthology of personal writings); *The Bathhouse* (in print and CBC Broadcast radio broadcast); and "I Lost Me" (Alzheimer article).

Brian Mullally is the author of four novels, and a selection of his short stories was recently published under the title *A Patch of Blue*. He lives on the north shore of Lake Ontario with his artist wife, and is currently working on a sequel to his latest novel between visits from his eight grandchildren. Check out www.bluedenimpress.com for more information.

Sherrie Murphree, Odessa, Texas, wife of Mel and mom of Marlon and Valerie, is a Bible teacher, church musician, and writer of inspirational articles and devotionals. Published in 30 different magazines and nine book compilations, she loves to encourage others.

Leah Murray is a rural-based photographer, writer, and small business owner in Hastings, Prince Edward, and Northumberland Counties, Ontario, Canada. A lifelong interest in rural life and small-to-medium sized businesses in rural Ontario led to expansion of her imaging business into office automation and business process services in support of the small business owner. Leah's personal work focuses on documenting rural and small-town Canada in post-millennium years along the shores of the Great Lakes.

Juanita Wier Nobles is a retired schoolteacher and pastor's wife living near St. Louis, Missouri. She published *A Heritage of Faith* in 2010 and her work was published in the *Love is a Verb* 2011 anthology. Her articles and puzzles have been in several magazines and newspapers and on-line.

Betty Ost-Everley is an internationally published author living in Kansas City, Missouri. When not leading the church choir or advocating for her neighborhood, she works as an administrative assistant. Betty is a member of the Heart of America Christian Writers' Network.

Linda Patchett is a high school teacher and mother of three sons. She lives on Otter Lake, Ontario, with her beloved cat Ollie, named after her favourite poet, Mary Oliver. Linda has had poems published at *Bywords.ca*, *Grandmother's Necklace—an Anthology* (in support of The Stephen Lewis Foundation), and *Drumbeat* magazine. Linda is most grateful for all things small—*snowflakes and butterflies/acorns and moonbeams.*

Sheri Pattillo enjoys writing, especially poetry, as an expressive outlet following time spent in corporate America and then the trenches of nonprofit work. She is a wife and the mom of two teenage boys who provide constant inspiration for her writing. Her other interests include running marathons and studying wine.

Sharen Pearson, Cottonwood, Arizona, is a pastor's wife and mother of five. She is the founder/teacher of Goof & Giggle Mom/Tot classes and the host/creator of Baby-FirstTV's Baby D.I.Y. program. Visit her at www.sharenpearson.com.

Cherry Pedrick, Lacey, Washington, is the coauthor of seven books, including *The OCD Workbook, Third Edition* and *The Habit Change Workbook.* She has written articles for *Northwest Witness* and other periodicals.

Linda Dawn Pettigrew is a grandmother and developing writer. Over the past decade she has written, edited, and published articles, essays, and educational resources. *My Grandmas, A & P* published in *Grandmothers' Necklace* was the first publication of her autobiographical work. *I Remember Mamma* will be the second.

Tammy Pfaff of Prospect Park, Pennsylvania, is a wife and mother of four children. A member of the Philadelphia Christian Writers Fellowship, she studies jornalism, and enjoys gardening, scrapbooking, and spending time with family and friends. For more information about her, log onto www.tammypfaff.com.

Dixie Phillips and her husband Paul have served the Gospel Lighthouse Church in Floyd, Iowa, for 30 years. They have four grown children and four grandchildren. Dixie loves throwing tea parties with her girlfriends and southern gospel music. You can read more about the Phillips' ministry at www.floydslighthouse.com.

John Pigeau is the author of the acclaimed novel *The Nothing Waltz*, founder of the First Edition Reading Series in Perth, Ontario, and owner of Backbeat Books, Music & Gifts in the same lovely town.

Elsie H. Platt, Tucson, Arizona, has a B.A. in Elementary Education from Juanita College, Huntingdon, Pennsylvania, an M.Ed in Speech Pathology from Penn State University, and is certified in Learning Disabilities at the University of Arizona. She now teaches a Bible class at a nursing home, an ESL class, and two pre-school music classes at her church. She also enjoys reading and travel.

June Carter Powell lives with her husband and fellow musician Michael and two cats rescued from street life. Recently published works include "Just Granny" written especially for the anthology *Grandmother's Necklace* and "Tea Leaves and Horses' Hooves" for *Blue River Dark Waters*.

Stella Mazur Preda's poetry has appeared in many Canadian—and some US—literary journals and anthologies. Her first book of poetry, *Butterfly Dreams*, was published in 2003. Stella is owner and publisher at Serengeti Press. Her second poetry book, *The Fourth Dimension*, was released in the spring of 2012.

Natalie Kim Rodriguez is a first generation Puerto Rican Hispanic female and mother to four children. She writes religious reflections on life and family. She volunteers, participates in community leadership, and is a teacher, social media marketing consultant, writing coach, and speaker.

LeAnn Rowse and her siblings grew up in India with their parents who were medical missionaries. They came back to the States for furloughs every five years. The incident in this book happened during their second furlough while visiting their paternal grandmother.

Joanne Sandlin, Prescott Valley, Arizona, says that sitting on a kitchen stool making cookies led to her lifelong interest in cooking and recipe collecting, and publishing her own cookbook *The Front Burner With Family and Friends*. A member of the Northern Arizona Word Weavers, she also writes a recipe column. Contact her at lazydays@cableone.net

Debbie Schmid has written four books, including two bestsellers, and numerous articles for various publications. She's been a keynote speaker at ladies' retreat and church seminars, and also enjoys leading Bible studies, mentoring young Christians, and nurturing hurting individuals.

Glen Sorestad is a well-known poet with over 20 volumes of poetry published including, his most resent book, *A Thief of Impeccable Taste* published by Sand-Crab Books. His work has appeared in over 50 anthologies and has been translated into a half-dozen different languages. The first Poet Laureate of Saskatchewan (2000-2004), Sorestad was appointed to the Order of Canada in 2010.

Dominic Spano, PhD., is an anthropologist who is interested in the dynamics of human behaviour. His previous work, *The Defendant*, is a story that looks at the behavioral nuances responsible for our daily patterns of interaction. His current work analyzes the sobering family dynamics as parents age and become infirm. Contact him at domspano@sympatico.ca.

Annmarie B. Tait resides in Conshohocken, Pennsylvania, with her husband Joe Beck. She is published in various anthologies including *Chicken Soup for the Soul*, *Patchwork Path*, the HCI "Ultimate" series, and *Reminisce* magazine, and has been nominated for a 2013 Pushcart Prize. You may contact Annmarie at irishbloom@aol.com.

Diane Taylor is the author of *The Perfect Galley Book* and forty magazine articles. She has taught English as a Second Language in Miami and Toronto, and also gives workshops in memoir writing, and creates oral histories for elders.
Visit her at www.dianemtaylor.wordpress.com.

Donna Collins Tinsley, wife, mother, and grandmother, lives in Port Orange, Florida, and has been published in several magazines and book compilations. Find her at http://thornrose7.blogspot.com/or join Somebody's Mother Online Prayer Support Group at http://www.facebook.com/groups/1194081880089314?id=244911885538943. Email her at ThornRose7@aol.com.

Freda Tong and her husband were missionaries to Taiwan for many years, and now live in Fontana, California. They have three adult children and six grandchildren. Freda has written one book and enjoys writing inspirational stories.

The loss of her oldest son four years ago jumpstarted **Coleene VanTilburg**'s desire to write and share, a healing process that continues. Co-leading an Aspiring Writer's group and working at the local high school as a special education student aide also keep her active and involved in many situations which bring inspiration.

Dorothy Wells is the third child in her family, and the writer.

Connie Poole-Wesala is a retired educator and author. She lives in Gilbert, Arizona, and is currently working toward a Creative Writing Certificate. Her two grown children live close by and are her favorite friends and travelling companions. Connie has been published in *The Gila River Review*, *Arizona Republic*, and *Celebrating Christmas... with Memories, Poetry, and Good Food* anthology.

Cassandra Wessel is a retired minister, currently living in rural Pennsylvania where Amish buggies rattle along the macadam roadways. She enjoys writing, supply preaching, her garden, and times spent with her family, friends, and church.

Jean Ann Williams has contributed to over three-dozen clips to magazines, plus articles in two book anthologies. She resides with her husband and their three pure-bred goats in a secluded valley in Southern Oregon. Every fall, Jean Ann picks blackberries for jams and her mom's blackberry stew.

Donna Wootton is a retired teacher and author of three books: one a small collection of short stories *A Proper Diagnosis*, another a novel called *Leaving Paradise*, and recently a work of creative nonfiction about her father called *MOON REMEMBERED, The Life Of Lacrosse Goalie Lloyd "Moon" Wootton*, published by Ginger Press. She is a member of the Writers' Union of Canada and the Spirit of the Hills Writers' Group.

Lois A. Wraight is a wordsmith and poet for whom words are both undisciplined play and serious discipline. Fascinated by her own and others' processes of aging, she plans to make this the subject of her next and perhaps penultimate chapbook.

Deb Wuethrich is a staff writer for the *Tecumseh Herald* in Tecumseh, Michigan. She has also published several devotions and magazine articles and is a contributor to *Cup of Comfort for Parents of Children With Special Needs*, and *Love Is A Verb* devotional, a Dr. Gary Chapman/James Stuart Bell project.

Anna Yin is a self-described geek and poetess. Her life in China was normal like the early stage of a butterfly in a cocoon, but passion for poetry bloomed after immigrating to Canada. Although an IT professional, she grew wings blending Chinese and Western cultures. Her winning awards and books are on Annapoetry.com

Another
Hidden Brook Press anthology
edited by
Donna Clark Goodrich

Celebrating Christmas
with Memories, Poetry, and Good Food

Order this or other Hidden Brook Press books on
any Amazon around the world.

or

Order from your local bookstore. Just give them the title and ISBN
and our contact info.
613-475-2368
writers@hiddenbrookpress.com